Elbridge Streeter Brooks

The Story of the American Sailor

In Active Service on Merchant Vessel and Man-of-War

Elbridge Streeter Brooks

The Story of the American Sailor
In Active Service on Merchant Vessel and Man-of-War

ISBN/EAN: 9783744747110

Printed in Europe, USA, Canada, Australia, Japan

Cover: Foto ©Andreas Hilbeck / pixelio.de

More available books at **www.hansebooks.com**

THE LIBRARY
OF
THE UNIVERSITY
OF CALIFORNIA

HEAVING THE ANCHOR ON AN AMERICAN MERCHANTMAN.

"A Yankee ship came down the river
Blow, my bully boys, blow!"

(*Page* 304.)

IN ACTIVE SERVICE ON MERCHANT VESSEL

AND MAN-OF-WAR

BY

ELBRIDGE S BROOKS

AUTHOR OF

THE STORY OF THE AMERICAN INDIAN

BOSTON

D LOTHROP COMPANY

FRANKLIN AND HAWLEY STREETS

PREFACE.

In all the mass of material devoted to the doings and the duties, the experiences, the adventures and the romance of the American sailor there is to be found no work that presents in consecutive narrative the progressive record of the seamen of America.

Such a narrative this volume seeks to tell. Jack's story, however poorly told, possesses a certain interest that must enliven even the dullest tale, for the American sailor has made his name the synonym of daring, of endeavor and of achievement. His arm has been the stoutest in sea-fight; his heart has proved the most undaunted in peril, the most faithful in time of stress, the most kindly in seasons of doubt, of trial and of disaster.

With so much material from which to draw, the sailor's story, compressed within the limits of one brief volume, must necessarily be fragmentary. Details have been skipped and only the general phases of his development, his progress and his decline have been here set into something like orderly array.

The glorification of any calling is not always its best defense. No class of the world's workers but has its negative side, none but has its phases of life and manners that are justly open to criticism, not one but may disclose the antagonistic elements of virtue and vice, of manliness and dishonor. No story is really a story that presents but one side.

But in spite of every drawback the American sailor has a story well worth the telling. And if from the gleanings and gatherings here set down the reader can evolve a plain and consecutive narrative the author will feel that the months of labor and of research spent in studying and sifting this accumulation of matter will not have been in vain. He does sincerely hope that out of the story at least may come lessons of manliness, of effort, of bravery and of honest work that may not prove altogether valueless to the American reader whose very comfort and existence have been rendered possible by the energy and the achievements of the American sailor.

In acknowledging the interest with which Mr. Bridgman has by his admirable designs entered into the spirit of the American sailor's story thanks and credit should also be given to the proprietor of the *Cosmopolitan* magazine who courteously placed at the service of the publishers the three illustrations that appear in the chapter devoted to American yachting, viz : the portrait of Mr. Burgess and the cuts of the Mayflower and the Volunteer.

CONTENTS.

CHAPTER IX.

CHAPTER X.

CHAPTER XI.

CHAPTER XII.

CHAPTER XIII.

CHAPTER XIV.

LIST OF ILLUSTRATIONS.

THE STORY OF

THE AMERICAN SAILOR

CHAPTER I.

THE EARLIEST MARINERS.

THE American sailor is the oldest of navigators. Agassiz declares that America was the " first-born among the continents — the first dry land lifted out of the waters, the first shore washed by the ocean that enveloped all the earth besides."

The story of beginnings is a difficult one to trace. But each fresh revelation of science throws new light upon the ways and manners of our predecessors of the long ago. Even before Europe was a completed continent America was an inhabited land; and here, amid the crash of Nature's conflicting forces, a savage race of men, we are assured, struggled for existence, with the uncouth, gigantic, and now long-perished forms of animal life that roamed the Western world where for centuries the great lakes had been storing their volumes of water and through whose central valley for a hundred thousand years the Mississippi had poured its muddy torrent toward the southern seas.

In just what distant age, however, of a prehistoric past the first American sailor launched upon river, lake or bay his clumsy log or frailer raft of bark is for the scientist and not the story-teller to discover. The problem is, as yet, far too misty and uncertain to suggest solution. But the beginnings of any craft or calling present an interesting field for study, while from the folk-lore of every land may be gleaned certain bits of fact that show how out of man's environment and man's most pressing needs come the slow but steady development of his inventiveness and ingenuity. In this peculiar domain America certainly is not lacking.

In the ancient days, so runs the Passamaquoddy legend, Mitchi-hess, the partridge, was the canoe-builder for all the other birds. And he built them splendid boats: a great shell for Kichee-plagon, the eagle, and a tiny one, a canoe an inch long, for A-la-mussit, the humming-bird. And when they all went on a trial trip truly it was a brave sight to see, so that when Ish-me-gwess, the fish-hawk, who lived on the wing and needed no boat, beheld this beautiful squadron standing out to sea he flapped his wings in amazement and cried "A-kwe-den skon-je!"—Ah, what a canoe is coming!

But, so the legend declares, when this expert boat-builder, Mitchi-hess, the partridge, essayed to build a canoe for himself he was so anxious to construct one that should be different from all others—a marvel; yea, a wonder such as even birds' eyes had never beheld—that he, like many another ambitious inventor, overshot the mark and constructed a canoe that would not go at all. Then for very shame at his failure he gave up boat-building forever and flying far inland became a hermit, hiding under the bushes very close to the ground. And the birds, because the partridge had made such a failure of his latest invention, distrusted all his earlier ones and giving up their beautiful canoes never attempted to be sailors thereafter.

Man, more persistent than the birds, was cast down by no failure and discouraged by no catastrophe. The unsteady log on which he sat astride and sought with hand or bough to paddle across the stream might, with a treacherous turn, roll him into the water; the frail canoe of over-lapping bark or well-stretched skins might capsize or burst asunder, and still with the marvelous patience of those far-off days the shipwrecked sailor would simply try again. Indeed with the rude ingenuity of those ancient times, the naked, half-brutal savage who, centuries ago, was the first American, would doubtless avail himself of whatever would float to carry him across the stream, or out into his shallow fishing-grounds. We may even picture one such using the upturned carapax of the giant glyptodon or the fluted shell of the great Damariscotta oyster as ferry-boat or fishing-craft upon some sluggish Louisiana bayou or some clear-flowing Maine river.

Gradually, as necessity suggested invention, the uncouth cave-dweller began with frequent burnings and much laborious digging with his rough stone tools, to hollow out the handiest logs into the rude semblance of a boat. Within this, when completed, he could sit and ply his equally crude paddle of well-scraped wood, floating himself and his companions over the waters that hemmed in his forest home. We know, from the researches of the archæologist, that the advancing intelligence of the more prolific mound builders connected their fortified towns that hint at a possible civilization with broad and well-made canals, and that along these water-ways the growing commerce of those misty days floated in log canoes — the earliest forerunner of those American merchantmen that in the later days of white civilization carried the products of American industry into every corner of the world.

The ceaseless assaults of savage and ferocious foemen destroyed these far-spread communities, scattered their peoples and laid waste their fortifications and their fields, but to-day, from the Ohio to the Mississippi may be seen traces of the great

BARBARIC SHIPBUILDING.

mounds which formed the basis of their busy cities, and remnants of the long canals that bore their simple commerce. Following them the communities of pueblo builders and cliff dwellers flourished and fell, but even when at last the land that had known these dead civilizations held only the roving red-man as occupant and owner, the hollowed log and the swifter bark canoe that those earlier peoples had so cunningly devised, still remained as the sole water craft of the American sailor.

The simplest forms may be variously developed. The floating log, as it gave to the primeval savage the first idea of navigation, has ever remained the basic form as to length and breadth out of which the art of ship-building has grown. Dr. Warre has given us the stages of evolution : the floating log — the raft of logs joined with brush wood or bundles of reeds — the hollowed log, or dug-out — the canoes of bark, or of stretched or inflated skins — the canoe or boat of strips of wood, fastened together with sinews, or thongs, or fibres of veg-etable growth — the vessel formed of planks stitched or bolted together with inserted ribs — the vessel planked upon an original framework of stout wooden ribs — and finally the elaborate iron shell that supplies the iron steamships or ponderous war-ships of this latest day.

The earliest American sailors were in the first stages of this evolution — the era of dug-outs and bark canoes. With the exception, perhaps, of the oblong, skin-covered boats of the mysterious Mandans, alike canoe and war-boat, balsa and kayak showed in their construction the original idea of the floating log which had first conveyed the earliest Americans over some deep and treacherous river. The size and method of construc-tion might differ, but the original idea as well as the present necessity were ever the same.

The bark canoe appears to have been the invention of the northern tribes who lived in the region of the *Betula Papyracea*, or paper birch — that tough-barked tree which is so durable that while the wood of the fallen tree may rot entirely away the outer covering of bark will remain strong and solid. This sort of boat which has been accepted as essentially and uni-versally Indian, was in reality confined to the tribes between the Ohio and the Saskatchewan, for while the aboriginal sailors of the far north had their light skin-boat, or kayaks, and their hundred-foot wooden war-canoes, the tribes of the south had their log dug-outs and their skin balsas. To both these the birchen canoe was unknown. " The Illinois," says Father Mar-quette, "greatly admired our little canoes, never having seen the like before."

We all remember how delightfully Longfellow's flowing verse describes the canoe-building of his mythical hero Hiawatha : —

Then he asked from the Cedar its boughs, from the Tamarack the fibres of its toughest roots, from the Fir-tree its balsam and its resin, and from Kagh, the Hedgehog, his "shining quills, like arrows." And with these he made the framework of his canoe, —

Then he sewed the bark together with the fibres of the tamarack, "bound it closely to the framework," closed the seams with the resin of the fir-tree, and wrought the quills of the hedgehog into his bonny boat to adorn and beautify it : —

At last his canoe was ready for launching.

> " Thus the Birch Canoe was builded
> In the valley, by the river,
> In the bosom of the forest;
> And the forest's life was in it,
> All its mystery and its magic,
> All the lightness of the birch-tree,
> All the toughness of the cedar,
> All the larch's supple sinews :
> And it floated on the river
> Like a yellow leaf in Autumn,
> Like a yellow water-lily.
>
> .   .   .
>
> And thus sailed my Hiawatha
> Down the rushing Ta-qua-me-naw,
> Sailed through all its bends and windings,
> Sailed through all its deeps and shallows,
> In and out among its islands,
> Cleared its bed of root and sand-bar,
> Made its passage safe and certain,
> Made a pathway for the people
> From its springs among the mountains,
> To the waters of Pau-wa-ting
> To the bay of Ta-qua-me-naw."

How nearly this poetical description of the building of a canoe accords with the reality may be seen by comparing it with Mr. McKenney's equally graphic description of the manner in which O-ku-na-ku-quid the Ojibway constructed his canoe near these very waters of Pau-wa-ting which Hiawatha navigated and which we know as the Sault Sainte Marie.

" The ground being laid off in length and breadth, answering to the size of the canoe (thirty-six feet long and five wide)," says Mr. McKenney, " stakes are driven at the two extremes, and thence, on either side, answering in their position, to the form of a canoe. Pieces of bark are then sewn together with wattap (the root of the red cedar or fir), and placed between those stakes, from one end to the other, and made fast to them.

The bark thus arranged hangs loose, and in folds, resembling in general appearance, though without their regularity, the covers of a book, with its back downwards, the edges being up, and the leaves out. Cross pieces are then put in. These press out the rim, and give the upper edges the form of the canoe. Upon these ribs, and along their whole extent, large stones are placed. The ribs having been previously well soaked, they bear the pressure of these stones till they become dry. Passing around the bottom, and up the sides of the canoe to the rim, they resemble hooks cut in two, or half circles. The upper parts furnish mortising places for the rim; around and over which, and through the bark, the wattap is wrapped. The stakes are then removed, the seams gummed, and the fabric is lifted into the water, where it floats like a feather."

But, though the bark canoe became eventually the Indian waterman's especial craft, other forms of the primitive dug-out long remained in favor among these earliest American sailors. In his fourth voyage Columbus encountered, off the Honduras coast, a capacious native sailing vessel * equipped with sails, awnings and crude steering gear. The Indian chiefs or "caciques" of the Mississippi embarked their followers on huge wooden boats "neatly made and very large," says Herrera, "and with their pavilions and standards looking like a large galley," and even to this day the Aleuts of Alaska and other of the far northwestern tribes make use of monster war-boats hollowed from the logs of the giant trees of that land of forests.

* "When the Adelantado was on shore," says Irving, "he beheld a great canoe arriving, as from a distant and important voyage. He was struck with its magnitude and contents. It was eight feet wide and as long as a galley, though formed of the trunk of a single tree. In the centre was a kind of awning or cabin of palm leaves, after the manner of those in the gondolas of Venice, and sufficiently close to exclude both sun and rain. Under this sat a cacique with his wives and children. Twenty-five Indians rowed the canoe, and it was filled with all kinds of articles of the manufacture and natural products of the adjacent countries." Another account of this American merchantman speaks of its being supplied with sails of palm fibres and a rude rudder.

The American Indians lived under the spell of superstition. They feared the elements and those forces of nature that they could not fathom or explain, and their dread of the water which could so easily devour them was not the least among these fears. They never ventured far upon it. They were "near-shore" sailors, and whether afloat for fishing, war or commerce they hugged the land and had little desire for discovery or adventure.

The fear of shipwreck was an ever present one. It tinges their legends and finds place in many a myth. The Thlinket legends of Alaska tell that once upon a time, ages ago, darkness fell upon the earth and it rained so hard that "it was as if the sea fell from the sky." The terrified natives rushed hither and thither until finally constructing a raft of cedar logs they sought to sail away from the tempest. But the mad waves beat so fiercely upon the raft that it was broken in two. Torn apart by the waters the voyagers never met again. But one section of the company thrown ashore upon Mount Edgecumbe, the great mountain that overshadows Sitka harbor, became the ancestors of the Thlinket race, while the other half carried southward became the parents of all the other nations. The "seven mythical strangers" (the Hoh-gates) of whom the California legends tell, living at Point St. George near San Francisco, essayed one day to harpoon a gigantic seal. But the wounded seal, flying seaward, dragged the boat towards the fathomless abysses "where dwells eternal cold." Suddenly the rope parted, the seal disappeared and the canoe was flung into the air so high that the Hoh-gates never fell to earth again, but remained in the sky changed into brilliant stars.

Though fearing the sea the Indian sailors were full of stories of the bravery of such of their race as did fearlessly brave its terrors. " Let us go on the sea in a canoe and catch whales by torchlight," said the Algonquin giant Kit-poo-sea-gun-ow to Gloo-skap the Mic-mac hero. And Gloo-skap, who was a mighty fisherman, consented. Now when they came to the beach, says the legend, there were only great rocks lying here and there; but Kit-poo-sea-gun-ow, lifting the largest of these, put it on his head and it became a canoe, and picking up another, it turned to a paddle, while a long splinter which he split from a ledge seemed to be a spear. Then Gloo-skap asked, " Who shall sit in the stern and paddle, and who will take the spear? " Kit-poo-sea-gun-ow said, " That last will I." So Gloo-skap paddled, and soon the canoe passed over a mighty whale; in all the great sea there was not his like; but he who held the spear sent it like a thunderbolt down into the waters, and as the handle rose to sight he snatched it up, and the great fish was caught. And as Kit-poo-sea-gun-ow whirled it on high, the whale, roaring, touched the clouds. Then taking him from the point, the fisher tossed him into the bark as if he had been a trout. And the giants laughed; the sound of their laughter was heard all over the land of the Wa-ban-aki. And being at home, the host took a stone knife and split the whale, and threw one half to the guest Gloo-skap, and they roasted each his piece on the fire and ate it.*

Naval battles among the early American sailors were seldom attempted. The Indian rarely fought " in the open." His conflict was one of ambuscade and stratagem, and he preferred the solid earth to the shifting surface of the water, and the shelter of tree and rock and underbrush to the exposed insecurity of the shallow canoe.

One naval battle between hostile tribes is however on record

* Told in Charles G. Leland's " Algonquin Legends."

and displays the water tactics of these unskillful men-o'-wars-men. Those bitter foemen the Ojibways and the Foxes were at strife. Four hundred Fox warriors floating down the Onta-nagun River in their bark canoes skirted the Lake Superior coast until they reached the island of La Pointe off the present town of Bayfield, in Northwestern Wisconsin. Here they surprised and captured four young women of an Ojibway village and making off under cover of a fog were so unwise as to vent their exultation within sound of the Ojibway town with derisive whoops and a stirring scalp-song. At once the Ojibway lodges were in an uproar. The aroused warriors pushed their large lake canoes from shore, and leaping into them silently pursued their foemen under cover of the fog. Twenty-two miles to the eastward of La Pointe along the rocky Wisconsin shore the Montreal River runs into the lake. Here, the Ojibways knew, the steep and slippery banks would give no foothold to the escaping Foxes, and they waited for the attack until they had overtaken the marauders at this point. Then, with a sudden onset, they paddled their heavier canoes straight into the Fox fleet upsetting the frailer boats. Leaping into the shallowing water Fox and Ojibway struggled in a hand-to-hand fight until the four hundred braves of the Fox war-party taken at such a disadvantage were all either drowned or killed.

Even in this lake fight it will be seen the Ojibways used the fog for their customary land tactics of ambuscade, while the frail and cranky river canoes of the inland Foxes could offer no resistance to the heavier lake-boats of the Ojibways, made to withstand the storms of Lake Superior, although both classes of canoe were constructed of the same pliant birch bark.

One other water combat deserves mention here. It was during the days of the earliest clashing of the two opposing races, the white man and the red. De Soto's glittering expedition for discovery and conquest had come to naught, and the intrepid but brutal leader slept in his unknown grave beneath the muddy waters of the broad Mississippi. The remnant of his ill-fated followers, a defeated and disappointed band, were flying for their lives, three hundred and fifty tattered fugitives,

A CANOE RACE.

all that remained of the Adelantado's thousand fighting men. In seven hurriedly-built brigantines the fugitives were feeling their hurried way down the Mississippi closely followed by their Indian foemen. The hostile fleet was composed of a great number of war canoes, of from fourteen to twenty-five paddles each and carrying, each, from thirty to seventy painted warriors.

With war-songs and terrific yells the Indian pursuers hovered near the Spanish brigantines, and about noon of the second day formed their canoes in battle line, as if for an attack. Swiftly paddling toward the Spaniards each division of the Indian fleet would glide past the hated pale faces discharging a shower of arrows and shouting their war-whoops and scalp-songs. For several days and nights this style of attack was followed up until the Spaniards, wearied with an ineffectual defense and scarcely protected by their shields and skin-made breastworks, were badly crippled and made but sorry headway. Harassed whenever they sought to land and forage, worsted whenever they strove to make a retaliatory attack, the Spanish refugees at last escaped from their tormentors after more than two weeks of this terrible river fighting and were only saved from destruction by their final arrival at the open sea, when, with parting shouts of defiance and a farewell shower of arrows, the Indian fleet gave up the pursuit and the miserable fugitives sailed westward across the Gulf to the Spanish settlements on the Mexican coast.

One of the most notable water-fights (which, after all, was no real fight at all) was that by which, if we may credit the account of Prescott, Cortez the *Conquistadore* obtained control of "the Aztec sea," during that last terrible conflict for the possession of the Mexican capital. Swift on the waters of the Tezcucan Lake, out of the bosom of which like another Venice rose the beautiful city of the Aztecs, swarmed the frail canoes and stouter war-boats of "the Indian flotilla"* rallying for the last defense of an invaded homeland. Even in this display of naval force the Indian tactics consisted rather in a show of force than in a real attack. The twelve brigantines of the Spaniards

* Bernal Diaz with his usual contempt of figures places the number of canoes in this "flotilla" at more than four thousand; Cortez himself estimated them at five hundred. The actual figures were doubtless even less.

massed for battle near the southern shores of the lake quietly awaited the Indian advance. But the Aztecs even in the supreme moment of danger hesitated to contend with vessels so much larger than their simple boats and with silent paddles kept fully a musket-shot away from the Spanish fleet. Suddenly a light breeze sprung up. Cortez expanded his battle line. His canvas filled with the favoring breeze; his men stood ready for the assault and then, under full sail, the fleet of the Spaniards bore down upon the startled enemy. A storm of stones and arrows greeted the approaching boats, but, undismayed, they held their course and the next moment had dashed into the Indian flotilla. It was an unequal fight. The stout prows of the brigantines crushed into the sides of the Aztec canoes smashing, overturning and sinking. "The water," says Prescott, "was covered with the wreck of broken canoes, and with the bodies of men struggling for life in the waves and vainly imploring their companions to take them on board their overcrowded vessels." The deadly lance-thrust and deadlier bullet of the merciless invader completed the work of destruction. Such canoes as were uninjured turned toward the city, and paddling desperately managed at last to escape from the terrible destroyers, but by far the greater part of the Aztec "navy" and its dusky sailors met their death in this last sea-fight of a conquered people.

These, and similar experiences, show the unskillfulness of the American Indian as a man-o'-war's man, and it is not to be wondered at that their astonishment at the "canoes with wings" in which the mysterious white man came from an unknown shore gave place to dread when, in actual conflict, they felt the inability of hollowed log and fragile strips of bark to withstand the shock of those heavy and unyielding prows.

But when they essayed to possess themselves of the " winged canoes" of their enemies their unskillfulness as sailors was all the more apparent. The story of the Narragansett Indians who boarded and appropriated Captain John Oldham's schooner is proof of this. The Narragansetts were skillful canoeists and near-shore sailors, but having murdered that " pest of the colony," Captain Oldham and his crew on board his own craft, they found themselves utterly at a loss to sail or steer their prize, and so were drifting helplessly out to sea when brave John Gallup spied them off Block Island. Running them down in his little fishing smack Gallup with his mate and two plucky fisher boys boarded the unmanageable vessel and assaulting the unprofessional pirates drove them into the sea and carried their prize safely into port.

Still another instance of the red-man's deep-sea misadventures is that story of certain Carolina Indians who, wearied of the white man's sinful ways in trade, thought themselves able to deal direct with the consumers across the " Big Sea Water." So they built several large canoes and loading these with furs and tobacco paddled straight out to sea bound for England. But their ignorance of navigation speedily got the best of their valor. They were never heard of more, and the remorseless ocean that had before their day engulfed so many other and more skillful navigators as remorselessly swallowed both the vessels and the crews of these would-be Indian merchantmen.

But for all his failures on the water both in navigation and in battle the American Indian was still a sailor. The lakes and rivers of his native land were well-known sailing courses to him, and his canoes bore the simple products of his skill and labor from tribe to tribe in a sort of rude system of inland commerce. From remote ages an extensive intertribal traffic existed in America, and to the services of the native canoeists was this traffic largely due. A system of barter linked distant and even hostile tribes, and articles from Mexico and Florida found their way in time to the far northern nations in Minnesota and New England and the Eastern sea.

But lake and river and that same broad sea held within them possibilities of usefulness too vast to permit them to be forever navigated by the crude methods and simple devices of a barbaric race. The prows of commerce and the keels of war were destined to cleave the waves and waters that washed the Indian's home-land. Even as canoe and dug-out gave place to the more intelligent developments of the same basic idea, so did the Indian race, itself scarce further advanced in the scale of human progress than were canoe and dug-out in the line of naval architecture, yield to the dominant influences of a higher civilization. To-day the Indian's canoe is the vehicle only for the sport or pleasure of adventurous idleness, while only in the waters of the farthest north does it find a spasmodic use by the now degenerate descendants of the earliest of American mariners.

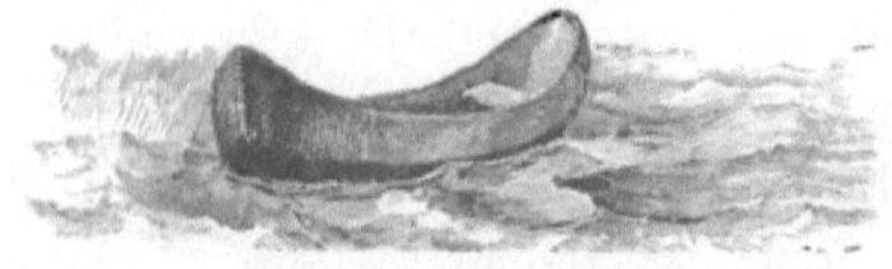

CHAPTER II

NAVIGATORS AND EXPLORERS.

HE first white navigators in these western waters can scarcely be considered as American sailors. The sons of a distant land they came here in foreign-built vessels for the purpose of adventure or of gain, and for many a year their homes and their interests were in those lands across the sea which they saw fade from sight in the wake of their departing barks or welcomed with eager eyes from the bows of their returning caravels. To Spain, to Holland, to England and to France their New World possessions were of value only for what could be brought away from them in treasure or in merchantable produce, and it was only when an actual and permanent colonization began that a race of native-born sailors was developed on the Atlantic coasts.

The mists of uncertain tradition closely shroud the earliest of these white navigators. The legends of a lost Atlantis — that fabulous continent of the mid-Atlantic, whose sea-kings sent their galleys to the east and to the west for conquest and for commerce — are not more vague and shadowy than are the tales that hint at but cannot verify certain marvelous voyages to the westward by the navigators of a still later day.   That old street in Moorish Lisbon, *Almagruvin,* " the way of them that go astray," might have had existence in every seaport town in maritime Europe, for from the Phœnician coasts to the fiords of Norway there had sailed westward into the " Sea of Darkness " ships and sailors that had literally gone astray — returning with marvelous tales of profitless adventure or returning never again to the homes from which they had sailed in search of treasure-filled Cathay.

It is conjectured that enterprising fishermen from the Bay of Biscay knew of the American continent and worked its exhaustless northern fishing-grounds years before the date of alleged Norse discovery.   Indeed there seems to be no valid reason why the same enthusiasm that reared the statue of Leif the Lucky in the streets of Boston should not with even more of certainty erect in some of our northern fishing ports the statue of a hardy, Basque fisherman of the ninth or tenth century, tricked out with net and reel and trawl and ancient fishing gear as the representation of the earliest European discoverer and the first white American sailor.

But after all neither Basque cod-fisher nor Northern Viking did anything to improve or develop their important discoveries. To all practical purposes America remained undiscovered until the faith of Columbus the Genoese braved all obstacles and gave the knowledge of the New World to the Old.

And not the great Admiral himself so much as his companions and his successors is entitled to the credit of real American exploration and discovery.   To the day of his death Columbus was ignorant of the true nature of his " find," and believed that he had touched the eastern shores of Asia.   There is reason to believe that Vespucci the Florentine, from whose

Christian name Amerigo the printer-monks of St. Dié drew the name America, was really the first modern discoverer of the main continent that bears his name, though the unchronicled voyage of that other Genoese, John Cabot " the Admiral," presses so closely upon that of Vespucci as to leave the real honor a matter of doubt.

The ships of these first discoverers flying the flags of Spain and England were quickly followed by others, impelled by the love of adventure or the hope of gain, while their patrons, rulers of the rival nations of Europe, in turn claimed the new-found lands by the right of discovery and possession. " Every rough sailor of the returning ships," says Mr. Gay, " was greeted as a hero when to the gaping, wide-eyed crowd he told of his adventures in that land of summer " and noble and hind alike became sailor, discoverer and explorer.

Most of these earlier voyages were made to the south, but some ran northward, and Harrisse affirms that " between the end of 1500 and the summer of 1502 navigators, whose name and nationality are unknown, but whom we presume to be Spaniards, discovered, explored and named the part of the shore of the United States which from the vicinity of Pensacola Bay runs along the Gulf of Mexico to the Cape of Florida, and turning it, runs northward along the Atlantic coast to the mouth of the Chesapeake or Hudson."

The story of all these voyages is full of incident, romance and excitement. The unknown sailor who first saw from the Pinta's deck the low-lying shore line of that yet unidentified island among the Bahama " Keys," was but a type of the thousands who were to succeed him, like him only to have both the glory and the reward filched from them by commanders even more ungrateful and appreciative than was Columbus the

admiral. The first terror dispelled there was no further need
for the impressing of seamen for the voyage across the western
sea. From every port and every part of Europe they came —
seaman and landsman, noble and vassal, rich and poor — all
flocking for service in the ships that were to sail to the westward, to "the land where the spices grow." "There is not a

IN SEARCH OF CATHAY.

man," wrote Columbus, "down to the very tailors, who does not
beg to be allowed to become a discoverer."

Too often "the very tailors" at whom the Great Admiral
so discourteously scoffed proved themselves not the least important men in the motley crew. In rags and tatters, naked
and hungry, wind-tossed and wave-tossed, many a ship's company was glad to cover their shivering, shipwrecked bodies with
the skins of wild animals or with strips of Indian fabrics fitted

to their needs by these very comrade-tailors that their renowned
" Admiral" so affected to despise. In cramped and comfortless
vessels, with but indifferent knowledge of navigation and none
whatever of the laws of health, with a heterogeneous company, ranging in degrees of goodness from the martyrdom-
seeking missionary to the booty-seeking cut-throat and jail-bird,
without authority and without discipline, with constant and
ever-growing rivalries and jealousies, and therefore with frequent
disturbances, strifes and mutinies, the voyages of the early explorers and navigators were begun in greed and too often ended
in tragedy.

But despite all the risk and all the drawbacks the fascination of the venture was irresistible. One successful voyage
blinded the adventurers to a score of failures. And there were
many such successes. Vessel upon vessel heavily laden with
the spoils of the New World, wrung from cheated and tortured
natives and smeared with the blood of victims, went over the
sea to Spanish, French and English ports. " Of eighteen vessels dispatched by my sovereigns with the Admiral Columbus
in his second voyage to the Western Hemisphere," says Peter
Martyr, " twelve have returned and have brought Gossampine
cotton, huge trees of dye-wood, and many other articles held
with us as precious, the natural productions of that hitherto
hidden world; and besides all other things, no small quantity
of gold."   Cristobal Guerra and Pedro Nino, earliest among the
traders of the Spanish Main, brought their little vessel of scarce
fifty tons burden into a Spanish port in April, 1500, " so laden
with pearls that they were in maner with every mariner as common as chaffe; " through the early years of that new century
heavily-freighted ships sent by the roystering bully, Vasco
Nunez, called Balboa, bore the " King's fifths " in great store

of pearls and gold from Darien to Spain ; and the murderers of the Peruvian Atahualpa and the Mexican Montezuma freighted galleon after galleon with the spoils of their deeds of blood until the treasury of Spain grew plethoric with its share of the ill-gotten plunder.

Such traffic awakened jealousies and desire in other than Spanish breasts. The Argonauts of England seeing in the laden galleons of their hated rivals of Spain, a Golden Fleece more magnificent than any their Grecian prototypes had coveted, turned marauders themselves and tracked the Spanish sailing courses with fire and with blood. Hawkins and Drake, Raleigh and Grenville, "and a host more of forgotten worthies," scoured the Southern Seas for Spanish prizes, and made their names a terror and a nightmare to the merchantmen of Spain.

Piracy thus protected by government easily gave rise to a free and unlicensed piracy, and the course of vessels across the Atlantic swarmed with marauders watching for their prey. Merchant vessels and treasure ships could only venture on their trips under strong escort, and the early days of commerce between the Old World and the New have given us a terrible record of mingled crime and cupidity, hatred, battle and blood.

But even out of the basest of motives may sometimes spring a virtue. This incessant warfare between unlimited greed and unlicensed enmity, developed a spirit of daring that has given to those old sea-fighters a setting that is strong and heroic. Cavendish, the boy-captain of an English ship, writing of his exploits among the colonies of Spain, says to his royal mistress Elizabeth, that queen and idol of English fighters: " I burnt nineteen sail of ships, small and great; and all the villages and towns that ever I landed at I burned and spoiled." John Hawkins, earliest of English slave-traders, attacked in the harbor of San Juan d'Ulua by the perfidy of Spain, in the year 1568, withstood for hours the fearful fire of the Spanish fleet and forts, and bore away two of his five little ships from under the very guns of the enemy. Francis Drake, with but one hundred and sixty-six men, in five small vessels, sailed Westward ho in 1577, ravaged the ports and merchantmen of Spain throughout the Southern seas, continued on with but one small vessel, the Golden Hind, and, after much discovery and much brave fighting against fearful odds (interspersed with so much of successful marauding that his men were "satiated with plunder"), made at last the circuit of the globe, received the honor of knighthood from his queen, and from the Spaniards, whom he had so often overcome, the title of " the English Dragon." Sir Humphrey Gilbert, friend of Sidney and Spenser, and beloved of his queen, faced danger and death in search of adventure; wrecked at last in a tempest off the New-foundland coast, he bravely met his death, calmly counselling his followers to trust and patience. It is of him that Long-fellow wrote : —

> " Alas! the land wind failed,
>   And ice-cold grew the night,
> And nevermore on sea or shore
>   Should Sir Humphrey see the light.

> " He sat upon the deck,
>   The Book was in his hand;
> 'Do not fear! Heaven is as near,'
>   He said, 'by water as by land!'"

Sir Richard Grenville — "our second Richard Lion Heart," Gerald Massey calls him *— one of the admirals of England,

---

* " A wise and gallant gentleman," says Kingsley, " lovely to all good men, awful to all bad men; in whose presence none dare say or do a mean or ribald thing; whom brave men left, feeling themselves nerved to do their duty better, while cowards slipped away, as bats and owls before the sun."

for fifteen hours, off the Isle of Flores, held at bay with his
single ship, the Revenge, fifteen great Spanish galleons, and
yielded at last only with his life to the press of overpowering
numbers.   Here is a poet's picture of the hero's end : —

> " Around that little bark Revenge
>   The baffled Spaniards ride
> At distance.   Two of their good ships
>   Were sunken at her side ;
> The rest lie round her in a ring,
> As round the dying lion-king
> The dogs, afraid of his death-spring.
>
> " Our pikes all broken, powder spent ;
>   Sails, masts to shred were blown ;
> And with her dead and wounded crew
>   The ship was going down !
> Sir Richard's wounds were hot and deep.
> Then cried he, with a proud, pale lip,
> ' Ho, gunner, split and sink the ship !
>
> " ' Make ready now, my mariners,
>   To go aloft with me,
> That nothing to the Spaniard
>   May remain of victory.
> They cannot take us, nor we yield ;
> So let us leave our battle-field
> Under the shelter of God's shield.'
>
> " They had no heart to dare fulfill
>   The stern commander's word :
> With bloody hands and weeping eyes,
>   They carried him aboard
> The Spaniard's ship ; and round him stand
> The warriors of his wasted band ;
> Thus said he, feeling death at hand : —
>
> " ' Here die I, Richard Grenville,
>   With a joyful and quiet mind ;
> I reach a soldier's end ; I leave
>   A soldier's fame behind,

Who for his queen and country fought,
For honor and religion wrought,
And died as a true soldier ought.'" *

These are but samples of the daring English valor that upheld the English name upon the western sea and laid the foundation of that later mettle that was to yield upon the shores they came to discover a race of hardy and intrepid

THE FIRST SIGHT OF LAND.

American seamen. At this remove we think less of their faults than of their virtues, and shrining their deeds of heroism in the stirring lines of poet and romancer, forget the flaws that

* The exact words of Grenville, here paraphrased by Gerald Massey, were: " Here die I, Richard Grenville, with a joyful and quiet mind, for that I have ended my life, as a true soldier ought to do, fighting for his country, queen, religion and honor." It is stated by some authorities that he held at bay in this memorable sea fight, instead of fifteen Spanish galleons, the entire fleet of fifty-three ships and ten thousand men.

history may discover in their characters, and reverence them rather as those types "of English virtue," as Kingsley declares them to be, "at once manful and godly, practical and enthusiastic, prudent and self-sacrificing," and which he has depicted with so much vigor and beauty in that noblest of all stories of the early adventurers, "Westward Ho!" the story of Amyas Leigh.

But not alone upon the Spanish Main were daring and valor linked with adventure and discovery. Far to the north, along that ragged Atlantic coast line, might be seen the white sails of navigator and explorer bent upon the finding of new worlds to conquer, to plunder and to people. They came in less number than to the Southern seas, but they came in sufficient force to complicate the claims of possession and to embroil nations in controversy and war.

Spaniard and Frenchman, Englishman and Dutchman in turn unfurled their flags in Northern waters and set up the arms of their respective countries in token of possession upon the self-same sand barren, the same rocky point, the same forest-covered slope. Bays were entered, harbors sounded and rivers explored, while along the entire coast from Labrador to Florida the same prominent coasting grounds received from various discoverers various names and titles. The jutting point off which Thorvald the Viking fought in 1003 his losing sea-fight with the "Skraellings" (Indians) and where to-day he lies buried,* looked out over Whittier's "turquoise bay" — that island-studded stretch of sea-water that the Norsemen of Thorvald's day called the Gulf of the Skraellings' land; the Spaniards the Bay of San Cristoval; the French explorers the Sea of Verrazano, or the Great Bay; the Dutch sailors on Captain

* "Krossaness" the "place of crosses" near Nantasket Beach or on Point Allerton.

Block's Onrust the North Sea, and the later English colonists Massachusetts Bay. So, too, that well-known arm of New England where with doubled fist Massachusetts, as Dr. Holmes says, "squares off at all the world," was the Keel Cape of the Norsemen, the Franciscan Cape of Cartier the Frenchman and the White Cape of that later Frenchman the intrepid Champlain; it was the Sandy Cape of the Spaniards, the Staaten Hoeck of the Dutch and the Shoal Hope and Cape Cod of the English. The Rio San Antonio of the Spaniard Gomez became the River of the Mountains of Verrazano the Frenchman, the "Great River" or the "North River" of the explorer Hudson, the "Great River of Prince Maurice" of his later Dutch successors and Hudson's or the Hudson River of its English masters. The greater river of the South appears upon respective maps as the Malbanchia of the Indians, the Palissado and Espiritu Santo of the Spaniards and the Mississippi of the French and the English. The pleasant capes of Maryland, the shifting sands of Hatteras, the flower-bordered coves of Florida in like manner took to themselves names in the language and according to the inclinations of respective and successive discoverers, and upon those very names and claims the white man's rivalries, animosities and greed visited the baptism of fire and of blood.

And in what "ships" those hardy mariners braved the terrors of the Western seas! Ships they could scarcely be called. "Very cockle-shells of boats," is what Irving terms them. The Santa Maria, the largest of the three vessels of Columbus, was but a craft of a hundred tons burden — sixty-three feet long, fifty-one feet keel, twenty feet beam and ten and a half feet draft of water; the Nina and Pinta were very much smaller — "open caravels" of scarcely fifty tons burden. In fact most of the vessels, so says Irving, "with which Columbus undertook his long and perilous voyages were of light and frail construction, and little superior to the small craft which ply on rivers and along coasts in modern days." The famous Victoria of Fernando da Magalhaens, or Magellan, in which that daring adventurer in 1520 circumnavigated the globe was of scare ninety tons burden. In "a small vessel" (the Matthew) John Cabot in 1497 "committed himself to fortune" and discovered the North American continent. The schooners of Verrazanno and Cortreal were scarcely more than fishing smacks. Neither one of the "ships" of Jacques Cartier, father of Canada, exceeded sixty tons burden; the Squirrel on which Sir Humphrey Gilbert went down to his death off the coast of Newfoundland was of but ten tons burden — scarcely more than a yacht; Sir Francis Drake's stanch little vessel, the Judith, with which he withstood the Spanish fleet at San Juan d'Ulua was of less than fifty tons burden; his still more celebrated ship the Pelican, which Queen Elizabeth ordered to be forever preserved as a memorial of his bravery, was a vessel of but a hundred tons, and Henry Hudson's famous Half-Moon was but a Dutch yacht or "vlie-boat" of eighty tons.*

When it is remembered that in the palmy days of the American merchant service the ships engaged in ocean ventures ranged from two hundred to five hundred tons burden, and the frigates of the naval marine from seven hundred to twelve hundred tons, some idea may be formed of the risks run by the early navigators in their attempting to thread the unknown

* "The splendid ships of the merchant marine of our day," says Dr. Francis L. Hawks, "render it strange to us that voyages should have been made across the Atlantic in such small craft as we have named. The largest vessel (the Tiger, in Sir Richard Grenville's fleet of 1585) was but of one hundred and forty tons, and some were of less size than a modern pilot boat. But even the caravel in which Columbus discovered the continent was of some thirty tons only; and the luxurious accommodations, the skill and safety of an Atlantic voyage now, furnish no proper picture of the risk and privations of the first European voyages to America. The humblest passeng / and most common seaman probably have more comforts now than had the Admiral Sir Richard Grenville in 1585.'

OFF KROSSANESS.

courses of a tempestuous ocean in such frail and insignificant vessels as those whose decks they so hopefully and yet so anxiously trod.

Still further toward the north the adventurers turned their prows. Firm in the belief that the way to Cathay and the Indian seas lay through the Northern Ocean, the lead of Cabot and of Cartier was followed by Frobisher and Davis who pushed their ships in 1578 and 1585 against the ice-packs of the Arctic circle. Their reports led still others to brave the rigors of the Frozen Sea, and Waymouth and Hudson, Button and Baffin in the opening years of the seventeenth century made the futile attempt to find a clear sailing course along the ice-bound Northern shores of the new continent. Forerunners of that intrepid army of explorers and navigators who have sought to solve the still unsettled problem of the Pole, their most practical discovery was the profitable outlet for the fur trade of the North that resulted in 1670 in the incorporation of the Hudson Bay Company, but from their day to this later era of Franklin and Kane and Greely "the open strait to Cathay" still remains undiscovered, closed against the hardy seamen of the Arctic zones by the impenetrable barriers of the Palæcrystic Sea.

So, north and south, through those early years of discovery, the navigators of Europe steered their little crafts. Each new voyage led to still other ventures, and the "able seaman" of one expedition became the captain or commander of a later one. The merchants and capitalists of England and Spain, of Portugal, Holland and France, advanced the moneys needed for each new attempt; hoping now for gold, now for slaves, or now for a profitable freight of pearls, or furs, or other coveted products of the Western world. Attempts at colonization might fail, still others were made; the jealousies of rival leaders or of hostile nations might wreck the hopes of one carefully-planned venture, another, spite of loss and death, was certain to follow speedily. On the Florida coast alike French Huguenot and Spanish Catholic fell victims to a war of creeds, and all along the Atlantic coast from St. Augustine to Pemaquid and Acadia each step in discovery and exploration was the source of international dispute and personal encounter. But still capitalists risked their much-loved gold, captains persisted and adventurers flocked to the western-bound ships, * undeterred by the tales of loss and ruin that came from over-sea, while from seaport and from country town sailors and landsmen hastened to enlist again for the search for gold along the far-off shores. To them there was no such word as fail: on the wrecks of earlier hopes they pressed to new endeavors confident, every one, that not the forecastle but the quarter-deck, not the farmhouse but the palace was to be his final goal; each as brave at heart and yet as full of boastful hopes as was Sir Thomas Stukely, the knight of Ilfracombe, who went pompously westward to people the land of Florida, boldly declaring to Queen Elizabeth that he had rather be sovereign of a mole hill than the highest subject of an emperor, and telling her plainly that, for himself, he, in that far western Eldorado, looked to be a prince before he died.

Poor fellows! They were but illy prepared to buffet the stormy seas and brave the rigors of an unknown coast. But, thinking only of possible gain, they embarked, sailor and landsmen alike, for service before the mast, lured on by the specious promises of gentlemen adventurers and half-piratical captains, into the mouth of one of whom — Captain John

* In 1543, 1544 and 1545, M. Gosselin declares, after careful studies of the old French records, "this ardor toward the New Lands was sustained; and during the months of January and February, from Havre and Rouen, and from Dieppe and Honfleur, about two ships left every day."

Oxenham of Devon, Kingsley puts this "listing call" before the tavern door of the "little white town of Biddeford," on the pleasant sea slopes of North Devon — then (in 1575) one of the chief ports of England : —

"Come ; come along ! Who lists ? Who lists ? Who'll make his fortune ?

> 'Oh! who will join, jolly mariners all ?
>   And who will join, says he, O !
> To fill his pockets with the good, red goold,
>   By sailing on the sea, O ! '

"Who'll join ? Who'll join ? It's but a step of a way, after all, and sailing as smooth as a duck-pond as soon as you're past Cape Finisterre. I'll run a Clovelly herring-boat there and back for a wager of twenty pound, and never ship a bucketful all the way. Who'll join ? Who'll join ? "

And when moved by such rude eloquence as this and by the misty promises of luck that seemed to lurk behind it certain of the more adventurous and ambitious ones came forward to "list," Captain Oxenham made them all the more determined by an apparent change of tone : —

" Now, then, my merry men all," he said, " make up your minds what mannered men you be minded to be before you take your bounties. I want none of your rascally lurching long-shore vermin, who get five pounds out of this captain, and ten out of that, and let him sail without them after all while they are stowed away in tavern cellars. If any man is of that humor, he had better to cut himself up, and salt himself down in a barrel for pork, before he meets me again ; for by this light, let me catch him, be it seven years hence, and if I do not cut his throat upon the streets, it's a pity ! But if any man will be true brother to me, true brother to him I'll be, come wreck or prize, storm or calm, salt water or fresh, victuals or none, share and fare alike ; and here's my hand upon it for every man and all ; and so —

> ' Westward ho! with a rumbelow,
> ' And hurrah for the Spanish Main, O ! ' "

And how often those hopes of good luck came to naught! Thovald the Viking laid his bones upon the inhospitable shores of Massachusetts Bay, the defeated leader of a profitless expedition. "There shall ye bury me," said he, "and set up crosses at my head and feet, and call the spot the place of crosses (krossanes) forever." Of the companions of Columbus scarce one but shared what Irving calls "the usual lot of the Spanish discoverers, whose golden anticipations too frequently ended in penury." Balboa, Narvaez, de Leon, de Soto, de Luna, and

ALONZO PINZON THE PILOT.
(A type of the old Navigators.)

other "hidalgos of Spain," ended their cruises for fortune in disaster and in death. Gaspar Cortereal, the Portuguese navigator, and his brother Miguel, seeking to discover a northern passage to India, sailed toward the Labrador coast, and were never heard of more. Verrazanno, the Frenchman, explorer of the easterly coast of the United States, and discoverer of New York, turned pirate and was hanged by the Spaniards, * upon whose commerce he had preyed. Sir Francis Drake, the " Dragon of England," conqueror of the Spaniards and discoverer of California, died on board his ship, sick with the fever, and of mortification at the failure of his last piratical

* Another account states that he was killed and eaten by American cannibals, in 1527. Either ending was sufficiently disastrous.

cruise ; Hudson and Gilbert still searching for the unattainable died, the one by mutiny and the other by shipwreck on the waters of the icy north. And the fate of these captains of notable name was but the end of hundreds of less note or of no renown, companions and followers, captains and seamen, who, sailing from old-world ports, with rosy expectations of success and gain, laid their bones upon the wreck-strewn coasts that ground their keels to powder, or found a watery grave beneath the waves that beat upon the new world's shores. Few, comparatively, of those old-time voyagers could exhibit such a "log" as was so jubilantly recorded by Captain Luke Fox from Deptford : " Caste anchor in the Downs on thirty-first October (1631), not having lost one Man nor Boy, nor Soule, nor any manner of Tackling, having beene forth neere six moneths. All glory be to God !"

Explorers and navigators speedily gave place to colonists. From ventures in the western and southern seas came the crude settlements along the coasts. From the insecure foothold came the successful occupation, and, despite all the disasters and sorrows of colonization, the stream of emigration steadily set in from the old world to the new. It grew with each new year ; homes were established around each stockaded point ; landing-places developed into harbors, and harbors into seaports ; growing necessities afforded new opportunities until, at last, along the Atlantic coast from the St. Lawrence to the capes of Florida the slowly increasing demands of colonial commerce gave rise to the new race of native American sailors.

CHAPTER III.

JUST when and by whom the first keel was laid and the first vessel built by European ship-carpenters upon the American coasts it is not easy to determine.

The half-legendary story of that early repair-work of the year 1004 that gave to Cape Cod its Norse name of Kjalarness or Kell-ness (the place or cape of the keel) has scarcely enough of proof to render it authentic. The raft of Nicuesa the Spaniard upon which, in 1509, he and his ship-wrecked crew vainly essayed to escape from the desolate West Indian "key" upon which they had been thrown could scarcely be esteemed a ship. Nor can we count as completed work the unfinished caravel commenced by the traitorous Olano, in 1510, at the mouth of the Belen River. We must therefore surmise that the four brigantines built in 1516 by Balboa on the Pacific side of the Isthmus of Panama from wood felled and transported across the mountains for the first Pacific "squadron" were in reality the first home-made vessels launched in American waters.

The two brigantines which Martin Lopez in 1520 built for Cortez seem to be the next constructions of record, but these all were surpassed by the fleet of invasion built by Cortez for the final conquest of a tottering empire: thirteen brigantines constructed by Martin Lopez at Tlascala and launched upon the Lake Tezcuco on the twenty-eighth of April, 1521 — "the first navy," says Bancroft, "worthy of the name, ever launched in American waters."

In 1528 Panfilo de Narvaez, self-styled governor of Florida and the Mississippi, scoured the coast of Florida for gold and slaves and paid for his perfidy toward the natives of that " land of flowers " with his death. Lured on by the rumors of an even greater Eldorado than Mexico — the golden city of Apalache — Narvaez and his men left their vessels behind them in or near Tampa Bay and struck inland only to encounter disappointment and defeat. Returning, after the greatest hardships, to the coast, they could find no trace of their ships and in their desperation set about to build themselves other vessels to take them away from this land of blasted hopes. But, says the narrative of Cabeza de Vaca, the treasurer of the expedition, " we knew not how to construct, nor were there tools, nor iron, nor forge, nor tow, nor resin, nor rigging; finally, no one thing of so many that are necessary, nor any man who had a knowledge of their manufacture. And, above all, there was nothing to eat the while they were making, nor any knowledge in those who would have to perform the labor."

Necessity, however, has ever proved herself the mother of invention. With nothing, apparently, to assist them in their undertaking, these stranded adventurers contrived after infinite exertions to build for their escape five rude and scarce seaworthy brigantines. To accomplish this they actually built themselves into their boats; for, stripping their persons of whatever they had of metal — their armor, swords, spears and horses' trappings — they forged these into tools and nails. Cutting down trees for the ribs and woodwork of their boats, they made their cordage from the manes and tails of their horses, killed (one every third day) for food. They calked the seams of their boats with the fiber of the palmetto-trees and pitched them with resin from the pine-trees. They sewed their shirts into sails; they tanned the skin from their horses' legs into water bottles, and after six weeks of unceasing labor they completed and launched their five home-made boats, each about thirty-three feet long, and embarked on the homeward voyage, fifty men crowding into each one of these frail crafts. Thus the very first ships built upon the coast of the United States were the work of a band of shipwrecked adventurers driven to desperate devices to escape in any way from the very land they had set out with so much of bombast and of hope to conquer and colonize.

It would seem as if so much energy and pluck should not have gone for naught. But disaster still pursued them. In a great storm, probably off the present harbor of Galveston, four of the boats were driven ashore and broken in pieces. Of the shipwrecked company all save four were soon drowned, killed or starved, and these four, of whom de Vaca was one, finally reached a Spanish settlement after long wandering and surprising adventures. The fifth boat, in which had sailed Narvaez the unlucky leader of a luckless expedition, was never heard of more.

De Soto, successor of Narvaez as *Adalantado* of Florida, succeeded also to his heritage of woe. His glittering company of a thousand men, dwindled to scarce three hundred. The leader himself, dying of hardship, disappointment and despair, closed his adventurous career in a midnight burial nineteen fathoms down beneath the turbid waters of the Mississippi. The survivors, anxious to escape from a country where they had known only woe, set about the building of seven brigantines to carry them down the Mississippi to the Gulf. These they constructed just above the mouth of the Arkansas River, after six months of hard labor, devoting to the work as had the followers of Narvaez, their armor, horse-gear and camp belongings, even to their store of shot and the chains in which they had hoped to lead away a multitude of Indian slaves. The bark of the mulberry-trees and the fibers of a hemp-like plant supplied them with cordage and oakum and the woven mantles of their Indian neighbors were taken for sails. Then after an exciting voyage of seventeen days down the Mississippi, fighting their Indian pursuers to the very last they reached the Gulf and cruised along the coast for fifty days more until they reached the Spanish settlements.

A SPANISH GALLEON.

Of a somewhat similar nature to these Spanish attempts at ship-building in the New World was that of the pinnace constructed, in 1562, by the French colonists, near Beaufort in South Carolina. Grown desperate because of their seeming abandonment by France (when the bloody feuds of Catholic and Huguenot drove from men's minds the remembrance of this struggling little colony over-sea) the escaping remnant of Ribault's colony with "slender victual" and "without foresight and consideration" hoisted upon their crazy pinnace their sails of sheets and shirts and put to sea. "No madder voyage," says one authority, "was ever undertaken." Storm-tossed for days in an unseaworthy craft, food and water were soon exhausted and life was only sustained by the horrible "death by lot," by which one comrade was sacrificed to appease the hunger of the rest. Rescue came at length from an English ship by which they were borne not to their French homes, but to English prisons.

Thus disaster followed disaster and scarcely a ship, built by unskillful hands, ever made the homeward voyage. Shipwreck in those sunny Southern seas was always imminent. The tropical hurricanes strewed the Florida coast with the fragments of many a Spanish wreck, and to tempt the waters in an unseaworthy craft was almost certain death. But man is always ready to try the one chance in ten. The beginnings of colonial ship-building in America were laid in defeat rather than in honest progress and can find with us little of approval save as they display the ingenuity of man when driven to desperate straits.

But at last the conquerors, coming as conquerors merely, gave place to the colonists. And in every colony were always to be found one or more ship-carpenters.

The "Popham colony" sailing westward in the spring of 1607 in the ships of its patentees, Sir John Popham and Sir Ferdinando Gorges, brought from England to the mouth of the Kennebec a company of one hundred and twenty persons. Among their number were entered besides artisans, carpenters, sawyers and laborers, a smith and a master ship-builder. This latter was Thomas Digby, and one of his first labors was to cut down sufficient timber, from which, when duly seasoned, he shaped the timbers, laid the keel and built for the use of the colony a small pinnace of thirty tons which was christened the Virginia. This was the first vessel built by Englishmen in American waters. She made several trips across the Atlantic, but the first use made of her was, it is said, to convey back to England before the close of the winter 1607-8 nearly two thirds of the Kennebec colonists, already discouraged by the severity of a winter on the storm-swept coast of Maine.

On a November night in the year 1613 the Dutch lawyer-captain Adriaen Block, lay off the southerly point of Manhattan island in his galiot the Tiger. He was awaiting the lading of a final cargo of furs from the Hudson River Indians before sailing for home. Suddenly there was a cry of fire. The Tiger was in flames, how or from what cause no one ever learned. Roused to action, as is the Dutch nature, none too speedily, captain and crew rowed ashore sad and homeless, and their good galiot burned to the water's edge. But if the Dutch nature is slow to action it is slow to acknowledge defeat. With no useless bemoanings of their ill-luck they set to work at once knowing that winter was closing in and that the Tiger was the last of the fur fleet for that season. So they built for themselves rude but substantial winter quarters at what is now No. 39 Broadway — the earliest beginnings of New York City — and these completed set to work on a new vessel with which to leave their winter prison when the spring should set in. It was a rude little craft — De Laet calls it a "yacht" — but it was a substantial one. It was thirty-eight feet keel, forty-four and a half feet deck and eleven feet beam. It was of sixteen tons burden and was the first decked vessel built within the limits of the United States. Captain Block called her the On-rust — the Restless, and in the spring of 1614 she was duly launched in the waters of the Upper Bay, sailed through the dangerous reefs of Hell Gate and coasted the shores of Long Island and Connecticut. Block in the Onrust is believed to be the first European navigator who ever sailed over the length of his "beautiful inland sea" — that sparkling stretch of salt water that men now know as Long Island Sound.

Slowly along the coast, as the colonies increased, the needs of commerce grew. The New England settlers and those of the Canadian shores drew so much of their living from beneath the waters, that they soon felt the need of fishing and trading craft. As the years rolled on many an honest keel was laid along the indented shore line from Maine to Maryland, and many a sloop and shallop, many a pinnace, bark and ketch, American built, were launched in American waters. The ship carpenter was an important artificer in every seaside settlement, and it is stated that at the breaking out of the Revolution there were more people in the northern part of New England (in Maine and New Hampshire) engaged in ship-building and in navigation than there were in agriculture.

But at the first this progress was slow. The colonists were poor, and altogether dependent upon the Mother Countries for their needed supplies. And the Mother Countries intended that they should be. Restriction of colonial trade meant profits for the home traders' pockets. The authorities at court, as we shall see in due time, made no move to help but instead sought to hinder the growth of American ship-building.

A COLONIAL ELEPHANT: LAUNCHING THE NIEUW NETHERLANDS.

This, however, was an industry that even kings and decrees could not stay. As has been said, every colony, every settlement ere long had its ship-carpenter.

One such established himself among the people of the Plymouth Colony in 1624, and though he died not long after his arrival, he still had strength and time enough to build for the colony two shallops. This was the name given to a sort of primitive schooner much used for the coasting-trade. The first of these two shallops made her trial voyage with a cargo of corn to the colonists at the mouth of the Kennebec, but it may be inferred that her crew were not too comfortably housed in their cabinless craft. She had, so says the old record, "a little deck over her amidships to keep ye corn drie; but ye men were faine to stand it out in all weather without shelter." The rough weather of the New England coast doubtless impelled the master and owners to make their open boat more habitable, for we read that the next year (1625) they " sawed her in ye middle, and so lengthened her some five or six foote, and strengthened her timbers, and so builte her up and laid a deck on her; and so made her a conveniente and wholesome vessell, very fitt and comfortable for their use; which did them service seven yeares after; and they gott her finished and fitted her with sayles ye ensuing year." Such a craft as this seems to have served the purposes of the colonists without immediate additions, for we read that in the year 1627 the whole tonnage of New England consisted simply of " a bass-boat, shallop and pinnace."

But before the seven years' service of this lengthened shallop were up two other and more ambitious attempts at ship-building were made in the colonies. On the Fourth of July, 1631, the first war-vessel built within the confines of what is now the United States of America, was launched into the Mystic River. This vessel was a bark of from thirty to forty tons burden, and was made from locust timber cut upon Governor Winthrop's farm — the "Ten hills" — near to the present town of Medford. Less than twenty years ago the identical ways upon which this bark was launched into the Mystic, were still standing and in a good state of preservation. Though not originally intended as a man-o'-war, as her rather poetical name, "The Blessing of the Bay," would seem to imply, this excellent sample of Master Walter Merry's honest ship-building work proved so staunch a craft that she was soon after her launching converted by the Massachusetts colony into a cruiser against the alleged pirates who were already preying upon the colonial commerce.

But by far the most notable venture in ship-building was made in that same year of 1631, in the six-year-old Dutch colony in the Manhattans. The fine timber that shaded that island colony was peculiarly adapted to boat-building, and we read, not infrequently, of carefully-selected masts made from the loftiest trees and sent by the colonists as gifts to their masters of the Amsterdam Chamber in Holland.

Two ship-builders from Belgium, attracted by the reports of the fine timber of the Manhattans, conceived it would be a profitable business to convert some of it into a great ship. The Heer Minuet, director-general of the colony, was speedily won over to their undertaking, and backed them with the funds of the Dutch West India Company. In good time the vessel was launched — a mighty ship of eight hundred tons burden, and carrying thirty guns. It was duly christened the Nieuw Netherlands, and furnished much food for boastful talk in shop and storehouse and on the neighbors' "stoopes."

And well it might, for it was indeed one of the finest examples of the naval architecture of its day. Not for fully two hundred years after the launching of the Nieuw Netherlands was so vast a vessel built in America. For when it was completed, alike the Belgian ship-builders and the Heer Director Minuet discovered that they had upon their hands as large an elephant as had the owners of the giant steamship, Great Eastern, two hundred and thirty years afterward. The expense of building far exceeded the original estimates. The States General of Holland censured the company; the company's shareholders grumbled at the directors; and the directors searching for a 'scapegoat pitched upon their ambitious director-general, and he was incontinently recalled to Holland and deprived of his office.

What was the future of the big ship the records of the time afford no trace, but its failure appears for a time at least to have put a check upon ship-building at New Amsterdam, for even after the Dutch colony became the English province of New York, we learn that though "a thousand shipps may ride here safe from wind and weather," there were in 1678 (over fifty years after the launching of the Nieuw Netherlands) only "five small shipps and a ketch belonging to New Yorke, foure of them built there."

The building of this large vessel by the Dutch colonists seems however to have given a certain impetus to the trade in the northern colonies. A Master Peter of Salem, in the Bay Colony built in 1640, a ship of three hundred tons burden, and forthwith the people of Boston, not to be outdone by their neighbors of Salem, built in the shipyard of Master Bourne, a vessel of a hundred and sixty tons. "The work," says Governor Winthrop, "was hard to accomplish, for want of money, etc., but our shipwrights were content to take such pay as the country could make."

Indeed, ship-building seems to have prospered in Massachusetts more notably than in any other of the American colonies of the English crown. For while in the Connecticut colony,

"THE TERRORS OF THE WESTERN SEAS."

as late as 1686 there were to be found as the property of the colonists but "a ketch or two and about six or seven sloops" and in New York, in the same year, only some nine or ten three-masters of not over a hundred tons burden, two or three ketches and barks and less than twenty sloops there were built in the Massachusetts colony as early as 1642 "besides many boats, shallops, hoys, lighters and pinnaces, other ships of a hundred, two hundred, three hundred and four hundred tons," while at a date just before the Revolution it is estimated that Massachusetts owned one vessel for every one hundred of its inhabitants.

Further to the south Maryland and Virginia, the Carolinas and Georgia, did but little in the real work of ship-building, trusting their commerce to English-built vessels rather than to home-made keels. Indeed, the restrictive policy of England, already referred to, impeded as far as it was able this necessary industry and the English parliament in the hundred and twenty years following its first decree of 1650, enacted thirty distinct and separate laws aimed at the destruction or at least at the restriction of the commercial trade of the colonies. By these statutes the export and import trade of the Colonies was largely restricted to English-built ships and no imports into a British colony were allowed save in an English-built ship "whereof the master and three fourths of the crew are English." It was the enactment of such arbitrary laws as these that constituted one of the leading grievances against England and stood as one of the causes for colonial revolution.

But, despite the tyranny of English masters and the greed of English capital, the commerce of the American colonies grew slowly but steadily. At the outbreak of the Revolution after one hundred and fifty years of occupation and gradual development, the coasting, fishing and carrying trade of America had assumed excellent proportions. The bulk of it, of course, was done by northern and especially by New England craft. The people of that sea-washed "dominion" in large proportion followed the sea. "Every port of the rugged coast," says Mr. Lodge, "had its little town from whose harbor issued the fishermen and coasters, who faced the storms of the North Atlantic, and did as much as any single class to build up the fortunes of the Eastern provinces." The foreign commerce of Boston alone in 1765 employed six hundred vessels, while more than a thousand were engaged in the fishing and coasting trade. The great "Long Wharf" of this old colonial metropolis, pushed out its two thousand feet of length into the blue waters of the beautiful harbor and was covered with handsome and substantial warehouses. From this famous dock sailed many a shrewd and venturesome Yankee skipper in his home-built bark loaded down with the fish of his native shores and bound perhaps for one of the far southern ports of the West India Islands. Arrived at the country of the "Dons" he would exchange his cargo of New England fish for one of West Indian products. This done, instead of returning home, he would steer over-seas to England where the chances were he would dispose of both cargo and vessel at a good round price. Then, chartering an English ship, he would come home laden with British manufactures to find a ready market among his own friends and neighbors and receive their congratulations upon his successful and profitable sea-venture.

The New York colony followed hard upon that of Massachusetts in its growing sea-trade. She had over five hundred vessels employed in the carrying trade; the cry of " From New York bound for " so and so came back in reply to the hail of the passing ship in many a foreign sea. One stout little sloop of scarce eighty tons built in an Albany shipyard made in 1785 the voyage to China and back with success and profit.

New Jersey's trade went out for the most part through New York and Philadelphia, though it carried on a small coasting and river traffic of its own in local ports.

In 1765 Pennsylvania employed in her shipping interests a fleet of nearly five hundred vessels and over seven thousand seamen. Ships were built in Philadelphia dock-yards for the use of the colonial traders and the commerce of the province was its most fruitful source of wealth.

The provinces to the south, as has already been said, depended largely upon northern or English ships for their commercial ventures. With fewer good harbors than had the rugged northern coast the southern cargoes of tobacco and of rice were shipped in English vessels and the arrival of the annual ship from England laden with goods which were sent by the London factor in exchange for a cargo of tobacco was the great event of the year to many a Virginia planter.

The carrying trade of North Carolina, so the journal of the garrulous Colonel William Byrd declares, was "engrossed by the saints of New England who carry off a great deal of tobacco without troubling themselves with paying the impertinent duty of a penny a pound."

The port and harbor of Charleston and the excellent system of trade that existed in that province previous to the Revolution brought in an annual revenue of seven hundred thousand pounds and gave employment to nearly two hundred vessels; and Georgia at the same period, employed in her commercial ventures more than two hundred vessels of which thirty-six were owned in the colony.

Hampered by the restrictive acts of an English parliament which, blind to its own interests, sought to limit and dwarf the growth of its foreign possessions the commerce of the American colonies received again and again blows that would well-nigh have destroyed less energetic and less determined peoples. But the pioneers of America had come to stay, and by fair means or by foul, for it must be admitted that the colonists sought by illegal practices to nullify the decrees of the mother country, its sea-trade grew apace. The ships of the traders and importers of colonial days were, says Mr. McMaster, "to be seen at Surinam, at Hispaniola, at the West Indies, at the Canaries, in the waters of the Mediterranean, and in the waters of the North Sea. Their captains drove bargains in the Levant, and bartered rice and indigo for rum and molasses in Jamaica. They sold great stores of corn at Lisbon and Madrid, and every year brought home five thousand pistoles for the liquor and grain purchased by the Dutch. The New England fleet numbered six hundred sail. The trade of the mother country with her colonies gave employment to eleven hundred ships and twenty-nine thousand sailors."

As for the American seamen of those colonial days we can gather some idea of their nature, their habits and their lives, from the old records that remain and the old stories that have come down to us. It was a time of courage and adventure. Those who came to a new world to try their fortunes must have possessed more of the bold and adventurous spirit than did the stay-at-homes; their sons and grandsons must have inherited some of this bearing, and have attained in the broad, free life of this great wilderness of a country the dash and daring that a hard sea-life requires. This we know the colonial sailors had; and we know too that the great sea that washed the shores near which their homes were built gave careers to a large portion of the boldest and most enterprising part of the population. It was not alone the dare-devils like Captain Argall and Captain Oldham — at times disturbers and at times defenders of the peace of the colonies — whose courage and audacity we remember. We recall also among the mariners of the earliest days the plucky French sailor lad of Ribault's slaughtered Florida colony who, spared by the butcher Menendez because he could play the flute, stole "a little boate" from his captors and pushing out toward Drake's English fleet, playing and rowing alternately, gave that shrill welcome to "the English Dragon" that cost the Spaniards their fort and their treasure chest on the River of Dolphins ; we recall, too, those anxious sailors from " Captaine White, his shipp," who made the Carolina woods echo with the shrill notes of their trumpet call and the dear home songs of England, hoping, yet all in vain, to find by this means their exiled kinsman of the lost colony of Croatan ; we remember the boastful expedition of the " five gentlemen, four maryners and fourteen saylors," of New-

port's Virginia Colony, that sailed away so gloriously up the James in a well-provisioned shallop to find the South Sea, and in less than a week came back again for all the world like the king of France's "forty thousand men" and quite as ingloriously. We remember also the stress and peril of the Sea Adventure, that ship of Sir Thomas Gates the Admiral, freighted with colonists for the Virginia enterprise, and how it was to the account of the storm and wreck as told by Master William Strachey, one of the passengers, that Shakespeare was afterward indebted for the motive of one of his greatest plays,

" The Tempest "; we recall the double defiance which the supercargo Jacob Eelkens in the English ship William and Captain De Vries in his own yacht the Squirrel gave to the fussy and choleric little Dutch director as they sailed past his fort at the Manhattans; how one of the trusty New Haven sailors on Captain George Lamberton's trading ship refused, though persecuted and put in irons, to yield to the bribe of the Swedish governor on the Delaware and accuse his own captain of unlawful measures; how, again and again, the " good Captain William Peirce " in his ship Lion appeared just in the nick of time to re-provision the starving colonists at Plymouth and Boston; how twenty Boston sailors sailed into " the Dutch-man's province " at the mouth of the Connecticut and tearing down the arms of Holland carved in derision on the self-same tree, in place of the shield of the States-General, a great, grinning face; and how, all along the Atlantic seaboard from Pemaquid to Florida, the early colonial sailors learned the dangers of a deadly coast only by bitter experience, shipwreck and death, or risked their all in fishing or trading ventures only to lose it by pirates, by Indian attack, or by the ever-present dangers of the deep. The story of those far-off days is one of mingled loss and gain from which the element of hazard was never absent.

And of the later colonial period, when all along the Atlantic coast the thirteen provinces of England were struggling toward position and independence, much could be written. With slowly developing strength and its attendant factors, trade and commerce, the America of the mid years of the eighteenth century was preparing for that career foreshadowed in the early " seventies " in the now famous prophecy of Timothy Dwight: —

" Here empire's last and brightest throne shall rise,
And peace and right and freedom greet the skies,
To morn's fair realms her trading ships shall sail
Or lift their canvas to the evening gale;
No dangers fright, no ills the course delay,
'Tis virtue prompts, and God directs the way,
And hark! what strange, what solemn breaking strain
Swells, wildly murmuring o'er the far, far main?
Down time's long lessening vale the notes decay,
And lost in distant ages roll away."

Leaving out of the account the warlike record of the American seamen of the later colonial period we find the sailor on coaster and on merchant vessel displaying even then the qualities that have marked the successful sailors of every age and clime. They were brave, as when in 1718, on board his little sloop, Maynard and his twelve Virginia sailors fought in hand-to-hand conflict and utterly defeated the terrible " Blackbeard " and his pirate crew; adventurous, as when in 1685, off the coast of La Plata, William Phips, the Boston ship-builder, bound upon what seemed to soberer men a wild-goose chase, found beneath the waters the wreck of the Spanish treasure-ship he had determined to discover and sailed away with a great store of bullion and of coin; timorous, as when the Providence ship-master Adderly to whom Phips confided a part of the treasure, was so filled with fear lest he be robbed of his cargo and so turned with elation at his success, that he went crazy and died of insanity at Bermuda; bold and determined, as when in 1744 certain New York fishermen, smarting at the recollection of their treatment by the English press-gang attacked and burnt the boats of an English frigate in New York harbor; humorous, even in their revenges, as when in 1757, a kidnaped Boston sailor sprang from his hammock in an English man-o'-war and soundly thrashed the sneaking commander thereof who had a way of spying in disguise among the common seamen of his ship; unscrupulous, as when, again and again, dissatisfied with their trading ventures they would seize their ships and turn rovers and pirates; superstitious, as when, in 1656, certain Maryland sailors conceived that because their unseaworthy vessel had become leaky there must therefore be a witch on board and so incontinently seized and hung poor goody Lee, one of their passengers, and flung her body into the sea; reckless, as when, in 1750, the hot-headed young Ricketts "of the Jerseys" put off from the wharf in New York harbor boldly flying his own " Birdgee flag " and sailed straight under the guns of the British man-o'-war Greyhound in direct defiance of the orders of the Lords of Trade commanding that all colonial vessels should fly a certain " Jack " of their appointing " and none other."

And so, in many a venture and on many a cruise, did the seamen of colonial days brave danger and death according to the varying fashion of their always fearless and sometimes wayward natures. But it was in this very school of experience that they developed and built up that sterling if stubborn character that in later years was to prove in many a sea-fight and on many a dangerous cruise the courage, ability, fearlessness and hardihood of the successful American sailor.

CHAPTER IV.

THERE is no service but has its share of lawlessness. And, firm as is our belief in these soberer nineteenth c e n t u r y days, in the wisdom of living up to the time-honored proverb that "h o n e s t y is the best policy" and to the sterner mandates of the eighth and tenth commandments, there is still to be found amid the mixed revelations of the early days of our national story a picturesqueness even if there can never be rightly discovered a justification in the devious ways of far too many captains, traders, merchants and sailors of colonial times.

This elasticity of morals found its excuse not only in the ways and methods of so-called " Christian " governments, but in the traditions of still earlier days. From antiquity, even, the pirate and the smuggler had been prominent features in the world's story. Greece and Rome had grappled with them in many a Mediterranean sea-fight and all through mediæval times they were now the enemies or now the courted allies of the tyrant states of Europe — themselves little better than banded smugglers or confederated pirates.

Singularly enough, piracy in America owes its origin to the Church. Spain, swooping down upon the Western world made the cross the symbol of possession even more than of proselytism. Backed by the religious edict or "bull" of a Spanish priest who happened to be the ruling pope at Rome, the king of Spain claimed the full proprietorship of America and dared assert his claims against the northern nations of Europe. France, England and the Netherlands at once protected. Discovery incited discovery and the hostile ships of the exploring nations pushed across the Atlantic bent on the double purpose of discovering new lands and defying the arrogance of Spain. England was especially aggressive and captains like Drake and Hawkins sailing under the commission of their sovereign counted every Spanish vessel a lawful prize and made their names the terror of the Spanish Main.

"The Queen of England," declared the royal Elizabeth, herself the chief instigator and abettor of this international sea-feud, "cannot understand why her subjects, or those of any other European prince should be debarred from traffic in the West Indies. As she does not acknowledge the Spaniards to have any title to any portion of the New World by the donation of the Bishop of Rome, so she knows no right they have to any places other than those of which they are in actual possession. Their having touched only here and there upon a coast, and given names to a few rivers and capes, are such insignificant things as can in no way entitle them to a property in those parts, any further than where they have actually settled and continue to inhabit."

With the least shadow of authority as an excuse men will

go to almost any length. That these legalized freebooters went at last to the length of a lawless and bloody piracy is the fault of those same Christian nations that, sanctioning them at first, sought in time, though almost ineffectually, to lay the storm they had raised.

The first discoverers had little respect for the claims of rival discoverers; the navigators who followed them and the

explorers who succeeded the navigators, in the absorbing search for gold, merged all their lesser desires into that of a conqueror, and a conqueror respects nothing but the heavy hand of a still stronger power. Finally, the struggle for possession in the New World resolved itself into a death-grapple between Spain and her rivals of Northern Europe. And even this waxed strongest and fiercest between England and Spain — bitter and unrelenting foemen in all that men held dear in honor or sacred in religion. "Spanish bloodhounds and English mastiffs" came to the tug of war in many a sharp sea-fight upon the Spanish Main. The picture that Kingsley draws of one of these same sea-fights in his story of "Westward Ho!" is not too realistic in its stirring lines: —

"Now then!" roared Amyas. "Fire and with a will! Have at her, archers: have at her, muskets all!" and in an instant a storm of bar and chain shot, round and cannister, swept the Don from stem to stern, while through the white cloud of smoke the musket-balls and the still deadlier cloth-yard arrows whistled and rushed upon their venomous errand. Down went the steersman, and every soul who manned the poop. Down went the mizzen topmast, in went the stern windows and quarter galleries; and as the smoke cleared away, the gorgeous painting of the Madre Dolorosa, with her heart full of seven swords, which in a gilded frame, bedizened the Spanish stern, was shivered in splinters; while most glorious of all, the golden flag of Spain, which the last moment flaunted above their heads, hung trailing in the water. The ship, her tiller shot away, and her helmsman killed, staggered helplessly a moment, and then fell up into the wind. "Well done, men of Devon!" shouted Amyas, as cheers rent the welkin. . . . . They grappled! . . . . . And then began a fight most fierce and fell: the Spaniards according to their fashion, attempting to board; the English, amid fierce shouts of 'God and the Queen!' 'God and St. George for England!' sweeping them back by showers of arrows and musket balls, thrusting them down with pikes, hurling grenades from the tops; while the swivels on both sides poured their grape, and bar, and chain, and the great maindeck guns thundering muzzle to muzzle made both ships quiver and recoil, as they smashed the round shot through and through each other. . . . . . So it raged for an hour or more, till all arms were weary, and all tongues clove to the mouth. . . . . . Thrice the Spaniards clambered on board the Rose; and thrice surged back before that deadly hail. . . . . . At last there was a lull in the wild storm. No shot was heard from the Spaniards' upper deck. . . . . . The Madre Dolorosa was heeling fast over to leeward. Her masts were all sloping forward, swifter and swifter — the end thus was come! . . . . . . The English cut away, and the Rose, released from the strain, shook her feathers on the wave-crest like a freed sea-gull, while all men held their breaths. . . . . . The Spaniard righted; but only for a moment and there, under the flag of Spain, stood the tall captain, his left hand on the standard staff, his sword pointed in his right. . . . . . She gave one awful lunge forward and dived under the coming swell. Nothing but the point of her poop remained, and there still stood the stern and steadfast Don, cap-a-pie in his glistening black armor, while over him the flag, which claimed the empire of both worlds, flaunted its gold aloft and upward in the glare of the tropic noon. . . . . A wild figure sprang out of the mass of sailors who struggled amid the foam, and rushed upward at the Spaniard. It was Michael Heard. The Don plunged his sword in the old man's body; but the hatchet gleamed, nevertheless; down went the blade through headpiece and through head; and as Heard sprung onward, bleeding but alive, the steel-clad corpse rattled down the deck into the surge. Two more strokes struck with the fury of a dying man, and the standard-staff was hewn through. Old Michael collected all his strength, hurled the flag far from the sinking ship, and then stood erect one moment and shouted 'God save Queen

Bess!' . . . . Another moment and the gulf had swallowed his victim and him and nothing remained of the Madre Dolorosa but a few floating spars, while a great awe fell upon all men, and a solemn silence."

It was by such fierce sea-fights as this — stern, stubborn and to the death — that England gained and maintained for many a year her supremacy of the seas, when the bloody ways of Spain in those cruel days of religious jealousies and bitter hatreds wrought all men up to the white heat of indignation and revenge. That other picture in Kingsley's graphic narrative telling how the English sailors surprised and took the great Spanish galleon off the coast of New Grenada, has in it quite as much of fact as of fiction. There is, too, even more of stern reality than of the novelist's romance in the terrible oath of Amyas Leigh as on the deck of the conquered galleon he heard the horrible story of how the Inquisition did to death the English seamen captured on the Spanish Main: —

" Harken to me, my masters all," he said, pale but stern of face, "and may God harken too and do so to me, and more also, if, as long as I have eyes to see a Spaniard, and hands to hew him down, I do any other thing than hunt down that accursed nation day and night, and avenge all the innocent blood which has been shed by them since the day in which King Ferdinand drove out the Moors! Henceforth till I die, no quarter to a Spaniard!"

To show how, through suffering and balked revenge and loss of all but life, this valiant sea-dog and hater of Spain learned even to forgive the nation against whom he had sworn so fearful an oath is by no means the least of the noble motives that mark this greatest of Kingsley's romances; but the oath serves also to show the spirit that animated the foemen who in the last quarter of the sixteenth century met in many a death grapple upon the Spanish Main.

But though England was foremost in this never-flagging hostility her neighbors of Northern Europe, though rivals in other matters, were her aiders and abbetors in this hatred of Spain. "A sailor in those days," says Mr. Shaw, "was expert with his weapons, and was almost a fighting man by trade. Spanish monopolies were the pest of every port from Mexico to Cape Horn; and the seamen who sailed the Caribbean were filled with a natural hatred of everything Spanish." So it came to pass that English, French and Dutch sea-captains made common cause against the cruisers and galleons of Spain and from this hostility sprung the Buccaneers.*

"The pleasures of a roving life grew to have for these alert and aggressive seamen a greater attraction than did a sober mercantile venture to friendly ports while the monotony of the routine was," according to Mr. Shaw, "broken by occasional skirmishes organized and led by Spanish officials. Out of such conditions," he continues, "arose the Buccaneer, alternately sailor and hunter, even occasionally a planter — roving, bold, not overscrupulous and not unfrequently savage, with an intense detestation of the power and the representatives of Spain."

It is a strange and altogether picturesque phase of American sailor-life that is furnished by the story of the rise and power of the Buccaneers. Banded together in a common purpose they became Americans all, sinking their several European nationalities in their mutual desires, and with something of the patriot in their uncompromising opposition to Spanish tyranny.

* The smugglers of the Spanish Main were accustomed to provision their ships at the island of St. Domingo because of its abundance of wild cattle. The flesh of these cattle was preserved by a crude treatment of fire and smoke by the natives of the island in their "curing huts" or *boucans*. The freebooters learning the process of "boucanning" from the natives finally received the name of "boucanniers" or "buccaneers."

But with each success they grew more hazardous. Thus was engendered a spirit of lawlessness until finally the Buccaneers lost the sturdy manliness of the sea-rover in the greed of the freebooter. For fully a century they held unquestioned power upon the Spanish Main — now the victors and now the vanquished in many a stubborn sea-fight. In time they combined their forces alike from politic motives and for mutual defence; they rendezvoused in certain of the smaller West Indian islands, fortifying some and colonizing others, and became the main reliance of the rivals of Spain in attempts upon Spain's American possessions. France, with their help, wrested the Tortugas from their Spanish masters; England, aided by them, conquered the Island of Jamaica. They have given a romantic, if bloody interest to every port and island on the Southern Seas from the capes of Florida to the mouth of the Amazon. At the height of their power (from 1671 to 1685) they were the undisputed dictators of the Caribbean, the acknowledged scourge of the Spanish American trade and dominions; and, crossing the isthmus, they made their name a terror along the Pacific coast from California to Chili.

Their career was full of brilliant successes and questionable actions, in which chivalry and brutality, munificence and greed were strangely mixed. The great expedition of their greatest commander, Captain Henry Morgan the Welshman, by which in 1671 with a fleet of thirty-nine vessels and a crew of two thousand men he conquered Panama and spread terror and death throughout the Spanish-American provinces was at once the most daring and the most important of the banded enterprises of these Free Lances of the Southern Seas. Marauder and murderer though he was, Morgan was at once a shrewd and able leader and ended his eventful career in honor and position,

"THE CURSE OF PIRATES."

becoming — by favor of his backer and (so it was charged) his business partner King Charles the Second of England — the governor of an English province and owner of the title of " Sir " Henry Morgan.

But such a continued reign of lawless and unlicensed power as was enjoyed by the Buccaneers was certain to fall at last. Public opinion and the better judgment of the very nations that upheld it were sure to work its ruin. The growth of a friendlier international feeling brought it into discredit. The courts of Europe grappled with the problem and finally by the peace of Ryswick in 1697, which changed so completely the whole status of colonial affairs in America, the confederacy of the Buccaneers was practically broken up and its scattered elements fell to the next lower position in the descending scale of ocean crime — that of piracy.

But, before we leave this picturesque era of the American pirate — for there was a time in the earliest days of the "ocean free-lance" when, as one author maintains, "the spirit of buccaneering approached in some degree to the spirit of chivalry in point of adventure " — we may linger awhile over the picture which Kingsley has drawn for us of the manner and the valor of these "avengers" as they termed themselves. Gentle English parson though he was, he could see the picturesque where a less artistic eye could only see the prosaic — the bold criminality of a lawless band of thieves. How deftly has he turned our sterner sense of justice into an almost unlawful sympathy, in his sigh of " The Last Buccaneer ": —

> " Oh, England is a pleasant place for them that's rich and high,
> But England is a cruel place for such poor folks as I ;
> And such a port for mariners I ne'er shall see again
> As the pleasant Isle of Avès, beside the Spanish Main.

"There were forty craft in Avès that were both swift and stout,
All furnished well with small arms and cannons round about;
And a thousand men in Avès made laws so fair and free
To choose their valiant captains and obey them cheerfully.

"Thence we sailed against the Spaniard, with his hoards of plate and gold,
Which he wrung with cruel tortures from the Indian folk of old;
Likewise the merchant captains, with hearts as hard as stone,
Who flog men and keel-haul them, and starve them to the bone.

"Oh, the palms grew high in Avès, and fruits that shone like gold,
And the colibris and parrots they were gorgeous to behold;
And the negro maids of Avès from bondage fast did flee,
To welcome gallant sailors, a-sweeping in from sea.

"Oh, sweet it was in Avès to hear the landward breeze,
A-swing with good tobacco in a net between the trees,
With a negro lass to fan you, while you listened to the roar
Of the breakers on the reef outside, that never touched the shore.

"But Scripture saith, an ending to all fine things must be,
So the king's ships sailed on Avès, and quite put down were we;
All day we fought like bull-dogs, but they burst the booms at night;
And I fled in a piragua, sore wounded, from the fight.

"Nine days I floated starving, a negro lass beside,
Till for all I tried to cheer her, the poor young thing she died;
But as I lay a-gasping a Bristol sail came by,
And brought me home to England here, to beg until I die.

"And now I'm old and going — I'm sure I don't know where;
One comfort is the world's so hard, I can't be worse off there;
If I might be a sea-dove, I'd fly across the main,
To the pleasant Isle of Avès to see it once again."

The king's ships did indeed "sail on Avès" and many another buccaneering port and the scattered bands of freebooters fleeing from the vengeance of their pursuers left the harried channels of the Spanish Main and distributed themselves along the entire American coasts, on either side the continent.

Driven to desperation by the change in their standing before the world they became pirates pure and simple and the glamour that had nimbused the buccaneer was lost in the brutality of the detested pirate.

Scarcely a port on the Atlantic coast in the colonial days but felt alike the pest and the profit of piracy. For it must be admitted that in far too many instances the pirate had his backer in some highly-respectable gentleman of means and position in the colonies who, equally guilty with his outlawed partner, shared the profit but not the perils of sea-robbery, plunder and crime.

There may, as has been shown, be conceded to the Buccaneers a certain excuse for their depredations upon Spanish commerce and even in their lawless acts may be found the basis of patriotism that had its place in those days of brutal international feud; but the spirit of chivalry that bound the buccaneering bands in the earlier days of their illegal forays gradually disappeared as their brotherhood declined from fighters to freebooters and the independence and rude honor that had marked the days of their supremacy degenerated at last into unmitigated vice and brutality.

Out of this condition sprung the pirate. Lawless, vindictive, greedy, cruel and savage the pirate of the past had not one of the redeeming traits of courage or lavish munificence that forms the inspiration of far too many of the stories and sketches that find an entrance into the literature for the young. The ideal pirate of the pages of fiction and the legends that gave these fictions life was a haughty, dark-browed, foreign-looking gentleman of great personal strength and with a personal exterior combining ferocity, fearlessness and force. The real pirate was in fact a coward and a craven. Scarcely one of the stories of fabulous wealth or princely gains accumulated by these salt-water burglars will bear investigation and a career of crime once begun as it took from the sailor who thus yielded to temptation all his manliness and all his better nature gave him in place of courage a blustering bravado and in lieu of the frankness of the seaman the craven brutality of the sea-thief.

And yet as the Church was in a measure responsible for the buccaneers, society was responsible for the pirates. The exigencies of trade yielded but slow profits to the colonial merchants and shopkeepers whereas their investments in piracy permitted them to purchase in a low market and sell in a high one. "Piratic expeditions," declared King William of England in the year 1695 to the Earl of Bellomont, "are fitted out from the colonies of New England and Virginia; and even the Quakers of Pennsylvania afford a market for their robberies."

Such, in fact, was the case. From Maine to Georgia every seaport town of the colonies was under the spell of the pirate. Newport, we are told, was reckoned as "a nest of corsairs"; the little ports of the Long Island coast harbored many a piratical captain who bought immunity from the English governors of New York by gifts and percentage. "The curse of pirates," says Mr. Lodge, "fell heavily upon Philadelphia. These outlaws brought trade and specie to the struggling colonists, whose virtue was not proof against the temptation. The pirate Evans," he declares, "owned land in Philadelphia, and the famous Blackbeard traded in their shops; while even the family of Penn's deputy, Markham, was mixed up with these illicit dealings." Further to the south Annapolis and Baltimore knew all too intimately the wiles and ways of the seductive sea-thieves; in North Carolina Captain Teach, the redoubtable "Blackbeard," had his headquarters; the secretary of the province was his ally and even the governor was corrupted; the port of Charleston was a favorite trading port with the pirates of the coast, " where," says Mr. Lodge, " they were popular and well-received because they spent money, and brought thither their ill-gotten gains to enrich the colony."

Around the names and fortunes of these lawless ocean rob-

THE PIRATE OF ROMANCE.

bers legend and romance have thrown a misty fascination. Their deeds and their daring have been magnified, their lives have been woven into song and story, their covetousness, brutality, cowardice and crime have spun themselves into heroics and lost all their repellent features in the atmosphere of excitement and mystery that has surrounded their memories. But stripped of all this fanciful adorning the pirate of "ye olden time" was but a low-lived, wicked and unattractive man. Captain William Kidd, greatest of all in name and renown, is now declared to have been in reality no pirate at all. His story is one of misery and failure from beginning to end. A New York merchant-captain with an hitherto honorable record, he sailed away in command of a piratical expedition against piracy. " By attacking the pirates," said King William to the Earl of Bellemont, governor of the New York province, "we shall accomplish a double object. We shall in the first place check their devastating operations, and we shall also fill our purses with the proceeds of the abundant spoil with which their ships are laden." With this questionable though kingly design as part of his sailing orders Kidd put to sea. A more dreary and less romantic voyage was never sailed. Unsuccessful from the very start Kidd's adventure ended in ignominy, disgrace and failure and his career had none of the brilliant exploits and none of the fabulous successes that have always been a part of his accepted story. The tales of buried booty that have marked the Atlantic coast with credulous treasure seekers digging for " Kidd's money" were all of them without foundation and his trial and execution were not for piracy but for the murder of a mutinous and insubordinate mate. There is every reason to believe that he died as a sort of scapegoat for certain highplaced and aristocrat partners in a scheme of plunder and a careful study of his case forces one to accept the opinion of Mr. Fernow who declares that " to-day that which was meted out to Kidd might hardly be called justice; for it seems questionable if he had ever been guilty of piracy."

But there were hundreds of others who were even more guilty than was Kidd and richly deserved a similar fate. The sea swarmed with these lawless characters and scarcely a voyage was attempted in those closing years of the seventeenth century in which "capture by pirates" was not the greatest risk that the voyager or the passenger ran.

But, though they were the terror of the seas, not one of these pirate captains did not lead a miserable and forlorn existence as far removed from the exaggerated stories of daring, excitement and success as can well be conceived. Avery and Stede Bonnet, Teach or "Blackbeard," Hawkins and Pond, Phillips and Few and others whose names are less familiar, ran their careers of crime in partnership, often, with men of position and influence in the colonies. Their successes were in much less degree than rumor has created for them and their ends in almost every instance were miserable and far from heroic. The piratical chapter in the story of the American sailor is one in which no lover of the sea and its dangers can take any pride and the possibility for its existence and long continuance is a sad commentary on the "crooked" business methods of "our honored ancestors."

Piracy on the high seas was at last stamped out alike by public opinion and by official vigilance. But illicit trading on the seas was not so easily ended. Piracy degenerated into the third and lowest phase of sea-crime — smuggling, and the descendants of the chivalric buccaneers became at last little more than craven sneak-thieves of the ocean.

For this again the State was largely responsible. The restrictions which England placed upon the commerce of its colonies were especially galling to a people whose sea-traffic was so full of promise and profit as was that of the coast-line colonies of America. In New England, in the middle of the eighteenth century, more people were engaged in ship-building and in navigation than in agriculture, and Massachusetts is said to have owned one vessel for every hundred of its inhabitants. When, therefore, Great Britain attempted by arbitrary laws to restrict the commerce of her American colonies decreeing by statute that nothing was to be allowed to be imported into a British "plantation" save in English-built vessels and by crews

A SMUGGLER.

three fourths of which must be English the Americans not only protested but proceeded to take matters into their own hands. Openly evading or secretly resisting the laws of the mother country they "smuggled in" the goods they desired to possess without the payment of the required duties and in direct defiance of the laws of England.

This secret traffic was carried on in every Atlantic port. The colonists became, in fact, "a nation of law-breakers."

"Nine tenths of their merchants," declares Mr. Wells,* "were smugglers. One quarter of all the signers of the Declaration of Independence were bred to commerce, to the command of ships and to contraband trade. Hancock, Trumbull (Brother Jonathan) and Hamilton were all known to be cognizant of or participants in contraband transactions or approved of them.

* See Chapter I of "Our Merchant Marine," by David A. Wells.

Hancock was the prince of contraband traders, and with John Adams as his counsel was appointed for trial before the Admiralty court in Boston, at the exact hour of the shedding of blood at Lexington, in a suit for five hundred thousand dollars penalties alleged to have been incurred by him as a smuggler."

But out of flagrant misdoings sometimes spring great results. Smuggling, originally participated in by the few for the sole purpose of gain and as the direct descendant of a stamped-out piracy grew at last into one of the principal methods by which an armed people protested against tyranny.

England's arbitrary laws by which she sought to cripple and restrict the native commerce of her colonies worked their own ruin by driving even the most loyal colonists into open violation of the law and were, in fact, one of the leading causes of the American Revolution.

The buccaneers, the pirates and the smugglers of colonial days though they were the negative and darker side of the life of the early American seaman still played their part in the process of his natural strengthening and development. The "tangled skein of good and ill" that enters into the lives of nations as well as of individuals has its place in a very marked degree in the make-up of the sailor. Temptation to wrong-doing is always strongest where the hardships of life are most aggressively present. The sea and its risks, the circumscribed life on ship-board and the lawless natures that, in those earlier days, were always to be found in every ship's crew all tended to weaken integrity when temptation came to suggest and allure. Mutiny and intimidation were ever-present possibilities for which the sea-captain must be prepared. "You are ruining us all," said mutinous William Moore to Captain Kidd, when

that vacillating skipper hesitated to attack a Dutch East
Indiaman. "You are keeping us in beggary and starvation.
But for your whims we might all be prosperous and rich."
And though the irate skipper forcibly reproved the abusive
gunner with an all too-handy bucket, and

"Murdered William Moore as I sailed, as I sailed,"

he still felt bound to consider and finally yielded to the clamors
of his men. In like manner many a master was forced into
piracy and smuggling by a lawless crew, or argued into it by
a covetous partner on land. The risks that were run and the
certainty of final detection and punishment counted for but
little to the men whose daily lives were a constant hazard amid
all the dangers and excitements of a treacherous and unstable
ocean.

CHAPTER V.

THE conflicting elements that entered into the occupation and colonization of the American coasts made sea-struggles inevitable. England, France, Holland and Spain endeavoring to achieve leadership alike in Europe and on the sea were in direct and constant antagonism. Claiming each the right of occupation in the new world their war-vessels and their privateers were always on the lookout for hostile sail and the story of American colonization is punctuated with sea-fights and naval battles.

In this school the American trader was early trained to a life of struggle. The colonial armadas sailing under orders for the capture of hostile settlements or the destruction of hostile fleets were often on the sea while the seaward-looking fort or the slender watch-tower, reared for the purpose of discovering the approach of the ships of the enemy were features of every seaport settlement.

It was the fleet of the Spanish Menendez that brought dismay and death to the French Huguenot colony on the Florida sands; in the fleet of the French commander, Gourges, came the avenging nemesis that slaughtered the Spanish colony of Menendez on that same Florida coast. It was the English captain Argall, half pirate, half soldier, who bore down in his little fleet upon the rival settlements to the north of Virginia pillaging and burning the huts of the French fishermen in Acadia and bullying the Dutch traders at the Manhattans. It was the Swedish captain Rysingh who sailing into the Delaware drove away the Dutch holders of Fort Casimir; it was the Dutch fleet from New Amsterdam that not two years later sailed to the south and conquered the only attempt at Swedish colonization made in America.

As colonization increased the disputes between the "parent" governments as to the boundaries and rights of occupation grew more fierce, but between none was the controversy more stubborn than between France and England. National feud was emphasized by personal quarrels. The dwellers on the American coast catching the spirit of resistance mingled political rivalries with personal ventures and alike French and English privateers sailed out of colonial ports to worry the commerce of their rivals upon the high seas or to descend with murderous intent upon unprotected settlements and illy defended ports. The spirit of the seventeenth and eighteenth centuries was one of personal conflict.

This era of antagonism though lawless and bloody proved also an excellent school for the sailor. It developed the fearless spirit in men and where the sailor must also be the fighter it made him watchful and wary, acquainted him with all the risks and hazards of a precarious existence and laid the foundation for a hardy, intrepid and excellently drilled race of seamen.

The New England colonies, for the most part, furnished the sea-fighters for the side of England; the Canadian ports supplied them for the cause of France. Castine and Pemaquid, on the broken Maine coast, strongly fortified by either nation were, according to Mr. Drake, "the mailed hands of each nationality, always clinched to strike."

Gradually as colonization grew the individual fighters combined for some special or carefully-planned expedition of attack, and colonial fleets, sailing now to the north or now to the south, developed into armadas for the reduction of certain of the stronger sea-fortresses of France or of England.

At first the feuds were personal rather than political. Such were the exploits of Sir Francis Drake against the poor little Spanish settlement on the River of Dolphins in 1586; of that unruly crew of Sir Humphrey Gilbert's ship, the Swallow, who in 1583 attacked, dismantled, robbed and "marooned" the crew of a French fishing vessel; of such "colonials" as Captain Hewes, the doughty Cape Ann fisherman who dared defy the choleric Captain Miles Standish; of the factious supercargo Eelkins who ran the wordy blockade of the "comic-opera" governor of Dutch New York, the Heer Van Twiller; of the blustering Captain Clayborne in the Chesapeake — Virginia against Maryland; of Richard Ingle, of Holmes and Winthrop and rascally Captain Oldham. But at last out of these private quarrels came the more pretentious expeditions by sea for the purposes of siege, reduction and capture.

First among these, in the order of time, was that authorized voyage of Captain Samuel Argall who, after his perfidious personal attack on Mount Desert in 1613 was, in that same year, dispatched by Governor Dale of the Virginia colony to complete his work of "punishing" the French. With three vessels

as his little fleet he sailed northward, ravaged and destroyed the
settlements at Mount Desert and Saint Croix and then, crossing to Port Royal, completed his errand of plunder. Leaving
the poor colonists to shift for themselves he sailed homeward
to Virginia pluming himself mightily upon having done a great
and glorious deed " for church and king."

Next, in 1636, came the semi-naval expedition of the Massachusetts colonists against the Indians of Block Island and Connecticut. This was under the command of grim old Governor
Endicott —

> " A grave, strong man, who for good or ill
> Held his trust with an iron will."

His trust in this matter was evidently "for ill," for it resulted
in a bloody and relentless Indian war from which the struggling
colonists suffered long and piteously.

The feuds of the French governors in Acadia, La Tour and
D'Aulnay — rivals alike in love and in dominion — renewed the
trouble along the northeastern coast and led to a Yankee expedition by sea hired by La Tour to help him against his rival.
This sailed from Boston in 1644, but returned rather ingloriously after destroying only a mill and some standing corn upon
D'Aulnay's plantation. For this assault D'Aulnay took dire
vengeance. Sailing with a flotilla and five hundred men against
La Tour's fort at St. John he reduced it, notwithstanding its
brave defence by the heroic Madame La Tour — known to
romance as Constance of Acadia — who died, only a few weeks
after her defeat, of shame and mortification over D'Aulnay's
success.

In 1654 there sailed from Nantasket, in Boston harbor, a
Yankee armada for the subjugation of the French possessions

in Maine. It consisted of four vessels and was under the command of Major Robert Sedgwick and Captain John Leverett —"two as marked men," says Drake, "as could be found in New England." This little armada had first been designed for the reduction of the Dutch settlements at the Manhattans, but peace having been concluded between Holland and England

ON THE WAY TO ACADIA.

the Puritans, Mr. Drake declares, "with true thrift launched their armament against the unsuspecting mounseers of Penobscot."

This expedition resulted in the temporary possession of Acadia by the English. The country was restored to France by the treaty of Breda in 1668. But the success of this expedition inflamed the New England colonists with that insatiable desire for the possession of Canada and more especially of Acadia * that ended only with the reduction of Louisburg and the capitulation of Quebec.

And now a new figure finds place in America's sea story — William Phips, the first native American sailor of note and renown. Born in 1651 on the rocky Maine sea coast near the mouth of the Kennebec the record of his adventurous life, almost from boyhood, reads more like a romance than sober history. One of the youngest children in a family of twenty-six, reared amid all the hardships and limitations of a frontiersman's home in those old days of bitter struggle this illiterate shepherd boy and ship-builder's apprentice rose in less than twenty years to the foremost position in the American colonies. Gaining fame and fortune " by fishing for shipwrecked treasure among the rocks and shallows of the Spanish Main " he was knighted by his king, led the first Yankee armada against the French power in Canada and received by royal appointment the post of " Captain General and Governor-in-chief of the Province of Massachusetts Bay in New England " — a dominion extending from Long Island Sound to the banks of the St. Lawrence. His life was full of adventure. Almost his first exploit was to rescue from Maine savages the fleeing fugitives of the Kennebec settlements and to bear them to a place of safety upon a ship that he himself had but just built. In the sharpest pressure of poverty he prophesied to his wife that he would yet obtain command of a king's ship and build for her " a fair brick house in the Green Lane of North Boston." And this he did within less than five years.

* By Acadia is to be understood the section now embraced in Nova Scotia, New Brunswick and the greater part of the State of Maine (east of the Kennebec).

He had long dreamed of recovering from the sea the sunken treasure of the Spanish galleons that had gone down amid the wreck and disaster of the stormy Spanish Main. Following up certain reports that had reached him he was at last able to vaguely locate one of these treasure wrecks off the South American port and thereupon boldly proceeded to England and laid his plans before the Admiralty Board.

The Quixotic scheme of an unknown New England sea-captain, by some mysterious means (perhaps because of his very bluntness and audacity *) secured attention and before the close of the year 1684 he was appointed to the command of the Rose Algier, a ship of eighteen guns with a crew of ninety-five men.

The story of his treasure-hunt is remarkable. With the most meagre information as to the position of the wrecked galleon, with an unruly and mutinous crew, amid all the dangers of Spanish attack and capture, with repeated failures to hinder and dismay he nevertheless stuck to his work manfully, finally discovered the wreck and fished up after only three days' work, bullion and coin to the amount of three hundred thousand pounds, besides precious stones and other valuable freight.

The partners in this remarkable enterprise took the lion's share in the returns and Phips after the accounts were all settled had as his portion of the prize only about sixteen thousand pounds and a gold cup for his wife. But King James gave him also the empty honor of knighthood and the promise of public position in England and this, in those days, was esteemed a just reward. Sir William, however, was loyal to his home-land.

* "Possibly the king intrusted to him," says Dr. Ellis, "besides the search for the sunken treasure, some other business on the high seas of a sort not to be entered on papers."

Returning to New England he built the brick house in Boston that he had promised his wife and was appointed by the king High Sheriff of New England.

In 1690 began the long series of European wars that lasted for nearly a century. They fell upon the colonies in America as border wars, as race wars and culminated finally in the successful struggle of the Revolution. King William's war, growing out of the revolt against the Stuart rule in England in 1688 and the occupation of the British throne by William of Holland, embroiled especially France and England and led to a struggle for colonial possessions in America. New England ached to attack Canada. Acadia as the nearest colony of France received the first blow. Its reduction was decreed by Massachusetts.

On the twenty-second of March, 1690, the General Court appointed Sir William Phips to the chief command of an expedition "against Nova 'Scotia and L'Acadie" and "of the shipping and seamen employed therein." Soldiers and sailors were enlisted for the enterprise and on the twenty-eighth of April the Massachusetts "fleet," consisting of one frigate of forty guns, a sloop of sixteen and one of eight guns besides four smaller vessels sailed from Nantasket for the ports in Acadia. Seven hundred men were embarked on this fleet of invasion which had orders to "assault, kill and utterly extirpate the common enemy and to burn and demolish their fortifications and shipping."

Acadia fell an easy prey to Sir William Phips, his seamen and his landsmen. Its coast-line was long, its defences few and imperfect. Port Royal (now Annapolis in Nova Scotia) its most important settlement was but poorly fortified. It yielded at the first assault and the entire Acadian coast from

Port Royal to Penobscot was speedily subdued and became a possession of England.

As to the "seamen and landsmen" attached to this first important expedition against Canada little is to be said in their favor beyond conceding to them bravery and determination. In manner and methods their conduct was quite within the line of that school of privateering and semi-piracy which largely governed the sea-struggle of their time. This expedition against Acadia was simply legalized plunder. The spoils of war were lawful property and many a New England home was enriched by the plundered possessions of Acadian firesides. As Mr. Bowen remarks "this doughty band seem to have plundered even the kitchens."

The complete success of this first expedition inspired the English colonists to a second and still more daring enterprise. This was nothing short of the complete subjugation of Canada. France must be driven from the American continent. There were soldiers and sailors in plenty who would rally for such an endeavor, and the success of Phips in Acadia proved what united action on the part of the colonists could achieve in the larger field of Canada. This was the popular opinion and it was speedily acted upon. Governor Leisler of the province of New York was the chief instigator of the enterprise and a colonial congress — prophecy of the historic congress of a century later — summoned at his call determined upon union of action. A force of five thousand men was raised for the invasion overland, supplemented by the alliance of fifteen hundred braves of the Iroquois. Quebec was to be the chief point of attack. Sir William Phips was given command of the expedition by sea and in the month of August, 1690, a pretentious fleet of thirty-two "extemporized war-ships" and a force of twenty-two hundred men — the largest colonial expedition yet attempted—sailed to the north from Nantasket, in Boston harbor.

How much sound sense lies in that old line of Massinger's,—

Inflated with their minor successes the colonies thought to achieve great things. But they were not yet ready for union. Their counsels were not fraternal. Local jealousies prevented unity of action. The land forces, wasting their time on petty and personal quarrels, miserably failed in co-operation. Montreal which was to be their first and peculiar prey was not even invested. The army of the colonies melted away so completely in the Champlain woods that the spies of the French commander could not discover even a trace of the invaders and Governor Leisler's military administration though conceded to be both " vigorous and spirited "* was rendered ineffective by the bickerings and jealousies of his allies and subordinates.

Deprived of the land support, the naval expedition under the command of Sir William Phips came to equal grief. In many respects this first important Yankee armada was a copy in miniature of its great Spanish prototype of a century before, when " Castile's black fleet " sailed northward for the conquest of England.

Like that, this later armada was born of bigotry and greed. The destruction of the Romish power in Canada and the control of the cod-fishery were its underlying motives. Prayers for its success, says Bancroft, " went up, morning and evening, from every hearth in New England." But this success was not to be. Lacking pilots who knew the devious ways of the St.

* Beside the land forces the New York colony through the energy of Governor Leisler contributed three vessels to the Boston fleet. The largest of this naval contingent was a well-built ship carrying twenty guns and was the first man-of-war ever fitted out in the harbor of New York. While the Boston vessels came back bootyless the New York " squadron " brought back to that city several valuable prizes.

"OGLETHORPE FOUGHT HIS WAY THROUGH THE ENEMY'S FLEET."

Lawrence channel, the fleet felt its way slowly up the broad river; the small-pox came as an ally to the French and even the elements rose to disturb and annoy. When at last Quebec was reached the French defences were found to have been thoroughly strengthened. Neither by a naval bombardment nor by a land attack was the flag of France to be dislodged from the embattled cliffs of Quebec, and the fiery Frontenac flung his contemptuous defiance in the face of the New England admiral. Disheartened and defeated Phips gave orders to retire and the fleet sailed homeward. A great storm arose to cripple and disperse it.

Here again was the story of the Spanish Armada repeated. Only the wreck of an ambitious expedition reached Boston. One vessel was lost never to be heard of more. Another, grounding on Anticosti, lost fifty-four of its sixty men. The six remaining sailors suffered incredible hardships and only reached Boston after a voyage of fifty-four days in a little skiff. Still another vessel was destroyed by fire and four ships were blown so far from the coast that they did not reach Boston until six weeks after the return of the fleet and when they had long been given up as lost.

The much-vaunted expedition was a failure and the colonists who had entered into it with so much of zeal now bewailed the financial burdens that this disaster entailed : but after the selfish manner of their day, they bewailed still more " this awful frown of God." It is safe to say however that the jubilant Frenchmen along the St. Lawrence held this same frown to be for them, instead, a merited and Divine smile. After all there is great truth in the words of Montaigne : People give the name of zeal to their propensity to mischief and violence, though it is not the cause but their interest that inflames them.

The discomfiture and chagrin that filled the Eastern colonies after the disastrous return of Phips' armament led to much boasting; but until the year 1704 little real action, so far as naval attempts against Canada were concerned, is recorded. In that year Colonel Thomas Church of the Massachusetts colony headed an expedition against Port Royal, now again in French hands. It proved an utter failure. So too did a second expedition sent from Boston in 1707 and it is asserted that the inglorious return of the invaders stirred even the staid and sober women of Boston-town to protests. " Why," one of them is reported to have exclaimed, when Captain Cyprian Southack and his " Province Galley " came sailing back, " our Cowards imagined that the Fort at Port Royal would fall before them like the walls of Jericho!" And another severe and sarcastic matron replied " Why did not the Blockheads then stay out Seven Days to see? What ail'd the Traitors to come away in Five Days' time after they got there?"

But failure is, we are told, " the highway to success." The Eastern colonists knew that there could be for them no safety until this " hornets' nest " in Nova Scotia was taken and in October, 1710, a final expedition sailed from Boston to Port Royal. This squadron consisted of six English and thirty colonial vessels manned by seamen and soldiers from Massachusetts, New Hampshire and Connecticut to whom were joined five hundred Royal Marines. This force meant business. So the French regarded it. The fortress at Port Royal was surrendered after a brief siege, the inhabitants in the vicinity were forced to take the oath of allegiance to the English Queen and that sovereign lady's name was given to the old French post which became thereafter and for all time Annapolis.

As in the day of Sir William Phips, success again led to

rashness. The fall of Port Royal awoke the old desire for all Canada. A strong memorial was addressed to the queen begging her "in compassion to her plantations to send an armament against Canada," and as a result there sailed from Boston harbor on the thirteenth of July, 1711, a fleet of fifteen English war-vessels with forty transports and a following of colonial sail. Captain Cyprian Southack, whose " Province Galley " on its return from that second unsuccessful attempt on Port Royal had aroused the ire of the women of Boston, was to retrieve his honor by leading the van as the fleet sailed up the St. Lawrence. There were five regiments of Marlborough's veterans in the fleet and the entire force of seven thousand men, half regulars and half provincials, was under the command of Admiral Sir Hovenden Walker.

As before, also, a land force from the middle colonies — consisting of fifteen hundred men and eight hundred Iroquois allies — was to invade Canada from the Champlain wilderness and conquer Montreal. So sure of success were all concerned that the English minister of war declared that "at last you may depend upon our being masters of all North America."

All bombast again. On the twenty-second of August the fleet feeling its way up the St. Lawrence was enveloped in a dense fog driven upon it by a strong east wind. The vessels driven on the northward shore, struck, many of them, upon the Egg Island rocks and the morning sun looked down upon a disastrous night's work — the wreckage of eight vessels with eight hundred and eighty-four men drowned. The "great fleet invincible " turned its battered prows homeward in full retreat. Quebec was not even sighted. The land forces were withdrawn. Montreal was not attacked and once again a Yankee armada sailed homeward in the shadow of ignominious failure, shipwreck and loss. while the English squadron that was to lead the fleet to victory returned at once to England.

But while at the north England and France were snarling at each other across the bulwarks of a ragged and broken sea-coast, to the south England and Spain were glaring at each other across a strip of sand. Oglethorpe's Georgia colony founded in so much promise gave peculiar umbrage by its very success to the Spaniards of Florida and the West Indies. The " black privateers " of Spain worried the growing commerce of the English south and Governor Oglethorpe's unsuccessful expedition against St. Augustine in 1740 spurred the Spaniards of the West Indies to a colossal revenge.

Orders were issued for the utter wiping out of the English colonies in Georgia and in the summer of 1742 a Spanish armada estimated to consist of fifty-six sail and seven thousand men sailed from Havanna to execute the prescribed vengeance.

It would seem as if expeditions of destruction conceived in wrath were never destined to succeed upon the coast line of the Western Atlantic. Not as in the north by the stupidity of pilots, the obstinacy of commanders and the crash of the aroused elements was the southern armada dispelled but by the tact, the ability. the generalship and the courage of one man — General James Oglethrope. With only eight hundred men at his command when the Spanish war-fleet appeared off Frederica on St. Simon's island he yet determined upon a desperate defence.

Word came to him that fourteen vessels from the Spanish fleet had tacked across to Cumberland Island and were threatening his fortification there. At once he put out with only three open "galleys" carrying men and ammunition to the relief of his sea-fort. With an intrepidity that appears almost foolhardy he pushed straight into the midst of the Spanish fleet. The over-timid Lieutenant Folsom who, so says the brave leader, "was to have supported me with the third and strongest boat quitted me in the fight and run into a river where he hid himself until the next day," but nothing daunted by this desertion the courageous Oglethorpe kept straight on, fought his way through the enemy, sank four of the fourteen Spanish vessels and relieved the sea-fort. The Spaniards were so taken aback by this display of English pluck that, so says the quaint report of the action, "the day after they run to sea and returned to St. Augustine and did not join their great fleet till after their grenadiers were beat by land."

By such courage and dash as this Oglethorpe conducted the defence of his colony. He prevented the landing of the invaders at Frederica, turned the defeat at "Bloody Marsh" into a victory and beat off a stubborn attack by the Spanish galleys upon the fortification at Frederica. Indeed, when the galleys withdrew, he himself led a pursuit in boats hastily manned by his soldiers and followed the fleeing Spaniards under the very guns of their fleet.

Utterly defeated by what Mr. Lodge well calls "as gallant fighting and shrewd generalship as the whole history of the American colonies can show" the Spaniards re-embarked in disorder and their great armada that was to utterly annihilate the English sailed back again to Cuba.

The next year, embarking a small force upon a few vessels, Oglethorpe sailed to St. Augustine and awed the Spaniards of Florida into such complete submission that from that time forward until the day when, in 1763, Florida was ceded to Great Britain, they never dared raise a hand against their English neighbors. "The memory of the defence of St. Simon's

Island and the southern frontier is," says Mr. Jones, "one of the proudest in the annals of Georgia."

The New England colonies, possessed by a desire for Canada that defeat could not weaken and disaster seemed only to whet, combined for another naval expedition against the possessions of France. To bigotry and greed was now added another

BEFORE LOUISBURG.

impelling influence — that of fear. A chain of French forts extended in a shrewdly-connected semicircle from the St. Lawrence to the Gulf of Mexico. Some day that semicircular encompassment might clinch itself into one decisive grip and crush within its grasp or thrust into the sea all the English that lay within the sweep of its iron fingers.

There was no question about it. Canada must become English or New England would become French. The feeling intensified with each new year. It burned fiercer by delay and finally burst into a crusade. In 1744 came "King George's War" in Europe and New England's opportunity.

The strongest French post on the ocean border, if not in all Canada, was that of Louisburg on the island of Cape Breton. Its situation was deemed impregnable. It had been called the Gibraltar of America. And yet against this stronghold the undisciplined fishermen and farmers of New England determined to hurl themselves. "It seemed," says Colonel Higginson, "an enterprise as daring as that of Sir William Phips, and as hopeless."

But it succeeded. Thirteen armed vessels carrying two hundred guns, with ninety transports and more than three thousand men rendezvoused at Canso, on the easterly end of Nova Scotia, in April, 1745, and prepared for the siege. William Pepperell, a New Hampshire merchant with but little knowledge of war, was commander. Captain Edward Tyng, a Boston sailor, had the direction of the fleet.

On the last day of April, 1745, this undisciplined force of seamen and landsmen came in sight of the great fortress they were to storm. For six weeks it was besieged by land and sea. At last it capitulated. The motto given by Whitfield the Methodist preacher to the expedition: *Nil desperandum, Christo Duce!* (Never despair, Christ leads you) gave the key-note to the effort and the victory. It was America's crusade, and the old crusading fervor blazed into final triumph. The gate to Canada was won and, as Bancroft says: "the strongest fortress of North America capitulated to an army of undisciplined New England mechanics and farmers and fishermen."

The coil was tightening about the French. Backed by the genius of Pitt, who saw in the conquest of America the chief glory and strength of England, the colonies consolidated for action. The objections of the Duke of Bedford * to the conquest of Canada were overruled; the terror of French invasion was passed. For, with the scattering of D'Anville's fleet in 1746 as it was sailing over-sea to the destruction of Boston, the last offensive move of France came to naught. Longfellow has told for us in pleasant rhyme the story of that last armada,† putting the record into the mouth of Mr. Thomas Prince, minister of the "Old South Church" in Boston: —

> " A fleet with flags arrayed
>   Sailed from the port of Brest,
> And the admiral's ship displayed
>   The signal: ' Steer southwest!'
> For this Admiral D'Anville
>   Had sworn by cross and crown
> To ravage with fire and steel
>   Our helpless Boston Town.
>
> " There were rumors in the street,
>   In the houses there was fear
> Of the coming of the fleet
>   And the danger hovering near,
> And while from mouth to mouth
>   Spread the tidings of dismay,
> I stood in the Old South
>   Saying humbly: ' Let us pray!

* The Duke of Bedford, the head of the British Marine office, objected to the conquest of Canada by the American colonies because of "the independence it might create in those provinces when they shall see within themselves so great an army, possessed of so great a country by right of conquest."

† Mr. Charles C. Smith thus describes this French "armada": " In June, 1746, a fleet of eleven ships of the line, twenty frigates, thirty transports and two fire-ships was dispatched for the destruction of Boston and the ravaging of New England. It was under command of Admiral D'Anville; but the enterprise ended in disastrous failure. Contrary winds prevailed during the voyage, and on nearing the American coast a violent storm scattered the fleet, driving some of the ships back to France and others to the West Indies and wrecking some on Sable Island." D'Anville died of apoplexy. His successor in command, Vice-Admiral D'Estournelle, committed suicide. The small-pox wrought havoc among the crews, and the officer next in command after scuttling some of the ships returned to France without striking a single blow. A second French expedition dispatched the next year was attacked by the English off Cape Finisterre and driven off with great loss.

" ' O Lord! we would not advise;
   But if in thy Providence
A tempest should arise
   To drive the French Fleet hence,
And scatter it far and wide,
   Or sink it in the sea,
We should be satisfied,
   And thine the glory be.'

" This was the prayer I made,
   For my soul was all on flame;
And even as I prayed
   The answering tempest came;
It came with a mighty power,
   Shaking the windows and walls,
And tolling the bell in the tower,
   As it tolls at funerals.

" The lightning suddenly
   Unsheathed its flaming sword;
And I cried : ' Stand still, and see
   The salvation of the Lord!'
The heavens were black with cloud,
   The sea was white with hail,
And ever more fierce and loud
   Blew the October Gale.

" The fleet it overtook,
   And the broad sails in the van
Like the tents of Cushan shook
   Or the curtains of Midian.
Down on the reeling decks
   Crashed the o'erwhelming seas;
Ah, never were there wrecks
   So pitiful as these!

" Like a potter's vessel broke
   The great ships of the line ;
They were carried away in smoke,
   Or sank like lead in the brine.
O Lord! before thy path
   They vanished and ceased to be,
When thou didst walk in wrath
   With thine horses through the sea."

English help, at first extended grudgingly, was now by the energetic measures of Pitt unsparingly given. In 1758 Louisburg (which the treaty of Aix-la-Chapelle in 1748 had given back to France) was captured by a great fleet under Admiral Boscawen and a land force under General Amherst. The next year Quebec fell; and as the ship of Admiral Saunders sailed down the broad St. Lawrence bearing homeward the dead body of the heroic Wolfe the last vestige of the French power in America that the brave Englishman had helped to break was blotted out in defeat and the day of colonial sea-struggle was over forever.

CHAPTER VI

AYS Samuel Smiles: "The sea has nursed the m o s t v a l o r o u s of men." The spirit of '76 created patriotism in America. Landsmen and seamen alike were to prove their mettle under the strain of a mighty impulse, and American seamen were to put to the test that valor which the risks of an ocean nurture along the Atlantic seaboard had given them. Heretofore, in time of stress and battle, they had relied too much upon the backing of English war-ships for success. Now, they were to contend against those very war-ships in the struggle for a free land and free homes. The Revolution had begun.

Very early in the conflict it became apparent that as England's supplies must come from over-sea such damage as could be done to England's transports and even to her men-of-war would be the most direct blow at her power and her resources.

Rhode Island, of all the colonies, was first to strike upon the seas, and it was from her chief port that Captain Abraham

Whipple took out the first armed cruiser in July, 1775, duly commissioned as a man-of-war by the legislature of Rhode Island. To Captain Whipple whose plucky reply to the British commander has become historic * has been acknowledged " the honor of firing the first gun in the naval service of the Revolution." But we have Dr. Hale as authority for the statement that even before Whipple's engagement the first naval battle had been won by the sailors and fishermen of New Bedford. Scarcely a fortnight after the fight at Lexington, they attacked and captured in one of the harbors of Martha's Vineyard one of the prizes sent in by the Falcon sloop-of-war and fifteen prisoners.

Following hard upon this exploit (on the twelfth of June next succeeding) came the capture of the king's sloop Margaretta and two transports by the sea-faring folk of Machias on the rocky Maine coast. The spirit of revolt was up: and all along the Atlantic sea-board the instincts of a people — to whom because of long acquaintance with England's obnoxious methods smuggling had seemed a virtue and resistance a duty — found easy expression in open attacks upon the vessels of a king against whom they had at length determined to rebel.

One by one the other colonies followed the lead of Rhode Island and commissioned war-vessels and privateers. The first real sounds of war that came to the ears of the continental congress assembled at Philadelphia were the echoing booms of the guns of the opposing vessels as the Pennsylvania flotilla

* Whipple had in 1772 headed a force of enraged Providence sailors against an English man-of-war sent into Narragansett Bay to enforce certain tyrannical British laws. On a certain stormy night in June, the Providence sailors embarking in their open whale boats surrounded and burned the offending vessel. Three years after Sir James Wallace, commanding the British frigate dispatched for the blockade of Providence, sent this message to Captain Whipple: " You Abraham Whipple on the 17th of June, 1772, burnt his Majesty's vessel the Gaspee, and I will hang you to the yard arm." To which courtesy Whipple replied: " To Sir James Wallace: Sir — Always catch a man before you hang him. Abraham Whipple." The plucky Rhode Islander was never caught and never hanged, but lived to capture many a British prize and to be called by courtesy " Commodore "

drove the Roebuck and the Liverpool down the Delaware River.

Washington, practical and far-seeing, was early impressed with the necessity for offensive action on the sea. On the second of September, 1775, he issued at Cambridge a commission, as commander-in-chief of the colonial forces, to certain Massachusetts captains to use their vessels offensively against all British supply-ships that should attempt to enter the harbor of Boston. His action was legalized by the Massachusetts colony and six vessels were at once commissioned for aggressive warfare on the high seas.

Ships being furnished sailors were not lacking. From the ranks of his citizen soldiery stepped at the word sailors enough to man his impromptu fleet. Broughton and Selman, Marblehead captains both, wrought with incautious haste such havoc in Canadian waters that even a zealous Congress was forced to reprimands and restitutions. With better good fortune John Manly, another Marblehead captain, waylaid in his schooner, the Lee, the British brigantine Nancy as she entered Massachusetts Bay, and took from her such store of the enemy's sinews of war as to fill the beleagured British in Boston with dismay and to give to the Americans corresponding delight and impetus. In the little navy that the Congress, before the close of the year, ordered and equipped this doughty Captain Manly found speedy and important place and performed many a valorous deed for the patriot cause.

This same continental navy, ordered by Congress at the close of the year 1775, deserves especial record here, for its thirteen ships of war were, says Dr. Hale, "the proper beginning of the navy of the United States." It is well to recall their names. They were the Washington, Raleigh, Hancock,

Randolph, Warren, Virginia, Trumbull, Effingham, Congress, Providence, Boston, Delaware and Montgomery. Before the close of the Revolution scarce one of all this valiant little fleet rode the waters as an American man-of-war. Fire and ship-wreck or the superior strength of the enemy had destroyed or captured them. But their memory should have grateful place in every American heart as the beginnings of that greater American navy that for a century thereafter upheld the honor of the stars and stripes on all the waters of the world.

The obnoxious sea-laws of England had for so many years dulled the consciences of Americans to the real iniquity of illicit ways in trade that smuggling and privateering were re-garded rather as duty than as crime. When, therefore, the active service of the Revolution called for a practicable navy those followers of the sea who responded to the call preferred the irregular life of the undisciplined privateer to the petty despotism that hedged the man-o'-war's man. Nearly every one of the thirteen newly-declared "States" issued commissions both to men-of-war and to privateers. The continental con-gress did the same. But the privileges and perquisites of the privateer, proved altogether too alluring. The regularly-consti-tuted navies found enlistments but slow work whereas the prize-money offers of the privateer captains attracted many a hardy seaman and many an adventurous landsman. Indeed it is asserted that at the close of the war the regular naval service of the United States possessed but a scant supply of men and vessels.

But what it lacked in men-of-war was amply compensated for by the privateers. Of these irregular war-vessels the sea-ports of the thirteen colonies furnished a great supply. They swarmed from Boston and from Newport, from Philadelphia and

Baltimore and Charleston and, acting either in conjunction with the continental "navy" or upon their own promptings and desires, they dealt sturdy blows for Freedom and their ever-open lockers and pockets. How considerable was this latter result may be judged by the assertion of Dr. Hale: " It has been said and probably truly that New England, the home of the pri-

RECRUITS FOR THE PRIVATEER.

vateers, was never more prosperous than in the last years of the Revolution, so large were the profits made in privateering enterprises."

We are accustomed to give but little consideration to the story of our navy during the Revolution esteeming it as a factor of but trifling value in the grand result of liberty. No mistake was ever greater. The fifty war vessels and more than five hundred privateers fitted out by Congress and the "States" during the war wrought almost incalculable damage upon England's commerce. Just how much in money this damage reached can never be reckoned, but it is a well-assured fact that the losses sustained by the commercial and manufacturing classes of England through the depredations of the American war-vessels formed one of the main reasons for the acknowledgment of independence at the close of the war.

The service was rough and undisciplined. Not even the semi-naval experiences of the Canadian sea-forays could give the continental service that tyranny of discipline that is at once the necessity and the arrogance of every properly organized man-of-war. The show and panoply of the English war-ship had but little place on the American vessels. The familiarity of association that springs from the close companionship of fishing-smack and trading-vessel, breeds certain contempt of station; it is impatient of any assumption of authority and laughs at pompous commands that savor too strongly of the quarter-deck. In how far the fisheries of the North Atlantic served as a school for the early American navy it is perhaps impossible to determine, but it was from these rough and ready captors of the cod and the whale that the first vessels of the new republic drew her adventurous seamen. The hazardous life of the banks and of the coast gave to the men who followed the lead of such captains as Manly and Whipple and Hopkins their dash, their stubborn ignorance of defeat, their determination, their bravery and their brawn.

And the men of the South were not behind their brethren of the North. With less of the sea life and the sea men than the Northern colonies possessed, they still had a proportionately large experience in the ways and struggles of a sailor's life. Wherever along the southern sea-board a little port looked off upon the wide Atlantic, from out its sun-lit harbor had, even before the days of revolution, gone many a vessel on errands of questionable trade and in open defiance of the laws of England. The old-time valor that had resisted Spanish encroachment and scuttled many a Spanish galleon on that historic main again asserted itself. The seaman who had already sailed as one in the crew of smuggler, pirate or honest sea-craft from the ports of Baltimore and of Charleston or the minor seaboard towns now signed his name to the shipping articles of the State or Government war-ship, or to the less conventional ones of the equally as acceptable privateer. In the annals of revolutionary endeavor the names of the men of Philadelphia, of Baltimore and of Charleston hold equal place with those of northern sea-ports. Upon the deck of the privateer, in the shrouds of the state war-ship or on board the more pretentious national cruiser northern and southern sailors proved their valor and their zeal. Not Massachusetts' state navy of thirty-four sail, nor Rhode Island's active and ever-ready home fleet did more valiant service than did the wary row-gallies of the Delaware or Maryland's plucky flotilla of state ships and "private armed vessels," Virginia's irregular "navy," or South Carolina's mingled flotilla of coaster, galley and launch.

New Hampshire's privateer General Sullivan, Massachusetts' cruiser Tyrannicide, Rhode Island's private vessel General Washington, the Connecticut brig Defence, New York's queer little fleet made up of " schooners, sloops, row-gallies, and whale-boats," and other of the "colony ships" (such as the Randolph of Philadelphia, the Defence of Maryland, and the armed schooner Peggy of South Carolina) all may stand, in the absence of space for a more general enumeration, as the representatives of that long roll of gallant sea-craft that helped to make revolution successful—a roll that gives equal place to the clumsy whale-boat of the North and the odd-looking " row-galley " of the South, to the swift-sailing privateer and the more pretentious national war-ship.

And the men who sailed the seas to fight under the flag of the new republic — what of them? They came from every section of the thirteen colonies, some trained to the ways of the sea, others, landsmen eager to sniff salt water, or to pocket unlimited prize-money. They manned the ropes, they reefed the white-winged sails, they pulled the clumsy flint-lock and wielded cutlass and boarding-pike with equal zeal and coolness, following the lead of commanders who felt that capture on the quarter-deck of a colonial cruiser meant for them a felon's trial and a pirate's fate.

But though fighting in the shadow of this assurance they never faltered. The list of these leaders on the seas is a long and honorable one. The generals in the Revolutionary armies may have eclipsed in glory and fame the commanders in its active if erratic navy, but not one of the nation's earliest war-chiefs is more worthy our remembrance and esteem than are its valiant sea-fighters. Theirs is a roll of bravery inscribed with many a name that rings with the story of gallant endeavor and success. Williams and Biddle and Mugford, Read and Barry and Conyngham, Wickes and Hopkins and Robinson, Hudson and Hinman and Nicholson, Rathbun and Talbot and Barney — these are some of the best known in that list of heroes; while last but not least on this now famous roll we read the name of John Paul Jones!

Of this most picturesque and most popular sea-fighter of the

Revolution very much could be written. Much indeed has been written that would scarcely bear the test of historic fact. A daring but unscrupulous fighter, a zealous but hot-headed partisan, a bold but often an uncertain captain, John Paul Jones was neither the demi-god of the cheap romancers nor the brutal pirate of British legend.

A Scotchman by birth and an American by choice and ambition Jones entered eagerly into the struggle against England and at its very beginning sought service in the navy of the new republic. From his earliest boyhood he had been a sailor. Born in Scotland, he had at the age of twelve taken to the sea, deserting for this adventurous life the home of his father—honest John Paul, the gardener of the Earl of Selkirk. From this time forward his life was filled with roving and adventure. By turns merchantman, smuggler and slaver in American ships, he developed into a skillful sailor, quitted the slave trade in disgust but rose through the sudden changes that marked the dubious sea-service of colonial days to be while yet a young man the captain of a swift West India trader. Falling heir to a Virginia property he became a Southern planter and supplemented his old Scotch name of John Paul by the additional though certainly not less prosaic one of Jones.

The Revolution roused him from his quiet life as a country gentleman and again he found himself on the sea. This time he was lieutenant of the cruiser Alfred, the little flag-ship of Esek Hopkins, first "commodore" of the new republic. Succeeding, in less than five months of actual service, to the post of captain, Jones, in the year 1776, sailed the Providence, a cruiser of twelve guns, on a summer war-cruise from the Gut of Canso to the Island of Bermuda, captured sixteen prizes and leaped into renown as a popular hero.

In the autumn of 1776 he took the armed ship Mellish,
freighted with supplies for Burgoyne's army, fought the frigate
Milford and received in the next year the command of the
cruiser Ranger. In this vessel he crossed the ocean and in
April, 1778, descended for purposes of plunder upon the coasts
of Scotland and England. It is one of the questionable phases
in the career of this popular hero that his first descent for booty
should have been upon the estates of that very Earl of Selkirk
where he had first seen the light as the son of John Paul, the
good Earl's gardener. There is however some satisfaction in
the knowledge that this doughty marauder's conscience was
sufficiently tender to cause him, when the booty of the mansion
on St. Mary's Isle was sold at Brest, to purchase the family
plate and return it to Lady Selkirk with a letter full of apologies and regrets.

Continuing his career of plunder with a boldness that was
doubly intensified by the knowledge that he would be uncere-
moniously strung up to the yard arm of the first English frigate
that could capture " so vile a pirate," Jones dodged the English
cruisers and raided the English coast with equal skill and intrepidity. When brought to bay at last off the Irish coast by
the English sloop-of-war Drake the dauntless " commodore "
turned on his assailant and after an hour of sharp fighting so
crippled and shattered her that, with forty of her crew killed or
wounded, the Drake struck her colors and surrendered to the
Yankee " pirate." Then Jones, grown still more bold by this
success, circumnavigated Ireland, increased his list of prizes and
sailed into the friendly harbor of Brest a greater hero than ever.

There never was a time in the old days of international
jealousy that France was not ready to extend aid and comfort
to the enemies of England. She was never more ready than

ON BOARD THE BONHOMME RICHARD.—"I HAVE NOT YET BEGUN TO FIGHT."

in this battle year of 1779. Revenge for the loss of Canada lent force to her "sympathy" with the colonies. She offered money, ships and men, and when Jones appeared at court the French government at once helped him fit out an expedition designed for the destruction of English commerce and flying the American colors.

This Franco-American squadron was as oddly-composed as it was, apparently, insignificant. It comprised five vessels — the Alliance, an American-built vessel with a cashiered French captain as its commander, the Pallas, a French merchantman, hired for the expedition by friends of the enterprise, and two small privateers (the cutter Cerf and the brig Vengeance). These latter went "on their own hook" hoping more for plunder than for glory. The fifth and most important vessel of the squadron was the admiral's "flagship." This was a ramshackle and unseaworthy old Indiaman, formerly known as the Daras but rechristened by Jones, in compliment to his friend Franklin, the Bonhomme Richard — the "Poor Richard" of the homespun philosophy of that day. This "flag-ship" was a two-decked frigate carrying forty guns, armed and equipped in almost ruinous haste and presented to Captain Jones by the French government.

The whole expedition was in fact little more than a business investment of a certain rich French banker who hoped for large profit in his share of prize-money. The crews of this rather shaky squadron were a curious mixture of all the odd and hard-looking specimens of sea-faring folk then to be found in a French sea-port. The captains and minor officers were inclined to be jealous and even insubordinate. The venture appears, in fact, to have been about as unpromising and dubious as could well be imagined. But the commander was a deter-

mined and daring man. He was "on his mettle." He felt that
he had a record to make, upon which even the alliance of France
and his own reputation might depend. He sailed out of the port
of L'Orient determined to win. To such a spirit defeat is the
last possibility. And so, out of the most unsatisfactory elements, John Paul Jones achieved one of the most memorable
and glorious victories in all the erratic sea-struggles of the
American revolution.

It was indeed a gallant encounter. Its story is well worth
recital. Sailing across the restless North Sea came the Baltic
Fleet of England — forty sail of merchantmen stretching out
to the southward from under Flamborough Head and convoyed
by two new and strong English war-ships — the Serapis, of
forty-four guns, and the Countess of Scarborough, an armed
ship of twenty six-pounders. Straight into this fleet dashed
the Bonhomme Richard with the Pallas at its heels. The
Alliance with its craven French captain and the two booty-
seeking privateers steered clear of danger. The merchantmen
scurried away toward safe harbor. The Pallas occupied herself with the Countess of Scarborough, and thus with the field
clear to themselves the poor old Richard and the lordly Serapis
engaged at once in what has been termed "one of the most
remarkable naval duels in history." It was like a fight between
a toothless old mastiff and a stout young bull-dog. At the very
first broadside so many of the miserable guns on the lower
deck of the Richard burst because of their poor metal that the
men on such of the other lower-deck batteries as had not yet
burst refused to work their pieces.

Night fell on the fight. The two ships grappled. Captain
Jones with his own hand made fast to the mizzen-mast of the
Bonhomme Richard the ropes that hung from the bowsprit of

the Serapis. With yards all entangled and with the hostile cannon actually touching muzzles the men of the Serapis rallied to board the Bonhomme Richard; but when they saw in the uncertain light the brave little Scotch-Yankee captain standing at the gang-way pike in hand and ready to receive them they fell back in dismay.

The broadsides of the Serapis had already told. The Richard was in a bad way. Sundry eighteen-pound shot had torn ugly holes through her side below the water-line. The lower-deck battery, as has been shown, had been abandoned. The battery of twelve-pounders on which Captain Jones placed his chief reliance had been utterly silenced and of all the forty guns only two spunky nine-pounders on the quarter-deck were available for service. There was a lull in the fight. "The Richard, ahoy!" shouted the English captain Pearson from the deck of the Serapis, "have you struck your colors?" And back came the reply of the plucky Yankee commodore in words that have become historic: "No! I have not yet begun to fight!"

Then the battle raged again. One more nine-pounder was added to the two pieces on the quarter-deck. The three guns poured their double-headed shot, their grape and canister into the Serapis, the marksmen in the tops bravely seconded the fire of this little battery and so hot grew the bombardment that the deck of the Serapis was raked fore and aft with this iron storm. No man could stand against it. Through three long hours the battle raged. The lower-deck battery of the Serapis — all ten-pounders — stove in the side of the Richard. Some of the timid fellows cried for mercy. "Do you demand quarter?" came the hail of the English captain. "No!" thundered back the intrepid gardener's son, and at it they went again with redoubled fury.

The mutinous French captain in the Alliance hovering on the skirts of the fight discharged a broadside full at the stern of the Richard. Again and again was this treachery repeated. The old ship was riddled. Fire burst out. One of the pumps was shot away. The leaks gained rapidly. The Richard seemed to be sinking. Again rose the cry for quarter, and a gunner ran to cut away the colors. But a shot from the Serapis carried away both the ensign staff and the gunner. The prisoners were set free, by some traitorous hand. But Captain Jones knew no such word as fail. In the face of absolute destruction he still fought on, drove the terrified prisoners to work at the pumps — and at last the crisis came. Some of the sailors on the main-yard of the Richard dropped their hand-grenades through the open hatchway of the Serapis, exploded a powder-chest and demoralized the British crew. Captain Jones himself aimed a doubled-headed shot straight at the enemy's mainmast, which stood out distinct and clear in the bright moonlight and the brighter glare of the burning shrouds.

It was a telling shock. The mainmast of the Serapis shook, tottered and went by the board. Her firing slackened and as a final fusilade rang from the deck of the sinking Richard the British colors were struck and John Paul Jones was victor.

The sequel to this savage sea-fight is soon told. The Countess of Scarborough had already surrendered to the Pallas. Both prizes were taken to a friendly Dutch port, but the poor old Richard, vanquished though a victor, could not be kept afloat beyond a few hours. Cut entirely to pieces between decks, with rudder and transoms gone, with quarters and coun-ter on the lower deck driven in, with all her lower-deck guns dismounted and the rotten timbers of the stern post almost torn away the decrepit old hulk slowly filled. The water rose to the lower deck and on the morning of the twenty-fifth of September, says Captain Jones, " At a little after ten, I saw, with inexpressible grief, the last glimpse of the Bonhomme Richard." But the waters that closed over her rang with the shouts of victory. The forty merchantmen, to be sure, favored by the morning fog ran safely into port ; but the moral effect of the victory was as great as if they had been captured. It established the power of the American navy in European waters and gave eternal fame to the name of John Paul Jones. The treacherous French captain of the Alliance only escaped his merited punishment of court-martial by a fit of insanity. Captain Pearson, the British commander of the Serapis, was knighted by King George for his gallant defense of the English frigate, and it is said that when Jones heard of this honor, he remarked, " Well, if I ever meet the commodore again, I'll make a lord of him."

This memorable victory, though the most notable naval battle of the Revolution, may serve as a type of those other determined and gallant sea-fights that helped to secure freedom for the American colonies. Other captains were fully as brave, other vessels as skillfully handled, other conflicts as stubbornly waged. Space will not permit the details, but from the first shot fired by O'Brien against the Margaretta, in 1775, to the last broadside fired by Barney from the Hyder Ali in 1782, the story of the doings of those undisciplined " blue jackets of '76 " is replete with incidents of personal bravery, daring and skill that equal and sometimes surpass even the stirring episode of Jones' fight on the deck of the crippled and sinking Bonhomme Richard.

The fire that burns in the stilted lines of the old song of

that day in which was celebrated the Hyder Ali's victory over
the General Monk could have been directed with equal force
upon the gallant deeds of many another Yankee captain striking for victory on the embattled waters: —

Captain Barney there preparing, thus addressed his gallant crew:
" Now, brave lads, be bold and daring, let your hearts be firm and true;
This is a proud English cruiser, roving up and down the main;
We must fight her — must reduce her, though our deck be strew'd with slain.

" Let who will be the survivor, we must conquer or must die;
We must take her up the river, whate'er comes of you and I.
Though she shows most formidable, with her eighteen pointed nines,
And her quarter clad in sable, let us balk her proud designs.

" With four nine-pounders and four sixes, we will face that daring band;
Let no dangers damp your courage, nothing can the brave withstand.
Fighting for your country's honor, now to gallant deeds aspire;
Helmsman, bear us down upon her!   Gunner, give the word to fire!"

Then, yard-arm and yard-arm meeting, straight began the dismal fray;
Cannon mouths, each other greeting, belch'd their smoky flames away.
Soon the langrage, grape and chain-shot, that from Barney's cannon flew,
Swept the Monk, and cleared each round-top, killed and wounded half her crew.

Captain Rogers strove to rally — but they from their quarters fled,
While the roaring Hyder Ali covered o'er his decks the dead.
When from tops their dead men tumbled, and the streams of blood did flow,
Then their proudest hopes were humbled by their brave inferior foe.

All aghast and all confounded, they beheld their champions fall;
And their captain sorely wounded, bade them quick for quarter call.
Then the Monk's proud flag descended, and her cannons ceased to roar;
By her crew no more defended, she confess'd the contest o'er.

It must not be supposed, however, that all the men who
fought upon the seas beneath the banner of the new republic
were of this heroic mold, or that all who lent their aid or
joined their fortunes to the infant navy of the United States

were actuated solely by patriotic motives. It is a sad truth, too often and too lightly passed over by history, that patriots are sometimes venal and heroes unheroic. The "gallant tar" and the "bold sea-dogs" of Revolutionary days whose deeds form so prominent a feature in the stirring sea-songs of Philip Freneau and other song-singers of the Revolution were often far from gallant and sometimes not even bold.

Too many of those early American sailors were led into the struggle rather by hope of plunder and prize-money than by thoughts of freedom and glory. We have the assurance of John Paul Jones himself that many of his men on board the Bonhomme Richard were mutinous, timid and even cowardly. Many, he says, "skulked below." Three at least of his under-officers were "cowardly and treacherous." Only the dominant courage and energy of the gallant commander and the fighting qualities of a portion of his crew brought victory out of defeat. And his experience was that of other often dispirited commanders. This lack of patriotism, indeed, affected the quarter-deck quite as much as the forecastle. It was due largely to the chaotic condition of the service and the still more mixed character and nationalities of the crews engaged. Long before the war was over Congress learned, so we are assured, "the danger of entrusting seamen of one nation to a commander of another." It was after all the minority of the home-born sailors of America whose vigor and determination, nurtured among the necessities and hardships of the fisheries and coast-trading life, stood steadfast amid discouragement and defeat and helped to give, at last, liberty to a nation.

But, in spite of these qualifying elements—discouragements, indeed, which every nation has at some time experienced — the record of the navy of the United States during its era of revolt

glows with examples of daring and heroism. It was Manly of
Marblehead who, by his capture of a British brigantine laden
with military stores, gave material aid to the poorly-equipped
camp about Boston. It was Mugford, another Marblehead

HELP FROM FRANCE.

captain, who, smarting under certain compromising charges,
dashed out in sight of the enemy's fleet and, in his little cruiser
of only fifty tons, boldly assaulted and captured a British ship
of three hundred tons and carried his prize into Boston, almost

under the guns of the English squadron. It was this same Captain Mugford who, when his prize had been safely delivered, again put out to sea, and being discovered by the now watchful enemy was attacked by thirteen boats from the British fleet. By desperate fighting the enemy was at last repelled, but the intrepid captain fell in the fight, shouting as his last command: " I am a dead man, but you can beat them. Don't give up the vessel."

It was Oliver Read, of Rhode Island, who, with other brave men, escaped from one of the dreadful Jersey prison-ships by springing into a boat alongside filled with British sailors. Overpowering them Read mastered the boat and made his way back to Rhode Island, shipped at once for offensive service and captured a British vessel commanded by the very same Tory captain who had treacherously sent him to the Jersey prison-ship. It was Seth Harding and Samuel Smedley who, with their little fleet of four schooners and a brig, captured off Cape Cod, after the sharpest fighting, three armed English transports and five hundred prisoners.

It was Lambert Wickes, one of the earliest of our naval captains, who took the first American cruiser across the Atlantic, carried Franklin, the first American ambassador, to France, spread havoc among the English shipping on the Irish Channel and in the Bay of Biscay, and, sailing homeward, went down in shipwreck, with all his crew, off the rocky coast of Newfoundland. It was Gustavus Conyngham who, in his clumsy lugger the Surprise, so annoyed and terrified the English marine by his rapid and unexpected movements, that he was hunted down as a pirate, but so skillfully eluded pursuit that England protested to France for harboring so fell a pest and compelled that country to send the bold privateer a-packing. Whereupon the daring Conyngham boldly put his lugger into an English port, refitted and victualed her there and, sallying out again, continued his victorious cruise.

In like manner it was the crew of the little cruiser Dolphin, the first American vessel to bear the United States flag in an ocean victory—who recaptured their own ship after she had been placed in charge of a prize crew; it was the crew of the privateer Ranger who, after a two hours' fight with a British war-brig, boarded her when victory seemed impossible and won her in a hand-to-hand fight; it was young Nicholas Biddle, a brave and daring commander, who, in the Andrea Doria, took so many British prizes off the New England coast, that he reached port with only five of his original crew; it was Captain Abraham Whipple who, as shrewd as he was daring, disguised his own vessel and, entering a convoy of English West Indiamen, for ten successive nights boarded and captured a ship a night and took eight of his prizes safely into Boston harbor.

The list could be largely extended. Of course American vessels fell a prey to British captors, but the honors in the struggle rested with the seamen of the new republic. Success however lay rather with the smaller craft and the free privateers than with the naval vessels. The national cruisers fared badly. At the close of the Revolution very few — only three in fact — remained as the basis for a new navy. But it was the destructive work of the commissioned and non-commissioned vessels in the service of the revolted colonies that helped swell the cry for peace that was raised in England after the French alliance and the repeated successes of the American arms. The courage of the American sailor, proved in many a stubborn sea-fight, showed that the will of a people determined to be free was not to be thwarted by British bayonets nor conquered by British broadsides. The pluck and endurance that could wrest a live-lihood from a stormy and forbidding ocean asserted themselves in a struggle for free coasts, free harbors and free homes. The American sailor, quite as much as the American statesman and the American soldier, in the crash of battle and on decks slippery with blood proved his claim to his birthright in the title-deeds of American freedom.

CHAPTER VII.

HE prestige of success is inspiring. At the close of the Revolution the Republic of the United States of America seemed scarcely in a condition to suggest strength, prosperity or ability to go alone. And yet the very fact that a confederacy of thirteen poverty-stricken colonies had successfully withstood the power and historic invincibleness of the British nation was of itself sufficient to give inspiration to the people and start the tide of European emigration in a westerly direction.

The new nation grew in numbers and in strength. Despite its trials from over-zealous patriots and would-be leaders, despite its load of debt, its yet uncertain federal union, its questionable standing among foreign nations and in foreign ports and the even more serious question as to its own future the American Republic girded itself for its struggle for place and recognition among the nations of the earth. Trade revived slowly; commerce as slowly expanded and the American sailor relieved from the dangerous demands of war betook himself to the only less dangerous pursuit of "following the sea," sailing under the flag of a new maritime service.

That such a service was at first domestic rather than international is scarcely to be wondered at. American commerce could venture abroad but at great hazard, for the sea was yet safe highway only to the strongest nations and the "banner of the free" had but the slightest show of national authority and national protection at its back. England was still the mistress of the seas, and England's statesmen had little faith in the ability of the "United States of America" to long maintain its high-sounding name. European nations, therefore, were slow to enter into commercial relations with what might far too soon prove to be no nation at all, and among the citizens of the republic themselves, for all their valorous boastings, there was doubting, confusion and great anxiety as to the future.

But there were some hopeful ones with sufficient faith in the future to assume certain risks. In the year 1784, less than four months after the surrender at Yorktown, the ship Empress sailed from the port of New York to distant China, and after a voyage of fifteen months brought back almost the first reports of that oriental fairy-land which, until then, had been scarcely better known to Americans than had the fabled and mysterious Cathay to the earlier navigators.

The voyage of the Empress led to other and similar enterprises. The New England merchants, harassed in European waters, determined to trade for their tea and their silks with China direct. In 1785 a second vessel bore the stars and stripes into Chinese ports and before the close of 1787 five ships had sailed for the "China seas." In the search for exchangeable commodities with the Chinese merchants two Boston ships — the Columbia and the Washington — doubled Cape Horn in January, 1788, collected a cargo of furs on the North Pacific coast and shipped this to Canton in the Columbia. This venture proved successful and on the tenth of August, 1790, Captain Robert Gray brought back the Columbia to Boston Harbor with a cargo of tea — "of all Americans the first to carry the United States flag around the world."

The next year, Captain Gray was again sailing the Pacific in the Columbia and, coasting along its northern shore-line for another cargo of furs, discovered the magnificent river that now bears the name of his gallant ship and "established the first claim of the United States to the soil of Oregon."

Such distant ventures, however, were for years the exception. The unfriendliness of the maritime powers and the antagonistic relations toward each other of the States themselves blocked the progress of a waiting commerce. There were quarrels and wranglings over the methods of "regulating trade." The commerce of the country was at the mercy of England, of France and of Spain. "Behind the Pillars of Hercules," says McMaster, "the Barbary corsairs were believed to lie in wait for American merchantmen." Danger and disaster stared in the face every American merchant who dared risk a foreign venture and their vessels were employed rather in the slighter exigencies of domestic commerce than in the almost certain wreck of foreign trade.

But, where men are determined and energetic, obstacles cannot forever remain insurmountable. America had vast resources of her own, and trade was certain to regulate itself, though nations were unfriendly and fellow-countrymen barred the way with clog and hinderance. Despite the controversy over imposts, and non-imposts, in the face, even, of conflicting and disastrous State regulation and disastrous rates of duty in foreign ports, trade grew in volume and extent. The stars and stripes first entered a British port at the masthead of a Nantucket whaler, laden with oil; and, little by little, the pluck and push of American sailors carried that flag into the ports of other powers and taught them to respect and welcome it.

The tonnage of the mercantile marine engaged in foreign trade steadily increased. In the year 1789, at the time of the formation of the Constitution, this registered carrying capacity was 123,893 tons; in 1797 it had risen to 597,777 tons; in 1807 it had grown to 848,307 tons. And this growth was in spite of foreign restrictions and of a vacillating home policy.

All this meant determination, energy and courage. The continuous European quarrels proved America's opportunity. Napoleon's mighty ambitions created American commerce. The carrying-trade in American vessels rapidly developed. Better ships were built each year. Yankee energy and Yankee seamanship struggled toward the lead. Sailors were allowed a share in far-away risks, and the sea, as a field for adventure and for profit, recommended itself strongly to ambitious lads. Bright young fellows rose quickly to command. The captain of a Salem trading-ship, off on a nineteen months' cruise to the Cape of Good Hope and the Isles of France and Bourbon in 1792, was but nineteen years old, his chief mate had barely reached that age, his second mate had but just passed his eighteenth birthday. And yet these boys succeeded so well in their important trust that the merchant who owned the ship sent them out again and again, and proudly boasted of the achievements of " his boys."

And the crews of those rough-and-ready days were no less

efficient. Every sailor of them all hoped at some day to be either East India merchant or captain. Many of them were as amply able to navigate their ships as were their captains. "When

GETTING READY FOR SEA.

a captain was asked at Manila," says Mr. Bachelor, "how he contrived to find his way in the teeth of a northeast monsoon by mere dead-reckoning, he replied that he had a crew of twelve men any one of whom could take and work a lunar observation as well, for all practical purposes, as Sir Isaac Newton himself."

To the pluck and ability of the seamen of that period Mr. Roosevelt, too, bears testimony: "There was no better seaman in the world," he says, "than American Jack; he had been bred to his work from infancy, and had been off in a fishing dory almost as soon as he could walk. When he grew older he shipped on a merchant-man or whaler, and in those warlike times, when our large merchant-marine was compelled to rely pretty much on itself for protection, each craft had to be well handled; all who were not were soon weeded out by a process of natural selection, of which the agents were French picaroons, Spanish buccaneers, and Malay pirates. It was a rough school, but it taught Jack to be both skillful and self-reliant."

It was, indeed, scarcely possible for the American sailor to be otherwise. Schooled by his Revolutionary experiences to a familiarity with a life of daring and adventure, bred among scenes and surroundings that made him at once fearless, ambitious and self-reliant, he was ready, in spite of foreign extortions and domestic bickerings, to run all risks and to brave all dangers for the sake of present possibilities and future profits. All along the seaboard the ports and harbors of his home-land offered him opportunities for his hardy calling. Portsmouth and Marblehead, Salem and Boston, Nantucket, Newport and New Bedford sent, each year, increasing fleets to the Indies or upon promising and productive whaling voyages. From the richer ports of New York and Philadelphia trading-ships sailed to all parts of the world, Baltimore dispatched many a swift-sailing "clipper" into French and German harbors, while from the lesser Atlantic ports sailed many a smart craft on ventures in the home-coasting trade.

It was a wonderful school for testing the mettle of men. The son of the wealthy merchant and his promising young clerk were both bred to a practical knowledge of the ways of foreign commerce and the risks of the sea before the mast or in the cabin of the ships of the "house." Along New England's broken sea-board few lads arrived at manhood ignorant of the stirring experiences that attended a voyage to the "Banks." "Long before a lad could nib a quill, or make a pot-hook, or read half the precepts his primer contained," says Mr. McMaster, "he knew the name of every brace and stay, every sail and part of a Great Banker and a chebacco, all the nautical terms, what line and hook should be used for catching halibut, and what for mackerel and cod. . . . By the time he had seen his tenth birthday he was old enough not to be seasick, not to cry during a storm at sea, and to be of some use about a ship, and went on his first trip to the Banks."

All along that hazardous coast, too, from Newfoundland to Montauk, cruised the watchful whalers, for the great spermaceti had not yet been driven far a-sea, and it was one of the legends of the Long Island ports that in those days of home whaling, "no man could marry till he had struck his whale."

"Wherever an American seaman went," says Mr. Roosevelt, "he had not only to contend with all the legitimate perils of the sea, but he had also to regard almost every stranger as a foe. Whether this foe called himself pirate or privateer mattered but little. French, Spaniards, Algerines, Malays — from all alike our commerce suffered, and against all, our merchants were forced to defend themselves."

The Algerine corsair called into being the American navy; the French republican first tested its strength. Of all the strange anomalies of history no one is stranger than this spectacle of a barbarous nation of illiterate pagans holding at call, like one of its own bashaws, the whole civilized world. And yet such was the fact. That group of North African nations known as "the Barbary Powers" — Tripoli, Tunis, Algiers and Morocco — were literally the rulers of the Mediterranean. Fierce, lazy, cruel and avaricious this nest of Moorish pirates preyed upon the commerce of that great land-locked sea and demanded tribute of all the trading nations. England, Holland, Sweden, Spain, Portugal, France and Germany supplied the corsairs with ships and naval supplies. Indeed, as Mr. McMaster remarks, "the idle Moors, with great shrewdness, obtained from one half of Christendom ships which they forced the other half to keep in good repair."

The coming of the American flag into Mediterranean ports suggested to these bandits of the sea a new source for tribute. The Dey of Algiers learned that this new nation across the western ocean had merchant ships but no cruisers and forthwith proceeded to waylay its vessels and exact the customary tribute from the American nation as its only relief from slavery and spoilation. One after another American vessels fell a prey to Algerine corsairs, their cargoes were stolen, their crews sold into slavery. The protection of American commerce was urged upon Congress and out of this demand grew the armed vessels that were the beginnings of the American navy.

The keels of six frigates were laid at once. At Boston the Constitution of forty-four guns; at New York the President of forty-four guns; at Philadelphia the United States of forty-four guns; at Portsmouth in Virginia the Chesapeake of thirty-eight guns; at Baltimore the Constellation of thirty-eight guns; and at Portsmouth in New Hampshire the Congress of thirty-eight guns — these with two hundred and fifty tons of balls and three hundred and fifty thousand dollars' worth of muskets, small arms and stores were ordered by the Congress and deemed protection enough against the pirates of Barbary and the invaders of any hostile power from across the sea.

This was in 1794; but in 1795 work was stopped. The United States, yielding to the timorous policy of tribute rather than war signed a treaty with Algiers by which at an expense of nearly a million dollars peace was purchased. It was a disgraceful truckling to a thievish power, but it was the fashion with other mercantile states and "peace at any price" was desired by the American traders.

After a while work on the new vessels was resumed and went slowly forward. By May, 1798, the frigates Constitution, Constellation and United States were afloat. A secretary of the Navy — Benjamin Stoddert of Maryland — was appointed and nine hundred officers and men constituted what was joyfully hailed as "the rising navy of America."

The first of these national vessels to be launched was the United States, built at the Southwark yards, near Philadelphia. Mr. McMaster has graphically described this event.

" In the long list of splendid vessels," he says, "which, in a hundred combats, have maintained the honor of our national flag, the United States stands at the head. After three years of unavoidable detention the first naval vessel built by the United States under the Constitution was to be committed to the waves. The day chosen for so great an event was the tenth of May (1797). The hour was one in the afternoon, and the whole city of Philadelphia, it was said, came out to Southwark to behold such a rare show. One estimate puts the number present at thirty thousand souls. . . . It was feared that a strong northwest wind, which had for several days kept back

BAINBRIDGE AND THE DEY.

the tides in the Delaware, would make the water much too shallow to permit the launch. Yet at sunrise on the morning of the tenth the best points of observation began to be occupied by an eager throng. By noon every hill-top and every house-top commanding a view on each side of the river, and every inch of space on the stands put up about the vessel and before the houses of Swanson Street, was covered with human beings. In the river a hundred craft rode at anchor, gay with bunting and richly-dressed dames. At one, precisely, the blocks were knocked from under her, the lashings of the cable cut, and, amidst the shouts of the great multitude, the United States slid gracefully down her ways."

Four months later, on September 7, 1797, the Constellation was launched at Portsmouth in New Hampshire. A month after, on October 21, 1797, the Constitution slid from the stocks at Charlestown — the Constitution, that historic frigate dear to so many generations of Americans, and a chipping from whose oaken bulwarks has been a coveted and notable relic to many a Yankee lad. Of all the gallant craft that have floated the flag of the Union and proved the valor of the American sailor in many a stubborn sea-fight none has been more popular or more dearly prized than this stout old frigate. And when after a half-century of service the rumor came that the old hulk was to be broken up * as unfit for further use thousands re-echoed the indignant protest of those stirring lines of Holmes which so many a Yankee schoolboy has since declaimed with spirit: —

> " Ay, tear her tattered ensign down !
> Long has it waved on high,
> And many an eye has danced to see
> That banner in the sky ;

* It is well to know that these lines written as Dr. Holmes now says, " in his fiery young days," had their effect. The Constitution was not destroyed as anticipated but was preserved in part as a relic. The old frigate is now an annex to the U. S. Naval Academy at Annapolis.

Beneath it rung the battle shout,
  And burst the cannon's roar;
The meteor of the ocean air
  Shall sweep the clouds no more.

Her deck, once red with heroes' blood,
  Where knelt the vanquished foe,
When winds were hurrying o'er the flood,
  And waves were white below,
No more shall feel the victor's tread,
  Or know the conquered knee;
The harpies of the shore shall pluck
  The eagle of the sea.

O, better that her shattered hulk
  Should sink beneath the wave;
Her thunders shook the mighty deep,
  And there should be her grave;
Nail to the mast her holy flag,
  Set every threadbare sail,
And give her to the god of storms —
  The lightning and the gale."

But though the plans for an efficient navy were halted awhile by the purchase of a dishonorable peace with the infidel Moors of Africa the work was destined to be speedily resumed by the rumors of war with the questionable Christians of France. It was a time of turmoil in that volatile land. The revolution of 1789 overthrew the government of the king and established the reign of the people. The tri-color of the republic displaced the white flag of the Bourbons on fort and at mast-head, and in the arrogance of success the French people, as had their kingly tyrants before them, claimed the supremacy of the seas as they boastingly asserted their supremacy on the land.

England and France were at war. America, struggling with financial and political problems, all the harder to solve because of the conflicting opinions of a yet unsettled people, sought to be neutral in the contest. France, relying on the help afforded during the Revolution for aid in her own quarrels, sought to invade this neutrality and force America to some overt act against England. President Washington saw the folly of such an attempt on the part of a weak and divided nation and refused to succor either combatant. Then France, combining insult and injury,* broke its treaty of alliance with the United States, banished the American ambassadors and proclaimed that hereafter the neutrality of America was not to be respected.

Harassed thus by both English and French cruisers the condition of the American merchant vessel was pitiable. There was safety nowhere on the seas, and to insure for its threatened commerce some degree of protection Congress pushed forward the completion of its war-vessels and in April, 1798, directed President Adams to hire or purchase twelve armed vessels in addition to the frigates then building. In May, orders were issued for the construction of certain lesser war-vessels and in June the President was directed to accept or purchase twelve more private armed vessels.

Under the spur of necessity action was speedy. Ship after ship put to sea, prepared for a forcible resistance to French cruisers and privateers. America's seamen were her strong reliance and the prompt measures of such naval commanders as Captains Stephen Decatur of the Delaware, Bainbridge of the Retaliation, Truxtun of the Constellation, Stewart of the

* Tallyrand himself, says Mr McMaster, had been heard to declare that " France had nothing to fear from a nation of debaters that had been trying for three years to build three frigates."

Experiment and Talbot of the Constitution moved France first to surprise and next to reconciliation. When, by another turn of the French kaleidoscope, Napoleon Bonaparte came into power one of his first acts was to reconcile the differences between France and America, and put a stop to the unfriendly ways of French naval commanders. But none the less was this result of an impending quarrel due to the firm front presented by America against French aggression and the valor and pluck of the Yankee blue jackets in their new and hastily improvised " navy."

This trouble with France hardly rose to the dignity of a war. It was scarcely more than a naval duel between two friendly powers who misunderstood rather than detested one another and its end was speedily and joyously announced. But the gallant manner in which the new frigate Constellation bore herself in the two decisive actions of the " duel " left the brightest and most popular memories of this brief international " disturbance." In the first of these the American war-ship captured the French frigate Insurgente ; and in the second she crippled and chased away the larger frigate La Vengeance. Commodore Truxtun of the Constellation was the hero of the hour. His brave fellows were loudly applauded, while the loyalty of the brave little " middy," Jarvis, who would not desert his post by the falling foremast but went down with it to death because there was his place in the battle was held by Congress to be worthy public recognition and esteemed by the people as deserving immortality.

This trouble safely over a respite came. Relieved of the hostile possibilities that had heretofore doubled the risk of every venture and emboldened by the knowledge that there did exist such a protection as an American navy, merchant-men again pushed out on trading trips and the tonnage of the mercantile marine increased steadily until, as has been noted elsewhere, it stood in 1807 at 848,307 tons. Daring captains, like Cleveland of Salem, pushed far from home into the new and unknown seas of the Western Pacific on long and hazardous ventures, while even the uncertainties of the sea that still existed only made the returns from such risks larger because of the few who could engage in it.

One of these hazards was at last to be removed. When in the year 1801 a change in administration made Thomas Jefferson president of the United States, the disgraceful tribute-peace with the robbers of the Barbary Powers was still kept up by the payment of "concessions" and by gifts. The new administration, like the proverbial new broom essayed to sweep clean. The navy of the republic, never sufficiently large, was reduced to what was termed a "peace footing." Seven of the thirteen national frigates were dismantled, the other public vessels were sold, the officers and men not absolutely required to keep up the meagre remnant were discharged, and the protecting power of the navy was rendered almost valueless by this unwise economy. Two of the six frigates kept in service were used for bearing American tribute to the African robbers. The better sense of America revolted at this semi-slavery. But the " interests of commerce " were thought to demand it. " No portion of our annals," says Mr. McMaster, " is more shameful than the story of the dealings of our government with the horde of pirates then known as the Barbary Powers."

American captains revolted at the orders that made them the bearers of hush-money to these contemptible robbers, but they were under orders and must obey. There was therefore something absolutely dramatic in the conduct of Captain Bainbridge. Ordered to Algiers in the frigate Washington with a part of the tribute to the Dey, he was astounded when he reached the robber stronghold to receive orders from the Dey to proceed with the Washington to Constantinople on the Dey's private business — for the Barbary Powers were themselves tributary to Turkey. The doughty captain protested that the Washington was an American ship and could not be used upon other than American service, but the Dey insolently asserted that the payment of tribute made the tributary nation a slave to the one receiving tribute. He demanded, furthermore, that the Washington should fly the Algerine colors at the masthead. Bainbridge's protests were ineffectual. The pleas of the American consul and the guns of the Algerine forts carried the day. The Washington sailed for Constantinople on the Dey's errand and the red flag of Algiers flew from the mainmast; but once out of range of the Algerine batteries the Moor's head banner came down from the peak at a run, and the stars and stripes flew in its stead. Arrived at Constantinople the disgusted Yankee captain dispatched a protest to his superior, the secretary of the navy, and added: " I hope I shall never again be sent to Algiers with tribute, unless I am authorized to deliver it from the mouth of our cannon."

While at Constantinople Bainbridge arranged for a dramatic revenge. He was politic enough to make himself agreeable to the Sultan, who had never even heard of the United States of America. Before returning to Algiers the shrewd Yankee captain obtained from the Porte a royal mandate, or firman protecting him from the insolence of the Dey. Then he sailed back joyfully.

His dramatic stroke succeeded admirably. The Dey had more business at Constantinople and the American frigate was

a convenient messenger. Again he ordered Bainbridge to
carry his message. To his astonishment he met with a curt
refusal. Enraged beyond measure, the Moorish ruler threatened the American captain with the direst punishment and his
nation with a relentless war, whereupon Bainbridge quietly

IN MEDITERRANEAN WATERS.

exhibited the Sultan's firman and the vassal of the Sultan
changed his tone instanter.

It was now Bainbridge's turn. With the air of a master he
demanded the instant release of all the Christian captives. It
was granted at once, and the victorious Yankee captain sailed
away from Algiers carrying with him all the French captives,
released at his order and without ransom.

Still the old disgrace continued. New complications arose.

Tripoli demanded an increase of tribute. The flag-staff of the American consulate was cut down. War was threatened. Congress at last awoke to a sense of its degradation. War-vessels were dispatched to the Mediterranean, and after much "palaver" and some hard fighting the Barbary Powers were humbled. The American sailor, behind the guns of American frigates, made the flag of his country to be both respected and feared and the commerce of the Mediterranean was freed from the peril of the African pirates.

The war had even greater results. It proved to the European powers the pluck of the American sailor and the strength of the small but spirited American navy. It put the half-acknowledged allies and abettors of the Barbary corsairs upon their good behavior, and it is even claimed that the success of the American cruisers in this African war broke forever the power of Venice as a maritime state.

It did even more. It broadened and strengthened the American sailor. It gave him greater self-reliance and convinced him of his ability to withstand, in equal or unequal fight, those whom he had heretofore rather dreaded to meet. As Mr. Abbot has said: " The political bearing of the Tripolitan war upon the war which afterward followed with Great Britain was slight ; but, as a discipline for the sterner reality of naval warfare with the nation long reputed to be mistress of the seas, the experience of the Yankee tars with the turbanned infidels was invaluable."

In this, therefore, as in previous conflicts the American sailor came off with honor. A naval war, waged, as a rule, at a removal from the home-centers contains greater elements of popularity than does the bloodier land conflict. There is a certain strain of mystery and consequently of glory attached to the fight that reddens the plunging decks with the blood of friend and foe, that sends the lofty mainmast crashing down in wreck, and hears, above the battle's blinding smoke, the clash of pike and cutlass or the hoarse shouts of a hand-to-hand conflict as, across the grappled bulwarks, the desperate sea-fighters meet in the deadly boarding-rush. So the sea-hero has always been a popular hero, from the days of the Vikings to those of Trafalgar and Hampton Roads. There was, too, an especial dash of romance about this Mediterranean conflict where Occident and Orient met in a new crusade, and Yankee and Muzlim grappled in deadly fight. The list of heroes grew with each fresh batch of news from the East. And from that three-hours' battle off the shores of ancient Carthage where Sterrett, in the little Enterprise captured the Tripolitan corsair, to that last encounter when Commodore Rodgers, before the walls of Tunis, humbled its turbanned Bashaw into final submission each new encounter gave renewed cause for glorification at home and brought fresh honors to the American navy.

Of course there was another side to it all. The old heroic spirit that had made the earlier followers of the Prophet as terrible as victorious had degenerated into the bully's bluster and the robber's greed. Such a spirit could not withstand the dash and courage of a race of hardy, freedom-loving seamen. The result could not well be other than it proved. But, for all that, the war with the "Barbary Powers" was a feather in Columbia's cap, and the whole nation echoed the sentiment that animated the spirited lines of one of Columbia's rhymsters: —

> " When fame shall tell the splendid story
> Of Columbia's naval glory,
> Since victorious o'er the deep
> Our eagle-flag was seen to sweep,

> The glowing tale will form a page
> To grace the annals of the age,
> And teach our sons to proudly claim
> The brightest meed of naval fame.
> In lofty strains the bard shall tell
> How Truxtun fought, how Somers fell !
> How gallant Preble's daring host
> Triumphed along the Moorish coast;
> Forced the proud infidel to treat,
> And brought the Crescent to their feet."

" Preble's daring host," indeed, gained in the way of laurels from the war more than any of their comrades. With his expedition went that gallant young Portland lieutenant, Henry Wadsworth, who, volunteering to blow up certain Tripolitan cruisers, as voluntarily perished with his comrades, " preferring death to slavery," and leaving thus a hero's memory gave his name as a precious heritage to his famous nephew — America's greatest poet.

With Preble went the younger Decatur, destined for still greater deeds, who with seventy-four brave young comrades, entered the harbor of Tripoli where lay the stranded and captured frigate Philadelphia, grappled with the derelict, drove its Moorish defenders overboard and then setting it on fire escaped almost uninjured through the terrible bombardment that raged all about him from infidel castle, batteries and corsairs. It was this same daring young Decatur, too, who running his gun-boat alongside one of the largest of the Tripolitan vessels speedily overpowered and captured her, grappled with the next largest, slew her gigantic captain in single combat, captured this second vessel and then rejoined his fleet, the hero of the day.

With Preble sailed the plucky midshipman Spence who, when the Siren was blown up by a Tripolitan shot that fired her magazine, coolly loaded the twenty-four pounder at the Siren's bow and as the waves were closing above the sinking vessel fired one last destructive shot at the enemy and went down into the water amid the cheers of his drowning comrades. It was Preble, himself, who, commanding that stout old ironsides, the Constitution, captured a Moorish frigate, forced an apology from the Emperor of Morocco, humbled the ruler of Tripoli, blockaded and bombarded Tunis, and fought so brave and successful a series of engagements with the Barbary Powers that he well-nigh ended the war and received on his return home the official thanks of the Congress and People of the United States.

The war was over. The treaty of peace concluded with the pirates of North Africa was not what the brilliant exploits of the navy should have warranted, but it put an end to further depredation. Not for years did the Algerian corsairs dare again to meddle with American vessels. The tone and efficiency of the American navy had been materially advanced by the successful conflict. Its need and value had been made apparent to the doubters at home; its valor was recognized by the powers abroad. In all this it was preparing the way for that greater and historic conflict with the strongest of the world's naval powers — a conflict which, in brilliancy and achievement was to add new laurels to its growing fame and give new lustre to the name of the American sailor.

CHAPTER VIII

"A—A—LL ha-a-a-ands! up anchor-r-r ahoy!"

It was the hoarse call of the mate summoning his new crew to action. They rallied to the call. Speedily the sails were loosed, the yards were b r a c e d, the anchor catted and fished. T h e last hold upon the home-land was broken, and down the roadstead, and into the open sea sped, let us say, the good ship Perseverance, or Aspasia, or Ontario, of New York, or Boston, or Philadelphia, bound for Hamburg, perhaps, or Copenhagen or some other far-off port with a promising Yankee venture, in the way of a cargo, of sugars and coffee, cochineal and other merchantable stuffs.

But it was seldom that the good ship, whatever her name and wherever bound, reached her destination in entire security. The logs of merchant captains in those opening years of the nineteenth century tell all the same story — heavy risks, constant losses and the ever-present danger of search and inpressment from English war-ships.

In those years England's supremacy of the seas was almost undisputed. In whatever waters her flag was found there was none to successfully dispute her sway. "Since the year 1792," says Mr. Roosevelt, "each European nation, in turn, had learned to feel bitter dread of the weight of England's hand. In the Baltic, Sir William Hood had taught the Russians that they must needs keep in port when the English cruisers were in the offing. The descendants of the Vikings had seen their whole navy destroyed at Copenhagen. No Dutch fleet ever put out after the day when, off Camperdown, Lord Duncan took possession of De Winter's shattered ships. But a few years before 1812, the greatest sea-fighter of all time had died in Trafalgar Bay, and in dying had crumbled to pieces the navies of France and of Spain."

What wonder then that the merchant service of America, protected by the most meagre of navies, should dread the power of England on the seas? Against the thousand sail of the British navy that of America could show but a half-dozen frigates and six or eight sloops and brigs.

Added to this show of superior force the British government had one especial and pernicious political dogma that fell with peculiar force upon American ships. This was the assertion that no British subject could change his nationality. "Once an Englishman always an Englishman — once a subject always a subject," this was the British creed. And, to enforce it, the boarding-officers of many an English frigate proceeded to measures that were unjustifiable, villainous and brutal.

It was in support of this assertion that Great Britain contended that "her war-ships possessed the right of searching all neutral vessels for the property and persons of her foes" and equally that she had the right to take from American merchant

vessels British seamen or seamen claimed to be such, whatever
their protest to the contrary or their ability to show proofs of
American naturalization.

"Any innocent merchant vessel," says Mr. Roosevelt, "was
liable to seizure at any minute; and when overhauled by a
British cruiser short of men was sure to be stripped of her
crew. The British officers were themselves the judges as to
whether a seaman should be pronounced a native of America
or of Britain, and there was no appeal from their judgment."

To this impudent "right of search" the English lords of
the sea added another outrage. They attempted to limit the
freedom of Americans to trade in French ports, although as
neutrals in the troubles between France and England the
American vessels had clearly the right of entry and trade.

So the trouble grew, and for every American merchantman
stripped of its crews by English press-gangs or deprived of its
cargo by English "adjudication" there was one more grievance
placed against England's account, one more vow of vengeance
destined at some time to be kept.*

But even English "decrees" and French "orders" could
not repress the commercial spirit that has always been the
corner-stone of the American character. To make a successful
venture in foreign seas was the hope that burned in the breasts
of many an ambitious lad in the seaport towns of the Atlantic
coastboard.

It has already been shown at how early an age such lads
went away to sea and how they occupied positions of importance on merchant vessels. It is asserted that in many of
these ventures into foreign seas not only the sailors, from cap-

* The reader of Cooper's "Miles Wallingford" can derive an excellent idea of this phase of English
aggression.

tain to cabin-boy, had a personal share but that even the fellow townsman of the merchant who fathered the venture, "not excepting the merchant's minister, intrusted their savings to the supercargo, and watched eagerly the result of their adventure."

How hazardous were these adventures and under what ever-present insecurities they were made can be learned from the log-book of many an American captain of those early days, and from the semi-occasional "Narrative of Voyages and Commercial Enterprises" that some garrulous captain would put through the press.

" Having escaped the pirates of all nations (for Government ships of the present day deserve no better name)," runs the opening line of one of the letters home of Captain Cleveland of Salem in the year 1810; and this but indicates the experience of many a brother captain of those troublous days.

The Embargo by which as an act of retaliation the United States government sought to punish her two most powerful persecutors, France and England, prohibited all vessels from leaving American ports. Its effect was disastrous. For, while it seriously affected the two powers against which it was aimed, it very nearly crippled American commerce.

Retiring from this untenable position Congress substituted for the Embargo the Non-intercourse Act. This prohibited commerce with France and England only. At once business revived. American vessels were again upon the seas and the American flag protected the home ventures in the ports of friendly powers.

To withstand the combined annoyances, however, of the two most powerful European nations was no small matter and this American merchant captains speedily learned to their cost.

The trouble with France in 1798 to which reference has already been made ended satisfactorily for America, thanks to Yankee grit and the friendliness of the great Napoleon. But English annoyance still continued. British cruisers "hove to" many an American merchantman and weakened her crew by their tyrannical "right of search." Sometimes however they were outwitted when by a valorous show of fight or by a diplomacy almost as plucky, the American captain would escape from his persecutor.

All this, though disheartening, was serving a good purpose.

A STERN CHASE.

It was developing the American sailor. For, as is often shown, it is only through the harshest experiences that the stoutest manliness can come. To be ever on his guard, to be ready for sudden action, to elude, to strike, if need be to fight to the death for his venture and his ship was the constant need of the American sailor, be he in fo'cas'le or on quarter-deck.

"Eternal vigilance is the price of liberty," and this vigilance was making the American seaman at once hardy, skillful and daring. Smarting under his wrongs he was burning for the time when he could revenge himself upon his persecutors, and enthusiastically echoed those patriotic words of Pinckney that so fired the American heart: " Millions for defence, but not one cent for tribute ! "

" The stern school in which the American sailor was brought up," says Mr. Roosevelt, "forced him into habits of independent thought and action which it was impossible that the more protected Briton could possess. He worked more intelligently and less from routine, and while perfectly obedient and amenable to discipline, was yet able to judge for himself in an emergency. He was more easily managed than most of his kind — being shrewd, quiet, and, in fact, comparatively speaking, rather moral than otherwise. Altogether there could not have been better material for a fighting crew than cool, gritty American Jack."

The actual demand for this "cool and gritty " material was to come sooner even than the most ardent patriot could imagine. Pushed to extremities by British insolence and outrage America at first protested and at last struck. The complaints of her merchants could not longer go unheeded. " In times like these." wrote Captain Cleveland in 1811, "there is no readier road to ruin than being concerned in shipping." And many a merchant well-nigh despaired of receiving protection from his government. But more potent than the British annoyance of merchantmen was British interference with American men-of-war. The unwarranted attack by the British squadron, in November, 1798, upon the American sloop of war Baltimore and her convoy of merchantmen, the still more dastardly attack by the British cruiser Leopard upon the United States frigate Chesapeake, in June, 1807, and the increasing and bur-densome aggressions of British privateers led to a climax at last in the year 1811, when Commodore Rodgers in the frigate President, took matters into his own hands, and severely punished a British cruiser that insolently answered his hail with a shot through the frigate's rigging. "Equally determined," said Commodore Rodgers in his report of the action, "not to be the aggressor, or to suffer the flag of my country to be insulted with impunity, I gave a general order to fire."

That general order was the signal for speedy action. Diplomacy was of no avail. England would not recede from her position as to the permanence of English allegiance, the right of search and the tyranny of impressment. It must be vassalage or war. The young republic decided for the latter and on the twelfth of June, 1812, formerly declared war against Great Britain.

How the American sailor received this important information may be learned from this entry in the diary of midshipman Matthew Perry, one of that famous family of American sea-fighters: " At ten A. M news arrived that war would be declared the following day against Great Britain. Made the signal for all officers and boats. Unmoored ship and fired a salute." The salute but typified the feelings of all the "blue jackets" in the service. So ready, indeed, were they for action that it is matter of record that on the very next day after young Perry's entry in his diary, and within sixty minutes of the arrival of the news of the declaration of war, Commodore Rodgers' squadron, consisting of five war ships — about one third of the entire American navy — put out to sea, eager to meet the enemy.

And what an enemy they were to face! The war of " eighteen twelve " was a modern reading of the old story of David and Goliath. In spite of all the allowance that should be made for our American tendency to be boastful and vainglorious the unequal proportions of the second war with England make its result a marvel. "The declaration of war by America in June, 1812," says Green, the English historian, "seemed an act of sheer madness. The American navy consisted of a few frigates and sloops; its army was a mass of half-drilled and half-armed recruits; the States themselves were divided on the question of the war." The country, in fact, was actuated by little of that spirit of patriotism that six-and-thirty years before had impelled its people to revolution. Its treasury was empty; its councils were divided. The agriculturists of the interior could not appreciate the woes of their brethren of the seaboard. "So great was the cowardly fear of British invincibility on the seas," says Mr. Griffis, "and so shameful and unjust were the suspicions against our navy that many counsellors at Washington urged that the national vessels should keep within tide-water and act only as harbor batteries. To the earnest personal remonstrance of Captains Bainbridge and Stewart we owe it that our vessels got to sea to win a glory imperishable."

Once committed to the war Congress used every endeavor to strengthen the navy, for it was speedily foreseen that upon that arm of the service must fall the brunt of the conflict. And, from the very outset of the struggle, the "blue jackets" showed that this reliance was not misplaced. More than one stanch frigate sailed to meet the enemy with the American sailor's battle-cry streaming from the masthead: "Free Trade and Sailor's Rights!" while the record of the deeds and the valor of the American sailor in what was pre-eminently his war prove how capable was the American Jack of "eighteen twelve" to meet and grapple with a great responsibility.

It is to be noticed that the British people, puffed up with pride over their long-continued superiority on the seas and misled by the attitude of certain timid folk in America, entered upon the war in a spirit of bravado that was only worthy of defeat. To them and to their press the American nation seemed only to awaken derision and the American navy to be only a subject for ridicule. The Americans, they declared, could not be kicked into a war: "they are spaniel-like in character: the more they are chastised, the more obsequious they become." The American navy to them had no right to the name. Its chief vessel, the Constitution, they characterized as a bundle of pine boards, sailing under a bit of striped bunting. "A few broadsides from England's wooden walls," so they averred, "would drive the paltry striped bunting from the ocean."

But they reckoned without their host. Other "bundles of pine boards" besides the gallant Constitution were to be forthcoming from the spaniel-like people they so affected to despise and the striped bunting was to float in triumph from the masthead of many a British vessel conquered in equal fight.

More than fifty frigates and war-ships of England struck their flags to American men-of-war. A constant stream of vessels were carried into port as prizes taken on the sea by American valor, while the conquests and destruction wrought by American privateers can hardly be computed. Politically, both the issues and results of this war between England and America were of small consideration in comparison with the vaster struggle for supremacy then being waged in Europe. But the naval triumphs of America broke alike the boasting and the tyranny of these so-called lords of the sea. "The effect of these victories," says Green, "was out of all proportion to their real importance; for they were the first heavy blows which had been dealt at England's supremacy over the seas."

And these blows were dealt, emphatically, by the American sailor. In spite of the claims of English historians that the American ships were largely manned by British sailors it is a fact that the crews were almost entirely composed of Americans. Three fourths of the common sailors, so says Mr. Roosevelt, hailed from the Northern States, one half the remainder from Maryland, and the rest chiefly from Virginia and South Carolina. Of the officers, he says, Maryland furnished the greater number, Virginia — then the most populous of all the States — ranking next, while four fifths of the remainder came from the Northern States.

A free people is not always amenable to discipline. And yet it is a significant fact that the personal superiority of the American seaman and his readiness to submit himself to his officers proved one of the main causes of his success in this the chief of America's ocean wars. The navy of the United States was not filled by impressment. Every Yankee Jack was a volunteer. The cause for which he was fighting was his cause. It was not that of any unloved prince or potentate.

"Never mind, shipmates," said brave John Alvinson as an eighteen-pound shot tore away his life, "I die in defense of Free Trade and Sailor's Rights," and with the American seaman's watchword upon his lips, he expired. "I left my own country and adopted the United States to fight for her," said the wounded Scotch sailor John Ripley, on the captured and crippled Essex Junior. "I hope I have this day proved myself worthy of the country of my adoption. I am no longer of any use to you or to her. I will not die in an English prison. Good-by!" And suiting the action to the word he threw himself overboard.

The American seaman, rough as he may have been, with a

certain independence of character that was sometimes unwelcome and even galling to those placed in authority over him, free-spoken with his superiors where the European man-o'-warsman was almost servile in his time-serving obedience, was always a patriot. He had, says Mr. Roosevelt, "an honest and deep affection for his own flag; while, on the contrary, he felt a curiously strong hatred for England, as distinguished from Englishmen. This hatred was partly an abstract feeling, cherished through a vague traditional respect for Bunker Hill, and partly something very real and vivid, owing to the injuries he and others like him had received. Whether he lived in Maryland or Massachusetts, he certainly knew men whose ships had been seized by British cruisers, their goods confiscated and the vessels condemned. Some of his friends had fallen victims to the odious right of search, and had never been heard of afterwards. He had suffered many an injury to friend, fortune or person and some day he hoped to repay them all; and when the war did come he fought all the better because he knew it was in his own quarrel."

It must be frankly admitted that the war of 1812 was brought to a conclusion not because England acknowledged herself defeated, but because the downfall of Napoleon and the adjustment of European affairs made further strife unnecessary. For this war with America was only esteemed by Great Britain as a sort of insignificant side-issue. The losses incurred by the British navy were scarcely noticeable in view of its vast proportions and its immense resources. Had Great Britain really been stubbornly determined to fight out the question of supremacy to the extent of her abilities the war might have had a different ending. And yet the fact remains that, though the treaty of Ghent which terminated the war made no men-

ON BOARD THE GUERRIERE.— "CAPTAIN HULL'S COMPLIMENTS."

tion of the causes that led to the quarrel, the encroachments of English cruisers upon American commerce were forever abandoned and the right of search and the impressment of American seamen became things of the past.

For three years was this war fought. Commodore Rodgers' opening gun — discharged by his own hand — was fired from the frigate President at the British frigate Belvidera off the Nantucket shoals, on June the twenty-second, 1812; the last broadside of the war thundered by command of Captain Biddle from the open ports of the Hornet in the South Atlantic on the twenty-third of March, 1815. And through all that desperate conflict for his right to the seas the American blue jacket conducted himself as a sailor and distinguished himself as a hero.

Space is not sufficient here to enter into the details of each encounter. But, more than ships and cannon, more than oak and iron, were the men who met in conflict and made their acts historic. "The Republic of the United States," says Mr. Roosevelt, "owed a great deal to the excellent make and armament of its ships, but it owed still more to the men who were in them. The massive timbers and heavy guns of Old Ironsides would have availed but little had it not been for her able commanders and crews." The story of those years of sea-struggle has been told by able pens and should prove inspiriting reading for all Americans. As one of these very chroniclers well remarks: "It must be a poor-spirited American whose veins do not tingle with pride when he reads of the cruises and fights of the sea-captains, and their grim prowess, which kept the old Yankee flag floating over the waters of the Atlantic for three years, in the teeth of the mightiest naval power the world has ever seen."

In the long list of naval heroes who made this war a brilliant era in America's story place and praise must be given to many an honored name — to Decatur and Perry and Jones, to Blakely and Biddle and Bainbridge, to Lawrence and Burrows and Allen, to Warrington and Stewart and Porter, while even above these gallant commanders must stand the names of Macdonough, victor on Lake Champlain, and of Isaac Hull, master of sea-tactics, "whose successful escape and victorious fight place him above any single ship-captain of the war."

The splendid defense by Captain Porter of the Essex against the combined attack of the British war-ships Phœbe and Cherub — an action in which our later hero Farragut, then a boy of barely thirteen, received his baptism of fire — finds scarcely a parallel in the history of the American navy; the rash but glorious action by which Lawrence lost alike the Chesapeake and his life won him eternal renown, even through defeat and death, as the " Bayard of the seas "; the successful conflict waged by Macdonough upon the land-locked waters of Lake Champlain proved him one of the greatest of American sea captains; Perry's victory on Lake Erie, from whence came that historic dispatch, "We have met the enemy and they are ours!" made his name more famous than is that of any other captain in the war; and, singularly enough, it was the masterly escape of the grand old Constitution, rather than her notable victory over the Guerriere, that has gained for Hull his greatest renown and made the affair by far the most remarkable occurrence of the war.

The story of that escape is well worth the re-telling. Cruising off the New Jersey coast on the seventeenth of July, 1812, while yet the war was young, the United States frigate Constitution found herself threatened by five of the ablest cruisers in the British navy. To fight was almost certain defeat. Captain Isaac Hull, commanding the Constitution, had under him a newly shipped crew of four hundred and fifty men (including officers), but few of them as yet familiar with the ways of naval war. Discretion was clearly the better part of valor, but even the discretion that retires seemed here unavailable.

To manœuvre a forty-four gun frigate out of the clutches of five well-equipped cruisers would tax the utmost skill of a master of sea-tactics. But Isaac Hull was as daring as he was skillful, and proved himself equal to the emergency.

Bearing down upon his lee quarter were the Belvidera and Guerriere; astern were the Shannon, the Æolus and the Africa. The wind died out. The ships were all becalmed. The enemy was drifting nearer and nearer. Capture was imminent.

What wind and sails could not accomplish muscle must do. At once Hull ordered out all his boats manned by his sturdiest oarsmen and bade them pull the ship out of her danger. Stout hawsers were run out and attached to the row boats. Willing arms and sturdy backs bent to the task and the Constitution began to edge towards safety. Not to be out-pulled the British ships resorted to the same tactics and the intervening distance was lessened. Preparing for the worst Hull dragged an eighteen-pounder as a stern-chaser to the spar-deck of his frigate, shifted one of his forecastle twenty-fours to the stern and ran two twenty-fours out of his cabin windows. "They near us at their peril," said plucky Captain Hull.

The Shannon, Captain Philip Broke's frigate, coming nearest in this towing contest essayed to open fire on the American but soon found herself out of range and gave it up. Calling all the boats of the squadron to his aid Broke bade the rowers

pull till the oars cracked but bring him within range of the
Yankee. The space was lessening again. Hull, with ready
wit, tried a new dodge. Splicing his hawsers until he had one
of the required length he attached a kedge-anchor to this and,
paying it out to his cutters, dropped anchor half a mile ahead of
his bows. Then came the order: " Clap on now, lads, and walk
away with the ship!" Ready and alert the Jackies on the
Constitution's deck sprang to the rope and hauled away for
dear life until the great ship was actually pulled up to the
kedge-anchor and out of all possible gun-range. Another half-
mile hawser was ready and the manœuvre was repeated. The
watchful Britons were at first nonplused, not at once "seeing
the point." As soon, however, as they did fathom the " Yankee trick" they immediately followed suit and began to " kedge"
also. For four hours did this slow-going game of sea-tag in a
calm continue, and still the Constitution was not caught. Then
a light breeze sprung up. The Constitution fired a good-by
shot at her nearest neighbor the Shannon, trimmed her sails and
called in her boats. The little puff of wind had brought the
Guerriere a trifle nearer the American and now she essayed a
broadside It fell short of the mark, as had the Shannon's shot
and the Constitution entirely ignored it.

The wind died out again. Hull lightened his ship by starting overboard two thousand gallons of water and set his stout
oarsmen to work on the tow-lines once more. The Shannon
did the same. And now with kedge and tow-line it was nip
and tuck between the two big frigates. But the Constitution
was the better handled of the two and kept just beyond the
danger range.

And now came the Belvidera's turn to play catcher. Working a double " kedge " she outstripped her consorts, gained con-

siderably upon the Constitution, and opened fire on her. But
she, too, was out of range and fared no better than had her predecessors. In the face, indeed, of the extra guns that Hull had
trained on his pursuers none of the British vessels dared to
come too near the Yankee fearing he would disable or sink
their tow-boats.

For fully twenty-four hours had the chase been going on.

It was tow and kedge, kedge and tow, but always just out of
gun-shot for the baffled British cruisers. Their sailors were
worn out with the unaccustomed labor. The capture of the
Yankee, seeming ever just within their grasp, really came no
nearer. And if they were wearied what must have been the

condition of the Americans?   But the brave blue-jackets
stuck manfully to their work; officers and men "spelled"
each other uncomplainingly, catching what bits of rest they
could, and wherever they could.

All night long the chase continued. Every puff of wind
was taken advantage of, alike by pursuers and pursued, to fill
their lifeless sails. At last, at half-past five on the morning of
the second day of the chase the breeze freshened, the boats
were again called in and with every stitch of canvas set the
race became a trial of sailing skill.

With his eye noting every move and flutter of his sails,
Captain Hull worked his ship so skillfully as to draw perceptibly
ahead of his foes. As the evening of the second day closed in
he was unmistakably gaining. The Belvidera was two miles
and a half in his wake; the Shannon was three and a half miles
on his lee; the Guerriere and the Æolus were five miles and
more astern, and the Africa was so far to leeward as to be practically out of the race.

Suddenly the sky clouded.   There came a change in the air.
The practiced eye of the Yankee captain detected signs of a
coming squall. "That shall bring us freedom," he declared.
And now again he added wit to forethought. "We'll make 'em
think there's a hurricane coming," he said. With a great show
of preparation for a coming gale, he furled his light canvas,
took a double reef in his mizzen topsail and brought his vessel
instantly under short sail just as the squall struck the ship.
The British, perceiving this evident haste of action to escape a
rising gale, followed suit as they had done before at every fresh
Yankee manœuvre, and began to take in all sail speedily and
to sail on different tacks to escape the storm. The ruse succeeded admirably. The storm and mist closed down upon the

vessels for an instant and then the squall passed off to leeward, but in that instant Captain Hull had sheeted home, hoisted his fore and main-top gallant sails and "with every rag out" was speeding away from his pursuers at the rate of eleven knots an hour. He had out-sailed, out-manœuvred and out-witted his foe! The disgusted Britons hastened to clap on all sail again and follow their escaping prey but the chase was virtually over. At sunset the American was far ahead; at six o'clock on the morning of the third day the British squadron was almost lost to sight and two hours later the hopeless chase was abandoned. Yankee grit had won.

One of the finest frigates in the American navy had been saved to the service when least it could have been spared by one of the most remarkable and most exciting sea-races on record. Becalmed, surrounded and threatened with almost certain capture, pitted against five well-equipped British captains — two of them among the ablest in the whole British navy — Isaac Hull had most skillfully out of the nettle danger plucked the flower safety, and in a three days' race for life had proven the superior skill and seamanship of the American sailor.

Within less than a month he had his revenge. Coming up with the Guerriere, one of the most boastful of his pursuers, on the afternoon of the nineteenth of August, he commenced action at once. No less skillful in battle than in retreat, he so handled his ship and so played his guns that after a desperate encounter, lasting only thirty minutes, the Guerriere was a defenceless hulk, rolling her main-deck guns into the sea.

"Captain Hull presents his compliments, sir," said young Lieutenant Read of the Constitution, springing upon the deck of the crippled frigate, "and wishes to know if you have struck your flag?"

"Well, I don't know," was the dry reply of Dacres, the captain of the Guerriere, "our mizzen-mast is gone; our mainmast is gone; and I think, on the whole, you may say to Captain Hull that we have struck our flag."

If such encounters as were these proved the ability of American commanders they showed, no less, the grit and fighting-stuff of the American sailor. "I honestly believe," says Mr. Roosevelt, "that the American sailor offered rather better material for a man-of-wars-man than the British, because the freer institutions of his country, and the peculiar exigencies of his life tended to make him more intelligent and self-reliant." And the fragmentary stories that have come down to us from that time of struggle bear out this statement.

"My brave fellow, you are mortally wounded," said the surgeon of the Constitution to Tobias Fernell, as the mangled sailor with both legs shot away echoed with a cheery shout his comrades' huzzas of victory over the captured Cyane.

"I know it, sir; I know it. I only care to hear that the other ship has struck."

When, during the engagement with the Guerriere, the Constitution's flag was shot away from the main-top, young John Hogan gallantly climbed to the top and, amid a storm of bullets, lashed it to the mast. When Garnet "as gallant as Nelson," fell, in Chauncey's fight in Kingston harbor, his men "prayed and entreated to be laid close aboard the Royal George only for five minutes, just to revenge Garnet's death."

Michael Smith, with his thigh twice shattered in the fight with the Penguin, lifted himself on the bloody deck of the Hornet "just for one last shot." Perry's pilot in the Lake Erie fight, jumped with his leader into the boat that was to make the perilous passage from the Lawrence to the Niagara declaring that he would stick by his captain to the last; James Anderson, in the Essex and Phœbe fight, with his dying breath bade his messmates "Give it to 'em, give it to 'em hard, lads; we're fighting for our liberty;" Seaman Thompson of the Chesapeake, hearing the call for boarders, alone sprang upon the Shannon when others held back from the leap, and finding himself unsupported bravely fought his way back to his own deck again. "Aim at the yellow, man!" cried Decatur to one of his gunners. The shot, thus aimed, struck the mizzen-mast of the Macedonian just as it was falling. "Ah-ha, my boy," said the excited sailor, slapping his watching commodore on the back, "we've made a brig of her!"

These, and countless other incidents of similar tenor that have come to us as "fo'cas'l' yarns" or as matter of historic record, may be treasured by all Americans as proof of the valor, the determination, the enthusiasm, and the patriotism of the American sailor. Nor should we forget the gallant record of that less regular but fully as efficient factor in the tale of naval warfare, the privateers of "eighteen twelve." Bent mainly on the accumulation of prize-money they nevertheless exhibited as much of courage, of dash and of patriotism as did their brothers of the regular service. The story of Captain Boyle and the Chasseur, of Captain Southcombe and the Lottery, of Captain Ordronaux and the Neufchatel, with many others of equal merit have given, alike to captains and crews of these irregular cruisers, as fine a record for bravery and skill as appears to the credit of the regularly commissioned seamen; the career of Captain Samuel Reid and his famous craft the General Armstrong is one continuous record of daring and of valor. "God deliver us from our enemies, if this is the way they fight," cried one Englishman, who witnessed the terrible defeat of the fourteen British boats, off Fayal, by Reid and his privateersmen.

War is always a sad alternative. The conflict of 1812 was unnecessary and might have been averted had but England been less arrogant in her claims of mastery and had America been less vacillating in her foreign policy. But when the war did come it was so gallantly fought out, at least upon the ocean and the lakes, as to give to the American sailor of eighteen hundred and twelve a notable place in the annals of naval warfare and on the rolls of naval heroism.

CHAPTER IX

NE would imagine that the growth of the ocean commerce, and therefore of the commercial marine of the United States would have been instant and rapid when once the American sailor had established his right to the seas. But this seems not to have been the case. Statistics show that during the years succeeding the close of the last war with Great Britain (notably between the years 1818 and 1825) there was not only no increase in what is known by merchants as "the registered tonnage " of the United States but a real decrease.

In the year 1807 this "registered tonnage " was, as has been already stated, 848,307 tons ; in the year 1837 it was but 810,000 tons — a falling off of over 38,000 tons, instead of the increase that one would suppose should have resulted from thirty years of American progress.

One explanation of this absolute decline in commercial energy is to be found in the fact that the almost ceaseless warfare between France and England, during the years that succeeded the formation of the United States of America, had thrown the carrying trade of the world almost exclusively into American control. The conclusion of this long-standing hostility enabled both Powers to take to themselves once again the transportation of their respective commerical ventures, while the blow dealt to American commerce by the dangers of war and the restrictions of embargo and non-intercourse was one from which recovery was slow.

The development of so new and so vast a country as was the United States offered to the enterprising youth of America an even more promising field for successful labor than the uncertain ocean could assure. Those who had heretofore looked longingly toward a sea-life found a stronger influence in the gleam of the axe and the crack of the rifle, while many a toughened tar whose life had been spent in the forecastle of a merchantman or on the deck of a man-o'-war now deserted his old associations for the life of the pioneer, and in these new and, at first, strange surroundings exchanged the cutlass for the ploughshare and the marline-spike for the pruning hook.

To this general statement one exception must be made. There was one class of seafaring-men who were not to be turned from their old pursuits by the allurements of Western forests or the golden promises of the fertile frontier. The fisher-folk of the East were proof against the fascinations of the West. For them the golden harvest field had no attraction. Beneath the tossing waters that washed their rocky shores lay as certain and as sure a harvest as Western grain-fields could give. "No whaler," says Mr. McMaster, "left his vessel; no fisherman of Marblehead or Gloucester exchanged the dangers of a life on the ocean for the privations of a life in the West. Their fathers and their uncles had been fishermen before them, and their sons were to follow in their steps."

As the result of these changing phases in American life the enterprise of the American sailor upon the high seas, for at least a quarter of a century, lay practically dormant. The coasting trade grew steadily and domestic commerce called for the employment of smaller craft and for good "near-shore" sailors. These home-stayers, however, the regulation ocean sailor always affected to despise.

But, all in good time, there came a change. The ceaseless tide of immigration and the constantly-increasing population of the American nation led to as rapid a growth of its commerce. That stagnant quarter of a century that closed with 1837 was followed by a sudden and marvelous advance. From 810,000 tons engaged in foreign commerce or ventures on the high seas — so the dry statistics tell us — the registered tonnage of the United States rose to 1,241,000 in 1847, to 2,463,000 in 1857, and, in 1861, had reached the successful-looking total of 2,642,000 tons. That year marked the culminating point of American commerce. For it is stated that in that historic and pivotal year of America's national life, the maximum tonnage of the United States — that is to say, the entire carrying capacity of the mercantile vessels of the United States engaged in foreign and domestic trade and in the fisheries — amounted to 5,539,813 tons. This was very nearly one third of the tonnage of the entire world, which had then reached a total of more than seventeen million tons. It was but a trifle below that of Great Britain, and was very nearly as large as the entire tonnage of all the other maritime nations combined.

That quarter-century of steady maritime growth — from 1837 to 1861 — is esteemed for America as the "palmy days" of its merchant service. The ships of the American republic sailed into every sea; her flag was a familiar sight in every port; her sailors were esteemed the most fortunate of all sea-farers; her service stood at the best and was held in the highest repute.

"In those days," says Mr. Nordhoff, "the American ship was the tautest, the best fitted, the best sailer and made the most successful voyages. The American shipmaster was by far the most intelligent of his class; he had also the air, as he had the habit of success; and he delighted in nothing so much as in a 'trading voyage,' in which he was not only master, but supercargo, and with a 'roving commission' went out to Africa, or the Indian Ocean, or the 'West Coast,' to barter American goods and Yankee notions for the produce of the country. . . . . In those days we Yankees counted ourselves the best men that sailed the seas."

One of the most famous of Longfellow's poems found its inspiration in these days of Yankee supremacy on the sea, — "The Building of the Ship" written in 1849. Of that poem President Lincoln said, as with tear-filled eyes and with cheeks still wet he listened to the closing lines, "it is a wonderful gift to be able to stir men like that." And surely a service that could inspire such lines must have been superb in it appointments, noble and manly in its calling:

> " Behold at last,
> Each tall and tapering mast
> Is swung into its place ;
> Shrouds and stays
> Holding it firm and fast!
>
> .   .   .
>
> And every where
> Her slender, graceful spars
> Poise aloft in the air,

And at the mast head,
White, blue and red,
A flag unrolls the stripes and stars.
Ah! when the wanderer, lonely, friendless,
In foreign harbors shall behold
That flag unrolled,
'Twill be as a friendly hand
Stretched out from his native land,
Filling his heart with memories sweet and endless!
. . . .

To-day the vessel shall be launched!
With fleecy clouds the sky is blanched,
And o'er the bay,
Slowly, in all his splendors dight,
The great sun rises to behold the sight.
. . . .

Then the Master
With a gesture of command,
Waved his hand ;
And at the word,
Long and sudden there was heard,
All around them and below,
The sound of hammers, blow on blow,
Knocking away the shores and spurs.
And see! she stirs !
She starts — she moves — she seems to feel
The thrill of life along her keel,
And, spurning with her foot the ground,
With one exulting, joyous bound,
She leaps into the ocean's arms!"

In those days of many ships and of stanch ones the
American sailor was a man of mark among those who "went
down to the sea in ships." As a result he was inclined to hold
himself above the seamen of other nations. A Yankee crew,
with a certain arrogance of its surroundings, was accustomed
to commiserate and even to despise those whom fortune or fate
had placed in the ships of other nations. "They looked down,"
says Mr. Nordhoff, "upon the 'lime-juicers,' as they called
English ships and sailors, as rather a stupid and semi-brutal

lot. They laughed at the 'parleyvoos,' or Frenchmen, as better
shoemakers than sailors. They despised the 'Dagoes,' or
Spaniards, as fellows who always lost in the race." The American seamen had also a certain aristocracy of service among
themselves. "The style and gentility of a ship and her crew,"
says Mr. Dana, "depended upon the length and character of

UNDER FULL SAIL.

the voyage. An India or China voyage was always the thing,
and a voyage for furs to the Northwest coast (the Columbia
River or Russian America) was romantic and mysterious, and if
it but took the ship round the world, by way of the Islands and
China, it would outrank them all." "One of the Pilgrim's
crew," he continues, "used to tell a story of a mean little cap-

tain in a mean little brig "— there were such, it seems, even then in the American service — " in which he sailed from Liverpool to New York, who insisted on speaking a great homeward-bound Indiaman, with her studding-sails out on her decks, and a monkey and paroquet in her rigging, ' rolling down from St. Helena.' There was no need of his stopping to speak her, but his vanity led him to do it, and then his meanness made him so awe-struck that he seemed to quail. He called out, in a small, lisping voice, ' What ship is that, pray ? ' A deep-toned voice roared through the trumpet, ' The Bashaw, from Canton, bound to Boston. Hundred and ten days out! Where are you from ? ' ' Only from Liverpool, sir,' he lisped, in a most apologetic and subservient voice. The humor of this," adds Mr. Dana, " will be felt by those only who know the ritual of hailing at sea. No one says ' sir,' and the ' only ' was wonderfully expressive."

Next to the Indiamen and other long-voyage vessels the packet-ships held honorable rank among the craft on the high seas. They were always well-built, well-officered and well-manned, and carried the choicest of cargoes — passengers from overcrowded Europe seeking life and opportunity in the great Western Republic. These were the " greyhounds of the seas," known as clipper ships, built in New York and Brooklyn yards and commanded by " true-blue " American officers. The commanders of these packet ships were, indeed, alert and energetic men, masters in their profession and ambitious to maintain the record for speed and promptness. " The master of the Montauk," says Cooper, in one of his novels descriptive of life on a packet ship, " had a proper relish for his lawful gain as well as another, but he was vainglorious on the subject of his countrymen, principally because he found that the packets out-

sailed all other merchant-ships, and fiercely proud of any quality
that others were disposed to deny them."

Built for fast sailing, with symmetrical proportions and ele-
gant appointments, the packet ship of fifty years ago, occupied
the place now filled by the superb vessels of the great foreign
steamship lines. Writers of that day are loud in their praise.
N. P. Willis in one of his descriptions of the New York water-
side speaks of " the superb packet ships with their gilded prows."
Cooper refers to them as " those surpassingly beautiful and
yacht-like ships that now ply between the two hemispheres in
such numbers, and which in luxury and the fitting conveniences
seem to vie with each other for the mastery."

It was the day of rapid sailing under canvas. The packet
ships were the fleetest of these sea-racers and every brilliant
record was noted with pride by press and people. Vessels like
the Palestine would often make the passage from New York to
the Isle of Wight in fourteen days, and the ambitious packet
captain anxious to keep up the record, would remain on deck
hour after hour crowding on canvas and taking advantage of
every possible change in wind and rain. " A fine sight it was,"
says a writer of that day, " to see a returning packet come up
the East River and anchor off her pier with all sails set. The
news of her arrival had been conveyed from Sandy Hook to
Staten Island and thence by another signal telegraph to New
York, though, perhaps, she had been two days in sailing her
last twenty miles from the Hook to the river."

The famous Dreadnaught was one of the most celebrated of
these Yankee clippers. Built in 1853. on her first return trip
from Liverpool she beat the Cunard steamer Canada into
Boston harbor. In 1859 she made the phenomenal run of three
thousand miles from Sandy Hook to Rock Light, Liverpool, in

thirteen days and eight hours, while, three years after, in 1862,
she covered the distance from Sandy Hook to Queenstown,
twenty-seven hundred and sixty miles, in nine days and seventeen hours. This feat by a sailing vessel stands without a
parallel. Steam, alas! that tolled the death knell of the ocean
packets shelved the noble Dreadnaught. But she sailed blue
water stoutly to the last. In the September gales of 1887, the
famous old clipper yielded to the enemy she had so long kept
under keel. In that fierce month of storm she went down in
wreck off the cruel coast of Newfoundland.

Far different from these trim and elegantly appointed passenger vessels in which the sailor found a snug berth, short
passages and fair pay, were the merchant vessels that made
long voyages to every point of the compass in the interests of
the special branch of commerce that their owners affected.
No better or more graphic description of life aboard such a
merchant vessel can be found than is detailed in that American
sea-classic by Richard Henry Dana, familiar to thousands of
readers as "Two Years Before the Mast." His experiences as
a common sailor upon two of the Boston hide-ships on the
Pacific coast — the Pilgrim and the Alert — touch both the
sun and shadow in the American sailor's life, and with all
the breezy flavor of a sea story combine the realism of daily
life aboard ship and the masterly touches of a well-equipped
student of human nature. No American boy should be
allowed to grow to manhood without having the opportunity
to read this unaffected and manly recital of an American
sailor's experiences "before the mast."

Life on the high seas, as countless books of salt-water
adventure and experience have pictured it, had in it more of
stern reality, of harsh requirements, and of unwelcome duties

than almost any other service into which a free man could voluntarily enter. "My lad," said one old sailor to a younger listener as the two stood by the hastily-made grave of a fellow-seaman, "log this down for your benefit: there is not much in a life that means hard work, poor pay, and ends like this; you drop it as soon as you can."

But there were few who did drop it until, after years of hard service, like battered hulks they drew ashore to slowly go to pieces in the safe harborage of home or, perhaps, within one of the numerous "Retreats" that philanthropy built for the kindly care of such human "flotsam and jetsam." With all its hardships and with all its risks there was always a fascination about this life on the heaving waters and the rolling deck that sent back to it again and again those who had thought to give it up forever when once they made their home port in safety.

The American sailor, in those "palmy days" when there were American sailors, retained his manliness and his individuality where the seamen of other nationalities were apt to be surly, grumbling, obsequious or time-serving, deceitful or insubordinate, according to their national characteristics or the nature of the service under whose flag they sailed. The American was more of a comrade, had less of the petty and personal jealousies that life in the confined compass of the gloomy forecastle was liable to create, and seemed to possess a higher idea of the real meaning of duty than had the seamen of other nations. "Now, Charley," said one of the shipmates of young Nordhoff, as that boyish sailor was about to ship into a new vessel as "able seaman; "now, Charley, this is your first voyage as seaman, and you mustn't let any one go before you. Wherever there's duty, there's likely to be danger, boy, and wherever there's danger, there do you be first."

It is a common remark that a ship on the high seas, in those busy days, was a floating autocracy in which the captain held the power of life and death, and where resistance was mutiny. But American seamen knew their rights and even tyrannical officers paid respect to the unwritten law of the forecastle.

One of these unwritten laws was said to be that no officer had a right to enter the " fo'cas'l' " without giving due notice of his intention and receiving the permission of its occupants. It once happened in an American ship, so the story goes, that an impatient mate finding the watch slow in answering his summons sprang down " below " to hurry them up. On the instant the flickering forecastle " glim " was " doused "; the object that happened to be nearest within reach of the outraged seamen — from boot to " scouse-kid " — went flying at the head of the offending officer and he, like a prudent man, made for the deck without further words and as rapidly as possible. Sea law was against him. He knew it, and he knew also that he had too good a crew to " risk a fuss." He simply held his temper and his tongue, while the men were sensible enough to seek for no further advantage from their victory. Another of these " fo'cas'l' " laws made it improper for new hands to be set to work before they had been " called aft " and " turned to duty." There is a story that a mate on an American vessel once, with oaths and hard language, ordered aloft certain of his crew who had just come aboard. At once the men, in a body, walked aft and, hats in hand, confronted the astonished mate. " Mr. Mate," said the oldest sailor, acting as spokesman, " we've shipped on your vessel as able seamen. We know our duty, sir, and mean to do it. If we don't, we know what to expect. But we're no 'sogers.' We mean to be treated decently and civilly as long as we do our duty. So look a-here. If you swear at one of us, he'll swear back. If you strike one of us, he'll kill you." This was forecastle law stoutly laid down. But the mate knew that, as custom ran, the men were in the right. He saw, moreover, that they were thorough seamen, and, without a word of hot reply he said simply, "Go forward, men, and turn to your duty. Two of you go aloft and cross the topgallant-yard, the rest of you stand by." And, in a long and tedious voyage, says the narrator, there was never a threat of trouble or abuse on board that ship. " Fo'cas'l' law " had been recognized and respected.

To the merchant service, indeed, as a school for training, was awarded by Mr. Nordhoff, who had himself served in both, the preference, as compared with the navy. The merchantman, he says, assumed interests and felt consequent responsibilities to which the "blue-jacket" was a stranger. There were fewer hands to do the work, and each sailor therefore, if he would save himself double duty in the end, was watchful, alert and ready to share the labors that fall to those before the mast. " And among every good crew," says Mr. Nordhoff, "there exists an *esprit de corps* which makes each man do his duty willingly, but present a front as of one man to the officer who attempts to exact more."

But forecastle law is brief and meagre when compared with the autocracy of the quarter-deck. Legislation has considerably modified this petty tyranny but, fifty years ago, the authority of a captain on board his ship had scarcely a limit. He was, indeed, "lord paramount." Although life on a merchant vessel was less hampered with rules and restrictions than on a man-of-war the sailors' privileges, even on the best of merchant ships, were few indeed. " Them men-o'-war captains is little kings," said an old sailor, contrasting life on a merchant vessel

ON THE HIGH SEAS.

to that on a war ship. But all the records show that even the bondage of the latter, so thoroughly hated by merchant sailors, was often equaled in severity by the slavery on the former. Punishments were frequent. Insolence and tyranny toward the over-worked sailors all too often led either to abject submission or to insubordination and a brutal captain could make his ship, as the sailors often called it, "a floating hell."

"Every one else," says Mr. Dana, after describing an unwarranted flogging scene on the ship in which he was one of the crew, "stood still at his post, while the captain, swelling with rage and with the importance of his achievements, walked the quarter-deck and at each turn as he came forward calling out to us: 'You see your condition! You see where I have got you all and you know what to expect! I'll make you toe the mark, every soul of you, or I'll flog you all, fore and aft, from the boy up! You've got a driver over you! Yes, a slave driver — a nigger driver! I'll see who'll tell me he isn't a nigger slave!'" Such treatment and such language were ill-fitted to make an American sailor submissive and obedient. A seaman of foreign birth would sulk under them and dream of a sweet revenge, but the American, with the sense of outraged manliness and the knowledge that at home he was a free man and a citizen, was stung by such treatment to a sense of degredation that his un-American comrade was incapable of. "I had no apprehension," says Mr. Dana, "that the captain would try to lay a hand on me; but our situation living under a tyranny with an ungoverned, swaggering fellow administering it and the character of the country we were in; the length of the voyage; the uncertainty attending our return to America; and then if we should return a prospect of obtaining justice and satisfaction for these poor men all filled me with dread;

and I vowed that, if God should ever give me the means, I would do something to redress the grievances and relieve the sufferings of that class of beings with whom my lot had so long been cast."

That he kept his vow we are well assured. Flogging on board American ships has long been a thing of the past. While the organized movement for its abolition was largely the work of such noble naval officers as Commodore Matthew Perry and his associates, it is not easy to calculate how much of the reform in this direction was due also to the silent influence of " Two Years Before the Mast."

Subjected to abuse of this sort it is little wonder that in persons of weak natures or of ill-balanced minds tyranny should lead to recklessness, and that, far too often, Jack should have developed into a drudge on shipboard and a sot ashore. Annoyances, deprivations, hardships and petty tyrannies often ruined many a poor fellow who had not sufficient strength of character to bear up under their strain. But it is equally true that where such treatment could be borne in silence or was manfully resisted the experience often served to bring out all that was strongest and most determined in a seaman's nature.

" Sailors are rough fellows," says Mr. Nordhoff, speaking out of his own experience, "and have their full share of the weaknesses incident to our common humanity ; but careless and light-hearted — and often positively wicked — as is your real tar, no man has a warmer or more easily-touched heart than he ; no one is more susceptible to the deeper and better feelings of our nature. . . . . Rough and plain-spoken as he is there is no tenderer heart than Jack's. There is no kinder nurse in sickness, no less selfish companion in the every-day pursuits of life, no more open-handed and free-hearted giver to the poor and needy, than he of the bronzed cheek and tarry frock."

So life on the high seas, in those "palmy days" of the merchant service, with all its hardships and with all its drawbacks, was full of the promise of adventure, of excitement, of change and of profit. Small wonder, then, that it could lure the dashing, ambitious and restless young fellow ashore into serving before the mast — hopeful, even to the last, of rising to the mate's berth or to the authority of the quarter-deck.

The demands of the merchant service gave employment, in those days, to thousands of busy workers on land as well as sea, and in every seaboard community, from Bath to Baltimore, and on to Charleston and New Orleans, the sound of saw and hammer, adze and plane testified to the growing spirit of commercial enterprise, as, down from the well-greased ways of many a ship-yard, slid the finished hull that had been for months busily preparing upon the stocks — a fresh proof of the clever and finished workmanship that gave to American vessels the palm for beauty, stanchness and speed.

East and west, south and north sped the stout ships, their white wings filled by favoring breezes, the flag of the Union flying at the masthead, and, tightly packed in capacious holds, the products of many a land and clime. The sailor loved his ship. Alike hardy seaman and hopeful merchant, as they looked with pride upon glistening hull, tapering mast and bulging sail, could praise the skill and the deft workmanship that had given so beautiful a creation to the sea. And both, too, could join with the shipbuilders in that song of their craft that Whittier, our poet of the people, had voiced for them : —

> "Up! — up! — in nobler toil than ours
> No craftsmen bear a part :
> We make of Nature's giant powers
> The slaves of human Art.

Lay rib to rib and beam to beam,
  And drive the treenails free;
Nor faithless joint nor yawning seam
  Shall tempt the searching sea!

Where'er the keel of our good ship
  The sea's rough field shall plough, —
Where'er her tossing spars shall drip
  With salt-spray caught below, —
That ship must heed her master's beck,
  Her helm obey his hand,
And seamen tread her reeling deck
  As if they trod the land.

Her oaken ribs the vulture-beak
  Of Northern ice may peel;
The sunken rock and coral peak
  May grate along her keel;
And know we well the painted shell
  We give to wind and wave,
Must float, the sailor's citadel,
  Or sink, the sailor's grave!

Ho! — strike away the bars and blocks,
  And set the good ship free!
Why lingers on these dusty rocks
  The young bride of the sea?
Look! how she moves adown the grooves,
  In graceful beauty now!
How lowly on the breast she loves
  Sinks down her virgin prow!

God bless her! wheresoe'er the breeze
  Her snowy wing shall fan,
Aside the frozen Hebrides,
  Or sultry Hindostan!
Where'er in mart or on the main,
  With peaceful flag unfurled,
She helps to wind the silken chain
  Of commerce round the world!

Speed on the ship ! But let her bear
　No merchandise of sin,
No groaning cargo of despair
　Her roomy hold within ;
No Lethean drug for Eastern lands,
　Nor poison-draught for ours ;
But honest fruits of toiling hands
　And Nature's sun and showers.

Be hers the Prairie's golden grain,
　The Desert's golden sand,
The clustered fruits of sunny Spain,
　The spice of Morning-land !
Her pathway on the open main
　May blessings follow free,
And glad hearts welcome back again
　Her white sails from the sea ! "

Unfortunately, however, if the truth must be told, too many a gallant ship in those busy days bore within her hold the " merchandise of sin."   Too often the sharp bows and square yards, the grace of outlines and tautness of rig that moved a sailor to admiration denoted the swift-sailing clipper that plied to and from the African coast bearing its accursed cargo of slaves, destined for the American or Cuban markets.   The story of the suppression of the African slave-trade is a picturesque and exciting one.   Says Mr. Griffis : " The business of slave export had in it plenty of gain, some lively excitement, but little or no danger.   Decoys were commonly used.   While a gunboat was giving chase to some old tub of a vessel, with fifty diseased or worn-out slaves on board, a clipper-ship with several hundred in her hold, with loaded cannon to sweep the decks in case of mutiny, and with manacles for the refractory, would dash out of her hiding-place among the mangroves and scud across the open sea to Cuba or Brazil."

Although the treaty of Ghent, which closed the war of 1812, had sounded the death-knell of this horrid traffic so far as the protection of the American flag was concerned, it is certain that far too often the swift clippers employed by the human traders

of Spanish America were Yankee built and sometimes Yankee manned. But it is also a pleasure to reflect that none were warier to track or swifter to destroy these piratical hunters of men than were the war-ships and the blue-jackets of the navy of the United States — a country not then itself free from the stain of traffic in human flesh.

And during all those years of peace that intervened between the last war with England and the struggles of the mid-century the little navy of the growing nation was seldom inactive. Her squadrons did duty in many a sea and bore the flag of the Union alike in petty conflict and in the interests of a wider knowledge of the possibilities of the globe.

The American navy, in those years of peace, drove from the historic waters of the Spanish Main the " Brethren of the coast "—those cut-throat robbers of the West Indian seas who, known to the sailors as " picaroons," preyed upon the commerce of every land and made their black flag the symbol of brutality and crime. So effective, under Commodore Porter's vigorous methods, was the work done by the American squadron in its punishment of the " Brethren of the coast " that those sea-robbers dared no longer fly their savage standard and, indeed, as Mr. Griffis says: " piracy on the Atlantic coast has ever since been but a memory. Unknown to current history, it has become the theme only of the cheap novelist and now has, even in fiction, the flavor of antiquity."

Lafitte, last of the Gulf pirates and most picturesque of all, aping the ways of the greater Morgan, sought to establish a piratical confederacy on Louisiana bayous and Texas beaches, but yielded at last, in 1821, to the guns of American men-of-war. Disappearing before their iron threats he left only the memory of a romantic and checkered career to pique the story teller and inflame the imaginations of all lovers of the marvelous.

The American navy, too, as has been shown, destroyed the iniquitous slave trade; it protected American commerce in the Mediterranean, ruffled with wars and rumors of wars; established the claim to superiority in beauty, strength, and excellence of build and discipline of the American " line-of-battle " ship; laid the foundation of that long-continuing friendship with Russia that still exists, spite of the diverse manners and methods of two such differently-constituted nations; forced the insolent Bourbon rulers of Naples to honesty and restitution; carried the stars and stripes, in the Wilkes Exploring Expedition of 1839, farther within the limits of the Antarctic Circle than the vessels of any other nation had ever penetrated; first hoisted the flag of possession in the "territory" of California; and bore the same "meteor flag" in peaceful exploration across the storied land of Palestine until it floated above the sacred waters of Galilee and the consecrated river of Jordan.

In the useless and inglorious, though victorious, war that the United States waged with Mexico the navy bore its part and gave to still another Perry the same meed of praise and pluck that has made that remarkable family famous in the naval annals of America. Tabasco and Tampico, Tuspan and Vera Cruz, Monterey and Los Angeles, with other and minor engagements, proved anew the daring and valor of the American blue-jackets and were a sort of medium ground whereon was displayed the mettle alike of the sea-fighters of an earlier school and those who were to win renown in the vaster conflict that was to come, before another quarter century had rolled away.

And, even greater in its significance than these deeds of blood and struggle, was the peaceful opening of Japan to the world — "one of the three signal events in American history," says Mr. Griffis "(the Declaration of Independence and the Arbitration of the Alabama claims being the other two), which have had the greatest influence upon the world at large." This was undertaken and accomplished by American seamen.

The mid-year of the century marked an era of change in America's life. Progress was the order of the day. But scarce any other phase of the world's ways and methods experienced so large a share of this advance and change as did the sailor's life on ship and sea. Steam revolutionized the service and gave to commerce a new factor of advance and strength. The temperance reform worked a moral change almost as great; by the influence of so thorough a seaman as Commodore Matthew Perry duelling, the grog-ration and flogging were removed from the naval service and largely eliminated, because of this, from the mercantile marine as well. Jack himself, affected by the spirit of change, was not of the same calibre as heretofore. Life on the high seas took on a vastly different aspect and while in many respects this was to be for the better it was also from this changing era in America's ocean story that what we are pleased to call the decline of the American sailor may be said to date.

CHAPTER X.

O wrest a precarious existence from the most unstable of elements; to face danger, privation, suffering and death for the sake of returns that would seem far too weak and insufficient to counterbalance the greater risks at which they are obtained: — these have for many a year been the duty and the destiny of the American fishermen. Followers of a calling that is esteemed as among the lowliest of all the occupations of man they are, more than any other craftsmen, ever loyal to their chosen field of labor.

And yet the very lowliness of this occupation of catching fish has ennobled it. From among the simple fisher-folk of Galilee, as if for the more emphatic denunciation of the arrogance of Levite and of Pharisee, did the Divinest of teachers choose his ministers for the enlightenment of a world; from the stench and slime of many a fishing craft has stepped a leader of men and in every land and upon every sea the fisherman has been esteemed the synonym of simplicity, honesty, hardihood and native common-sense.

The fisher-lads of the Atlantic coast have had a record of fully three centuries and a half of ceaseless endeavor, privation, poverty and loss. Storm and shipwreck have decimated their number, the fogs that have enshrouded their little craft and cut them off from all sight and sound of home are not more dense than is the cloud of social ostracism that seems to have kept them apart from the rest of the world; and while ignorance and moral obliquity have been part of the atmosphere of far too many American fishing-villages, love of home and of kindred has ever been the fisherman's lode-star. The stern realities of his daily struggle for existence are all the more stern because of this very regard for home and kin and the wail that rings through Kingsley's sad ballad : —

" For men must work, and women must weep,
And there's little to earn, and many to keep,
Though the harbor-bar be moaning," —

finds in the story of the American fisher-folk a kindred strain with that of their fellow workers of Brixham and Kinsale and the Hebrides, of Scheveningen and Tarragona and Etretet.

The United States of America exist to-day because of this lowly and dangerous calling. Indeed, had the eternal fitness of things held sway, not the rapacious eagle but the succulent codfish would be the national emblem of America.

It was because of this noble sea-food that the Western world was discovered. It was from one of these very Newfoundland fishermen that the great admiral received his first knowledge of the new world. Years before Columbus steered from Palos the daring fishermen of Northwestern France knew and frequented the American fishing banks from Labrador to Cape Cod. "This land," says Postel, "because of a most lucrative abundance of fish was visited by the Gauls, from the earliest recorded time and they were accustomed to frequent it for sixteen hundred years before." Sebastian Cabot, so Peter Martyr declares, "himself named those lands Baccalaos because that in the sea thereabout he found so great multitudes of certain bigge fishes, much like unto tunies (which the inhabitants call Baccalaos) that they sometimes stayed his shippes." Investigation, however, shows that the Indian word *baccalaos* was not of native coinage but was really, as Lescarbot affirms, "from the imposition of our Basques, who call a codfish Bacaillos." "As far back as there is any remembrance," says this same authority, "and for several centuries our Dieppe, Maloins, Rochelois and other sailors of Havre de Grace, of Honfleur, and other places had made regular journeys into these waters for the purpose of cod-fishing."

Known thus from the earliest ages, the pursuit and capture of "the imperial cod" has been for centuries the main cause of settlement, labor and strife along the North American coast. Even yet it is a bone of contention between the great Republic and the northern colonies of England. Protests and treaties, recrimination, retaliation and arbitration alike seem of no avail. And, indeed, until the inevitable happens and the English-speaking folk of the North American Continent are one confederated people, the problem of the coast fishery — its rights, its limits and its returns — will continue unsettled and unsolved.

But surely it has been a problem worth the solving. Steadily increasing in importance as population has grown and as appetite has been systematically developed the fishing industry of the United States is one of its most important means of livelihood. At the close of the Revolution it employed the services of 4,405 men and had a fleet of 665 vessels. In 1880 the number of men employed had multiplied many-fold, the number of vessels in the fishing service amounted to 6,605, and the smaller but necessary boats in use counted 44,805. These gave a total tonnage of 208,297 and called for an invested capital of nearly forty millions of dollars. The estimated value of

CODFISHERS HAULING TRAWLS.

the American fisheries on ocean, lakes and inland waters in 1880 was nearly fifty millions of dollars, in 1883 it was nearly one hundred millions.

This extensive industry now gives employment to almost a million men. In this estimate are included those who depend upon it for commercial support, those who follow it but a portion of the year and the families of the fishermen themselves.

And no craftsmen are more strictly American. Of the hundred thousand men who brave the seas in pursuit of its gleaming game scarcely more than ten per cent. are foreigners. *

From the very start the American fishermen have been the most national, the most loyal of men. From their number came the most daring fighters in the days of intercolonial trouble. They formed the nucleus of the navy of the new republic in its days of revolution; they proved the hardiest and most determined privateersmen in the struggle of "Eighteen twelve." Inured to a life of hardship, risk and trial, tossing and toiling in fragile boats on fickle waters, enveloped in fogs, bronzed by wind and sun, versed in the language of cloud and wave and sky, an unscientific but no less correct reader of the secrets and teachings of the sea, the fisherman where he should be the most versatile is the most uncommunicative of men. There is but little humor in his soul. Where the "jolly Jack tar" of the merchant service and the "blue-jacket" of the navy are careless, happy-go-lucky, improvident and companionable fellows the fisherman is reticent, introspective, and clannish, with but few "yarns" as compared with his brethren of the "fo'cas'l'" and the mess-table — the creature of a craft that is peculiarly a thing by itself apart.

Much of this is doubtless due to the nature of the calling. The stern realities of a life that grows hard and monotonous as it is dangerous and depressing leave but scant room for that lightness of heart that comes only with a diversified occupation and a freedom from anxiety. The terrible death roll of the New England fisheries covers many a domestic tragedy and

* The recent reports as to the presence of large numbers of " Province " people — Nova Scotians and others — on American fishing vessels would seem to qualify this statement. But, even acknowledging such a Canadian invasion, it is doubtful if there would be any marked difference in the aggregate. And, in time, perhaps, even Canadians may not be counted as foreigners.

many a grave of ambition, of hope and of anticipation. The cod-fisher of the Northern Banks and the whale-fisher of the Pacific coast have but little time for the amenities and the humors of life. They stand too often face to face with death.

But he who thus often faces the worst is none the less self-sacrificing, brave and heroic. Self-preservation may be the first law of the fisherman's nature, but it is one that none is readier or more willing to break, when occasion offers. Not all are of that selfish mould in which was cast Skipper Floyd Ireson of whom Whittier has sung :

> " Small pity for him!— He sailed away
> From a leaking ship, in Chaleur Bay,—
> Sailed away from a sinking wreck,
> With his own town's-people on her deck!
> 'Lay by! lay by!' they called to him.
> Back he answered, ' Sink or swim!
> Brag of your catch of fish again!'
> And off he sailed through the fog and rain!
>   Old Floyd Ireson, for his hard heart,
>   Tarred and feathered and carried in a cart
>   By the women of Marblehead."

For, though the *sauve qui peut* rings far too often on the fisherman's field of battle when wind and wave and treacherous fog combine to threaten and destroy, and though Skipper Ireson has his modern counterpart in such small-souled men as that Maine fisherman who deserted his helper afloat in a dory in a killing fog just when he should have stood by to save him because he had his fare of cod and was in haste to make port and a market, it is a fact that such lookers out for number one are but the unfrequent exceptions to the rule. They quickly get the cold shoulder. And, where Wall Street would judge such a nature as sharp, shrewd and Napoleonic, Marblehead and

Gloucester, the Hamptons and Cape Porpoise regard it as
" worse than infidel."

The day of the fishing village as such is past. The tendency to centralize that is so distinctively American has touched
the fishing industry as it has every other phase of American
life and the distributing facilities of the larger cities have sent
many a once prosperous " fish wharf " in some little sea-settle-
ment to ruin and decay. But wherever a community of fisher-
folk still is found, where every " elderly sailor-man " is " skipper "
by courtesy if not by actual rank and out from which, day after
day, go the solitary occupants of dory or of whale boat to set or
pull their trawls, there still exist many fireside legends of the
bravery, the self-denial and the heroism of their fellow-craftsmen
of to-day or of their ancestry in the days gone by.

More exciting than the deep-sea fishery if not more hazardous ; more fascinating if not more profitable is the chase and
capture of the whale. It is to cod-fishing as is the hunting of
the lion and the elephant to that of the bear and the buffalo.
Both sea-pursuits are full of the element of adventure but the
actual danger that attends every whale chase invests that noble
ocean sport with more of the attributes of daring and of risk
than does the catching of cod, of halibut and of hake.

The startling cry from the look-out of " There she blows ! "
the rapid lowering of the boats with each man ready and alert
for action, the race for the prey, the whirring harpoon, the stubborn tug of war 'twixt man and fish, the monster's death-strug-
gle and the cheers of victory ; or, perhaps, the deadly retaliation
of a monster brought to bay, boats wildly tossed in air, hunters struggling for life in the sea, and the wild cries of despair
and defeat — these surely partake more of the heroisms and
hazards of the battle-field than of a prosaic and money-getting

A FIGHT WITH A GIANT.

mercantile venture. The harpoon outranks in the romance of the sea the entangling seine and the hundred-fathom trawl.

The whale-ship, or as seamen call the whaleman's craft, the "spouter," has for many a year been one of the peculiar features of ocean life. Dirty, evil-smelling, reeking with the marks of blubber, soot and grease, the "spouter" of the Atlantic and of the greater Pacific is and has ever been the home of danger, of endeavor, of risk and of final gain or loss.

Even as the humble but laborious fisherman has been esteemed as lower in the social scale than one who goes before the mast in some little coasting vessel, so has the sailor on some trim merchantman or some stately man-of-war ever held in a certain contempt the less ship-shape and less cleanly "spouter" and her crew.

"As soon as her anchor was down," says Mr. Dana, describing one of these oil-getting craft encountered at sea, "we went aboard, and found her to be the whale-ship Wilmington and Liverpool Packet, of New Bedford, last from the 'off-shore ground,' with nineteen hundred barrels of oil. A 'spouter' we knew her to be, as soon as we saw her, by her cranes and boats, and by her stump top-gallant masts, and a certain slovenly look to the sails, rigging, spars, and hull; and when we got on board, we found everything to correspond — spouter fashion. She had a false deck, which was rough and oily, and cut up in every direction by the chimes of oil casks; her rigging was slack, and turning white, paint worn off the spars and blocks, clumsy seizings, straps without covers, and 'homeward-bound splices' in every direction. Her crew, too, were not in much better order, but looked more like fishermen and farmers than they did like sailors."

Indeed, so adds Mr. Dana in a foot-note to this sailor's judgment given after a lapse of many years, "long observation has satisfied me that there are no better seamen, so far as handling a ship is concerned, and none so venturesome and skillful navigators, as the masters and officers of our whalemen. But never, either on this voyage or in a subsequent visit to the Pacific and its islands, was it my fortune to fall in with a whale-ship whose appearance, and the appearance of whose crew, gave signs of strictness of discipline and seaman-like neatness."

But untidiness, though it may be a crime in the sailor's calendar, is by no means a bar to all the virtues. By the very nature of his pursuit a whaleman can keep neither himself nor his ship free from the marks of his calling. Results, rather than appearances are the chief aim of the whaler's life of long absences and much toil and danger; and the record of the palmy days of the whaling trade show how great were these results. In the year 1854, when the whaling fishery of the United States touched high-water mark, there were engaged in that industry six hundred and two ships and barks, twenty-eight brigs and thirty-eight schooners with a maximum tonnage of over two hundred thousand. More than ten thousand seamen were engaged in the pursuit and the yield in sperm oil, whale oil, whale bone and sperm candles ran well into the millions.

From the very earliest days the American sailor had risked his all in this promising but dangerous pursuit. It had lured the wary Indian from the security of his home waters, as with crude wooden weapons in frail canoes of bark or log he braved the terrors of the open sea he so detested in the excitement of the chase and the hope of capture. Good Master Weymouth in the account of his voyage to America in 1605 says of these native whalers: "One especial thing is their manner of killing the whale — which they call *powdawe;* and will describe his form: how he bloweth the water; and that he is twelve fathoms long; and that they go in company of their king with a multitude of their boats; and strike him with a bone, made in fashion of a harping-iron fastened to a rope which they make great and strong of the bark of trees, which they veer out after him; then all their boats come about him as he riseth above water; with their arrows they shoot him to death; when they have killed him and dragged him to shore they call their lords together and sing a song of joy. And those chief lords whom they call sagamores divide the spoil and give to every man a share, which they hang up about their houses for provisions."

This co-operative system of whaling in vogue among the aborigines, appears to have been adopted among their white successors, for in every whaling venture of record every one employed, from master to cabin-boy, seems to have gone in on shares. In the earlier days when the great fish had his home in native waters the chase was followed almost in the shadow of the home-tree. But, as demand grew, the home supply diminished and year by year the pursuit of the whale was carried farther and farther away from the old home fishing-grounds. The cruises grew longer and longer. Days turned to weeks, weeks to months and months grew to years as fishing-grounds became more remote and ships sailed away into almost unknown seas. The young fellow who had left his country home and shipped as a green hand on the "spouter" came back from a two or three years' whaling cruise an experienced and hardy whaler, well-stocked with yarns drawn from his three years of absence, labor and adventure.

And how much of labor, danger and adventure a three years' whaling cruise meant the voluminous records of the service and the still greater mass of unwritten "yarns" of the

sailors themselves amply testify.   They tell of long cruises far
away from home, of weeks — of months even — of profitless
and unrewarded search for game, of the inspiriting cry that at
last announces the prey, of the call to the boats, the attack, the
struggle and the capture; they tell of the laborious process of
cutting, extracting, trying and barreling; they tell, too, among

THE HEAT OF BATTLE.

all the minutiæ of a whaleman's life, the more stirring and
dramatic phases: the danger, the daring and the fight for life
that so often enters into the whaler's experiences.

Of these latter incidents records and "yarns" are full.   But
none is more interesting than that graphic account of his hand-
to-fluke fight for life told by an old whaler, hailing from one of

the Long Island " Hamptons." It was off somewhere in the Northern waters that his second mate fastened to one of the big fellows known as a " right " whale. " The critter was disposed to be ugly," says the old skipper, " so I pulled up and fastened to her also. I went into the bow and struck my lance into her shoulder-blade. It pierced so deep into the bone that I couldn't draw it out. The whale gave a great quiver and squirm and, turning a little, she cut her flukes and took the boat amidships. The boys all jumped for it as the boat rolled over with her broadsides all stove in, and I cut the line just in time to save being run under with a kink. I crawled up on the bottom of the overturned boat with the rest of the boys and sung out to the second mate who wanted to cut his line and pick us up, to go ahead and kill the critter; 'we're all right,' says I. But the next minute I was ready enough to sing a different tune. For, all of a sudden, the big fish turned and coming up on the full breach struck our wreck a blow that sent us all sky-high. As we came down into the water the whale's whole bulk came down on us sideways, like a small avalanche. Right and left she cut the corners of her flukes in a regular spite and in the fuss and clutter and 'white water' that she made two of my poor fellows went down.

" Here was more than I bargained for; but worse was yet to come. That whale seemed to have a special spite against me. She came feeling around for me with her nose and as she passed me where I was trying to swim out of her way I grabbed hold of the warp and let her tow me along a little way until she slackened speed. Then I dove under just in time to clear her flukes while she threshed away in a fury at the broken boat. She had just about finished smashing the wreck into splinters when she caught sight of me again and made for me on a half breach. Bang! that great head dropped on me again, driving me half stunned, deep under the water. So the fight kept on. Again and again would she run her head in the air, fall on my back and drive me bruised and battered far down under the water. Sometimes I would dive to clear her fluke and sometimes I would grab the line attached to the maddened brute and hold on for dear life until a sweep of the flukes sent me under. The boats could get no chance to pick me up; the minute that whale saw them coming for me she would leave off worrying me and make a dash at my rescuers. How I kept alive is more than I can understand. My legs became paralyzed, my strength gave out, I could not catch hold of the lines that were thrown out to me, everything was growing dim and far-off, when with a sudden rush the mate's boat made one last dash for me and by just the narrowest squeak hauled me into the boat more dead than alive. Then the mate who was a plucky chap and had 'got his mad up' put me on board ship and went for the fish again. Watching his chance he got a set on the whale just over her shoulder-blade and sent the red flag into the air. This tamed her. She lagged around awhile and then settled away dead. It was weeks before I grew well from my hurts — but then, you see, we got that oil."

It was such pluck as this that followed the whale into every sea, that ran every risk so grand a chase presents and that made the mettle of the American whaler known and respected among his fellows. Unsuccessful voyages, shipwreck, privation, and all the terrors of the sea could not deter the "spouter" from his accepted calling and only the decline of the whale-trade itself, as new discoveries gave to the world something of more value and less expense than oil and whalebone, drove the American whaler from the seas.

This was the pluck — recklessness and hardihood, some might call it — that exhibited itself in one muscular American whaler who, off St. Helena, deliberately " tackled " a " right whale " with only a single lance and harpoon in his boat. Carried overboard by the kinks he was given up for drowned, but he clung to the submerged line and was dragged into the boat by his comrades. " Well, Jube, how did you like it down there?" he was asked after he had come back to life. " Well, boys," he replied coolly, " it's a lonesome road to travel; there's neither mile-stones nor guide-boards as I could see."

An old whaling captain still lived in Nantucket a few years ago who could boast that the keel of his ship had never touched bottom, that he was never at sea a day without going aloft except in a gale of wind, that he had never lost a man by accident or abandonment, or had one off duty by sickness for more than a week, that he had never lost but one spar though making many short and quick voyages, that he had never returned without a full cargo of sperm oil, and that he had instructed and trained to his own calling sixteen apprentice-boys taken from the lower walks of life every one of whom had risen to rank and standing in the whaling service. This was an exceptional record and yet it has been equalled in one way or another by scores of American captains who saw, in the ships and the crews they had handled, many a craft of which to be proud and many a man who could add weight and distinction to the name of the American whaler.

Years ago in the South Pacific, so says Mr. Scammon, an English, French, Portuguese and American ship lay becalmed within a mile of one another. A whale was raised, and at once from each ship a boat started in pursuit. By superior pulling the American passed in succession the Portuguese and the

French boats and at last came within ten rods of the English crew. A mile and a half ahead rose the whale. " There she blows !" came the cry from the boat-steerer. "An eighty-barrel one ; dead ahead ! Give way, lads ; give way !" " The English boat and ours," says the American boat-steerer from whom Mr. Scammon had the story, " had exactly the same number of stout, active hands. Seeing us pass the other boats the Britishers put all their strength and force to the oar. Slowly but surely we gained on them and so great was our excitement over the race that we were almost over the spot where the whale had last blowed before we thought of it. As the two boats came abreast the English boat-steerer dropped on to my peculiar way of throwing extra weight upon my oar and attempted the same tactics. But he threw too much force upon it and almost immediately snapped it off short at the lock. Thus disabled he could only growl at his bad luck while we shot by him like a flash. At that moment the whale blowed again only a few rods away. The next moment we were fast; and as a reward for our race we were able to stow down eighty-five barrels of oil and shorten our voyage by two months."

Many another yarn could be spun hinting at the pluck and peril, the dangers and distresses, the worries and the victories of a whaler's life : Of boats dragged off at a fearful pace by the struck whale, of ships " stolen " and towed away bodily, of boats crunched like egg-shells in the massive jaws of an infuriated whale, of overturned sailors actually clambering on the back of the monster fish and clinging there for dear life, of many a moving accident and hair-breadth 'scape, of streaks of luck and months of failure and defeat.

The American fisherman, be he cod-fisher or whaler, has played an important part in the history of his country. He has

"FOR MEN MUST WORK AND WOMEN MUST WEEP."

founded States, established towns and cities, and been a source at once of profit and of advancement to a growing nation. Gloucester and Marblehead, New Bedford, the Long Island Hamptons, Nantucket and Hudson all owe their origin and development to the toil of the hardy fisher-folk. The commonwealth of Massachusetts was a direct outgrowth of the fishing industries of an early day. It was a serious question with the first settlers whether the Cape Cod peninsula should not be made the main place of settlement because of its many advantages as a fishing and whaling station. Upon the Atlantic seaboard many a flourishing community has been the out-growth of the labors and the need of this class of American seamen, while on the Pacific coast the great city of San Francisco to-day counts its fishing trade as supplying one tenth of its fifty millions of annual exports.

The deep-sea fisheries of the North Atlantic " Banks," the once enormous whaling interests of the towns of Southeastern Massachusetts, of the Long Island and Connecticut ports, the shad fisheries of the Hudson, Connecticut, Delaware and Potomac rivers, the oyster beds of Chesapeake and Delaware bays, the now declining menhaden fisheries of the Long Island and New Jersey coasts, the fisheries for red snapper, mullet, pompone, grunt and Spanish mackerel on the Southern and Gulf coasts, the yet undeveloped but vastly promising salmon, seal and cod-fisheries of the Pacific coast, and the great lake fisheries of Erie, Huron, Michigan and Superior make and have made for many and many a year the American fisherman one of the most important factors in the progress and development of America's story. His welfare and his conflicting interests, as against those of his rivals and Canadian neighbors, have formed the subject for much diplomacy, much international dispute, and

much wasted eloquence in congress and in parliament. His
" rights" have furnished the basis for four treaties with England
(those of 1783, 1818, 1854 and 1871) while still another, that of
1887, hangs undecided in the balance.

Third in the order of the fish-producing countries of the
world the United States contributes one seventh of the grand
total of one hundred and twenty-five millions of dollars that
stands as the annual value of the maritime and inland fisheries
of the globe.   And spite of the decline of much that was once a
leading factor in the great fisheries of the world, the American
sailor who pursues on river, lake and sea his humble but time-
honored calling of a catcher of fish, may feel that still to-day the
words of the English statesman Edmund Burke, though inspired
by the position of the American fisherman of a century ago,
have bearing and application to himself and the brethren of
his craft: " No sea but is vexed by their fisheries.   No climate
that is not witness to their toils.   Neither the perseverance of
Holland, nor the activity of France, nor the dexterous and firm
sagacity of English enterprise ever carried this most perilous
mode of hardy industry to the extent to which it has been
pushed by this recent people."

On fishing-smack and whaler, on sloop, on schooner and on
black-hulled sealing steamer, on dory, whale-boat and diminu-
tive lake and river craft, careless of his condition and reckless
often of his life, the American fisherman busies himself at his
dangerous calling, content with little and never expecting much
in this world's goods.   While politicians wrangle and dispute
over his " rights " and rumors of war spring from the conflicting international interests involved in his exact position he still
serenely sets his trawl or flings his harpoon wherever the " harvest of the sea " seems most fair and promising.   His has been

a record of centuries of toil and patient endeavor that the greatest of nations may well esteem as worthy commendation and reward. And yet so philosophic and reticent is the fisherman's nature that, whether his "rights" may embroil two nations in war or be determined only by long and exhaustive arbitration this deep-sea hunter is apparently the least interested party to the strife. Unruffled and undisturbed, he pursues his calling — voicing in his own peculiar way that seldom finds expression in words, the contented spirit that Whittier has put into verse:

> "Our wet hands spread the carpet
>   And light the fires of home;
> From our fish as in the old time,
>   The silver coin shall come.
> As the demon fled the chamber
>   Where the fish of Tobit lay,
> So ours from all our dwellings
>   Shall frighten Want away.
>
>
> Though the mist upon our jackets
>   In the bitter air congeals,
> And our lines wind stiff and slowly
>   From off the frozen reels;
> Though the fog be dark around us
>   And the storm blow high and loud,
> We will whistle down the wild wind,
>   And laugh beneath the cloud.
>
>
> In the darkness as in daylight,
>   On the water as on land,
> God's eye is looking on us,
>   And beneath us is his hand!
> Death will find us soon or later,
>   On the deck or in the cot;
> And we cannot meet him better
>   Than in working out our lot.

When the account is made up in the orderly story of the centuries that is yet to be written the historian, as he weighs and epitomizes all the industries of man that have been factors in the gradual development and upbuilding of a world, must accord not only praise but honor, not only respect but glory, to these patient, laborious, simple-mannered and stout-hearted sea-folk who have made successful and important the calling and the name of the American fisherman.

CHAPTER XI.

YOUR thorough-going sailor, rude and unlettered though he may be, never allows himself to be esteemed an ignoramus. The confinements and restraints of shipboard may make him careless as to the proprieties when ashore, but his manifold experiences in knocking about the world, his habit of thoughtfulness induced by the long watches at sea and his protracted isolation from the rest of the world result, naturally, in no small amount of native common-sense, a certain feeling of superiority over the " poor chaps ashore," and a readiness to find a reason for all things.

Illogical and superstitious he may be, crude in his methods and lame in his theorizing, but the sailor is still a good deal of a philosopher, and may sometimes teach even those who esteem themselves as far above him in worldly wisdom. He has, too, underneath a certain expressed contempt for all landsmen and for the ways and methods of the world at home, a real admiration

for " book larnin' " and the things it teaches. The records of
every voyage for purposes of exploration, research or scientific
investigation show how ready is the sailor to ship for such a
voyage and how deeply interested he becomes in the objects of
the expedition.

The seamen on the ships of Columbus doubtless deemed
themselves able to give the great admiral " points " as to his
venture and from the days of the Santa Maria to the Blake no
expedition for other than strictly mercantile purposes but has
had its seamen ready to descant upon the merits of the cause
to which the voyage was pledged, with certain deductions there-
from which would astonish the learned men in whose interest
the ships have sailed away.

There came as passenger to the Pilgrim — now famous as
the ship in which Mr. Dana made his memorable voyage — a
certain Harvard professor bent upon studying the botany, con-
chology and ornithology of the California coast. At first, says
Mr. Dana, he was a problem to the crew. They called him
" Old Curious " from his zeal for curiosities and some of them
said that he was crazy, and that his friends let him go about
and amuse himself in this way. Why else, they argued, a rich
man (sailors call every man rich who does not work with his
hands, and who wears a long coat and cravat) should leave a
Christian country and come to such a place as California to pick
up shells and stones, they could not understand. One of them,
however, Mr. Dana declares, who had seen something more of
the world ashore, set all to rights, as he thought. " O 'vast
there! " he said. " You don't know anything about them craft.
I've seen them colleges and know the ropes. They keep all
such things for cur'osities, and study 'em, and have men a-pur-
pose to go and get 'em. This old chap knows what he's about.

He a'n't the child you take him for. He'll carry all these things to the college, and if they're better 'n any they've had afore, he'll be head of the college. Then, by and by, somebody else 'll go after some more, and if they beat this one he'll have to go again, or else give up his berth. That's the way they do it. This old covey knows the ropes. He has worked a traverse over 'em and come 'way out here where nobody 's ever been afore, and where they'll never think of coming." This explanation, says Mr. Dana, satisfied Jack; and as it raised the Professor's credit and was "near enough to the truth for common purposes" he did not disturb it.

Scientific societies, governments and interested individuals are, as this old salt declared, always ready to "work a traverse" over other societies, governments and individuals and hence the information of the world progresses and sailors are given opportunities to ship on queer cruises into strange latitudes. The records of such expeditions for scientific research as those of the Beagle, the Challenger, the Bibb and the Blake show the interest that even the commonest sailor on board took in the voyage and its results. Professor Agassiz, in his latest book (" Three Cruises of the Blake ") bears testimony to the interest displayed by the crew in the professor's dredging for the flora and fauna of the "abyssmal realm" of the deep sea — a duty, as he says, "so foreign to their usual routine."

Where once the sailors of Columbus and the earlier navigators needed to be driven on board the caravels that were to bear them upon a secret errand to an unknown shore the seamen of to-day are ready and anxious to ship on expeditions that are to open new realms to commerce, to discover new forms of nature and to wrest the closely-locked secrets of some vaguely-known or inaccessible land.

It was the seemly and courteous behavior of the blue-jackets of Perry's squadron that in 1852 helped to make of a great and mysterious nation a friendly power and to open Japan to civilization and the world; it was quite as much the interest and efforts of the seamen as of the officers that made so notable a success of Commodore Wilkes's expedition of search and discovery to the far southern seas, in 1838 — the first maritime exploring expedition ever undertaken by the United States Government; that circumnavigated and surveyed the "sacred river" Jordan and the Dead Sea; that laid the first Atlantic cable; carried the "mercy ships" Jamestown and Griswold to famine-stricken Ireland and to starving Lancashire; and pushed again and again the prows of exploring squadrons against the icy ramparts of the northern pole.

It is in this latter field of enterprise that the American sailor has especially distinguished himself. The problem of a northwest passage has for centuries interested the world. From the days when, seeking "a nearer avenue to Southern Asia," Sebastian Cabot understood "by reason of the sphere that if I should sail by way of the northwest I should by a shorter tract come into India," and when Martin Frobisher declared this to be "the only thing left undone in the world whereby a notable mind might be made famous and fortunate," the determination of this nearer avenue to Asia through the waters of the frozen North has been a labor in which many a venturesome mariner has risked life and courted death.

The half-mythical "Boston ship" of 1639, the Philadelphia schooner Argo in 1753, the Virginia expedition in the Diligence in 1771, and Captain Taylor's Rhode Island sloop of 1753 seem to have been the earliest of the strictly American explorations in search of this baffling passage to the West.

IN ARCTIC SEAS.

In the year 1845 the sudden and mysterious disappearance of Sir John Franklin and his ships roused the world to a fresh interest in the secrets of that terrible land about the pole and gave the name of the lost English captain a foremost place on the tragic but honorable roll of the martyrs to science. At once expeditions for his recovery were organized in England and America and what is known as the " First Grinnell Expedition " sailed from New York on the twenty-second of May, 1850.

This, though sailing under the sanction of the United States Government, was really a personal contribution to the twin causes of mercy and science by Mr. Henry Grinnell. He was a philanthropic merchant of New York City, who supplied the two vessels and the means for the voyage, or as his memorial to Congress expressed it : " Your memorialist has from his own resources provided for the principal expenses of the expedition. It would strengthen his hope of ultimate success and facilitate greatly the object in view, if the act of Congress should authorize the word to be passed in the navy for volunteers among the men, as well as the officers, limiting to fifteen the number for each vessel. Should the pay and naval rations be deemed insufficient by the crew, your memorialist wishes to give from his own purse such additional sums as may be proper and satisfactory to the volunteers."

Such an example of philanthropy was not to fail of recognition. The " word was passed " in the navy for volunteers and it was answered, as Mr. Grinnell says, " with a zeal and nobleness of spirit beyond praise, without the promise or hope of reward." Indeed it is a tribute to the manliness of the American sailor that finds expression in the remark of Admiral Osborn, one of the most distinguished of England's

Arctic navigators: " I was charmed to hear that before sailing, officers and men had signed a bond not to claim under any circumstances the twenty thousand pounds reward which the British Government had offered."

The first Grinnell expedition failed of its main purpose — the discovery and relief of Franklin. So too did the second Grinnell expedition dispatched in 1853 under the command of that dauntless physician in the United States Navy — Elisha Kent Kane. It failed, but the name of Kane is inseparably linked with that of Franklin and the cause of Arctic discovery.

But as Professor Nourse says, the "overruling circumstances detract nothing from the worthiness of the original purposes of these expeditions, or from the fidelity of the officers and men engaged in them." These and the succeeding efforts to find the open polar sea or to rescue lost explorers, cast away in the cold, have added to the scientific and geographical knowledge of the world, have encroached more and more upon the stubborn fastnesses of the icy North and have strengthened that bond of international charity and good-will that must, in time, obliterate the strifes and jealousies of men. To these results the American sailor has contributed his share in fidelity, patience and manly endeavor and though the record of Arctic discovery is marked with disaster and checkered with death not one of the brave fellows who sailed northward in the causes of research or relief would, if they could, regret the impulse that led them to volunteer for such peculiar and dangerous service.

Following the " Second Grinnell Expedition " to the Pole in which Dr. Kane laid the seeds alike of his death and of his fame, came the Relief Expedition for his recovery, sent out by Congress in May, 1855, under the command of Lieutenant

Hartstene in the bark Release and the propeller Arctic.   This, as we know, was successful.   In August, 1855, Commander John Rodgers in the sloop of war Vincennes, passing northward through Behring Strait, located Wrangel Land in the high latitudes to the northwest of Alaska and, returning, marked the soundings of Behring Strait for the guidance of succeeding mariners.   In July, 1860, Dr. Isaac I. Hayes who had already penetrated the " Land of Desolation " with Dr. Kane led an exploring party to the northeast in the fore and aft schooner United States, discovered what he believed to be the " open Polar Sea," unfurled the American flag on Cape Lieber (in latitude eighty-one degrees and thirty minutes), the highest northern point then reached by man, and sighted still further to the north the inaccessible headland of Cape Union.

The next American attempt to storm the pole was the romantic and tragic endeavor of Captain C. F. Hall.   A landsman and not a sailor, earning only a bare livelihood as an engraver in the far inland city of Cincinnati, his sympathy for the lost Englishman Franklin awakened within him " an enthusiasm for the search and for Arctic Exploration which failed only with his life."   Three times he made the effort.   His first trip was made entirely without companions, vessel or crew from the port of New London in Connecticut in May, 1860, whence he was conveyed North with his slender outfit of boats, sledges, instruments and provisions by the generosity and financial help of two American merchants, Grinnell of New York and Haven of New London.   His second expedition undertaken solely on his own responsibility and made by himself and two Esquimaux sailed from New London in July, 1864.   His third and final expedition was made in the year 1871 in the United States steamer Polaris, sent out under the authority of Congress and with the landsman, now "Captain" Hall, as commander. With it sailed a competent scientific corps and a crew of fourteen seamen. This national recognition was in itself a triumph of patient enthusiasm. The results of Hall's three voyages, occupying nine years of exploration and effort, gave an impetus to Arctic discovery, added much to the knowledge of the land of ice, carried the American flag to the farthest north, discovered traces only, of the fate of Franklin and his men and added yet another to the list of those indomitable explorers who have died martyrs to science for the good of man.

Lieutenant Schwatka in 1878 with four comrades penetrated far toward the pole still searching for the remains and records of the Franklin expedition and in July, 1879, Lieutenant G. W. De Long, with a crew of thirty-five officers and men sailed from San Francisco to the Arctic Ocean on the bark-rigged steam-yacht Jeannette, backed by the private enterprise of James Gordon Bennett. The expedition ended, as so many others had done, in disaster and death. Crushed in a relentless ice-pack to the northward of Behring Strait, the Jeannette was abandoned and a long and miserable flight for life ended for De Long and his gallant company of American sailors in starvation and death on the desolate shores of Siberia.

To discover and relieve the lost Jeannette three expeditions were dispatched to the North, and following these the expedition of Lieutenant Greely to the eastern gateway to the pole and of Lieutenant Ray to the westward, with the relief expeditions dispatched for their succor and return, complete the list of American endeavors to force the secret of the great Northern land.

Whether or not the benefits derived from these expeditions in behalf of scientific and geographical information are com-

"JIM BLUDSO."

mensurate with the terrible cost at which they have been obtained, it is certain that the end is not yet. The "saddening shadows" of the Jeannette and the horrible experiences of Greely cannot dampen the ardor of the explorer or the enthusiasm of the scientist. "Volunteers from naval and civil life," says Professor Nourse, "are still ready to offer themselves for the fascinations of the most daring Arctic adventure and Arctic exploration will not soon be abandoned." The attractions of the unknown overtop caution, comfort, danger and the risk of death.

To this long record of honorable labor in behalf of the world's enlightenment the American sailor has contributed the greater share of endeavor, endurance and fortitude. Commanders might plan and philanthropists assist but without the work and the willingness of the common sailor little could have been accomplished. From the pioneer days of American Arctic discovery when, one hundred and thirty years ago, Captain Swaine of Philadelphia was twice repulsed by the icy barriers which he sought to force in his little schooner Argo to the hour when in May, 1882, Lieutenant Lockwood flung the stars and stripes to the icy breezes at the farthest northern point ever reached by man, the story of the American sailor's share in the advance of polar exploration is one continual record of earnest and willing endeavor in the face of hardship, privation, peril, starvation and death.

It is a relief to turn from this picture of desolation and disaster to one of marvelous progress and success ; and, surely, no completer transition could be made than to read, after the story of the ever-frozen seas of the far North, the story of the never-frozen seas, land-locked within the great American continent.

Northeasterly, through the narrow water-way that separates

the State of New York from the Province of Ontario pass ever, with ceaseless flow, three quarters of all the fresh waters of the globe. The great St. Lawrence River, so says Sir Charles Hartley, "taken in connection with the great lakes, offers to trading vessels the most magnificent system of inland navigation in the world."

And these "trading vessels" have certainly availed themselves of the river's generous offer. In 1887 the shipping of the United States on the great lakes included 1,286 sailing and 1,225 steam vessels, 549 canal boats and 84 barges — a total of 3,144 water craft with a total carrying capacity of 783,722 tons. Canada's lake shipping swelled this total by some nine hundred vessels and 120,000 tons.

Add to these figures the shipping statistics of the Mississippi and other Western rivers, which in 1887 showed a total of 1,293 sailing craft with a carrying capacity of 327,405 tons and the inland commerce of the United States shows an aggregate footing of nearly forty-five hundred vessels capable of carrying over eleven hundred thousand tons.

This inland commerce has been mainly of recent growth. At once the cause and the result of Western immigration the navigation, commerce and fisheries of the great Northern lakes and Western rivers have called into existence a class of busy workers as distinct from the sailors and fishermen of the ocean courses as are the white fish, the pickerel and the sturgeon of the lakes distinct from the cod, the halibut and the whale of the great salt seas.

Indeed the salt-water sailor is quite as ignorant of the manners and methods of the fresh-water mariner as is the landsman himself. And he holds, withal, a certain unconcealed contempt for the inland seas which his unsalted brother navigates. The times have not materially changed since that dogmatic seaman, old Cap, of Cooper's Leather-Stocking Tales, sneered at Ontario.

"As for this bit of a lake," he growled to his niece as he looked out upon it from the deck of the Scud, "you know my opinion of it already, and I wish to disparage nothing. No real seafarer disparages anything; but hang me if I regard this here Ontario, as they call it, as more than so much water in a ship's scuttled-butt. . . . . . . And look at that water! It is like milk in a pan, with no more motion now than there is in a full hogshead before the bung is started. No man ever saw the ocean like this lake." And when his niece would have called his attention to the ripples on the shore and the surf on the rocks the old sailor broke in contemptuously: "All poetry, girl! One may call a bubble a ripple if he will, and washing decks a surf; but Lake Ontario is no more the Atlantic than a Powles Hook periagua is a first-rate." Then looking at their young lake skipper, old Cap remarked: "That Jasper is a fine lad. He only wants instruction to make a man of him." "Do you think him ignorant?" asks Mabel, who is far from holding that slighting opinion of the young sailor. "He is ignorant," her uncle responds; "he is ignorant as all must be who navigate an inland water like this. He can make a flat-knot and a timber-hitch, it is true; but he has no more notion of crowning a cable, now, or of a carrickbend, than you have of catting an anchor."

But all readers of "The Pathfinder" must remember how old Cap modified his censure and changed his opinion when, after he had nearly wrecked the Scud on a lee shore in a furious lake gale, young Jasper assumed command and saved the vessel.

That very incident alone, conceived by one who had known

and studied the great lakes from boyhood, is an indication of the difference between fresh-water and salt-water navigation.

Indeed, the peculiar nature and composition of these inland waters call for a seamanship quite as skillful and fully as daring as do the ocean currents.

Since first, two hundred and ten years ago, the Chevalier La Salle beat up across Lake Ontario in his little vessel of ten tons — "the first ship that had ever sailed on that fresh-water sea"— the dangers and difficulties of lake navigation have brought many a ship and sailor to grief and educated a race of brave and hardy inland sailors. Necessity triumphs over every obstacle; and the growing demands of occupation and development have created an inland marine that outranks in extent and efficiency all the other fresh-water shipping of the world. Great cities have sprung into existence upon the lake shores. Buffalo is the commercial centre of the inland seas of North America. Chicago is the largest grain and pork market in the world. In 1883 over twelve thousand vessels cleared from Chicago's harbor. Sandusky has the largest fresh-water fish market in the United States. Detroit is the centre of a great and growing foreign and coastwise commerce. Milwaukee's shipping entries and interests equal those of Baltimore, of Boston or of Philadelphia. And Duluth, "the zenith city of the unsalted seas," is rapidly fulfilling the prophecies that, made not so many years ago, excited only laughter and ridicule.

To all this progress the American sailor of the inland marine has contributed an important share. If his voyages are shorter than those of the ocean "tar" his work is more laborious, for he must be both sailor and stevedore. The growth of steam navigation has, on the lakes as on the sea, materially lessened the proportionate increase of sailing vessels but the white wings

ON INLAND WATERS. (OFF THE CITY OF ERIE.)

still outnumber the smoke-stacks. Alert and watchful when winds arise and dangers threaten the fresh-water sailor is as skillful in emergency and as brave in actual peril as is his brother of the sea and the record of heroism in storm and in shipwreck can yield no greater meed of praise to the one than to the other. There have been terrible scenes of wreck and disaster on the lakes and the story of the loss of the Lady Elgin on Lake Michigan is as full of terror and as eloquent in manliness and heroism as is that of the Arctic, of the Austria or of the Ville de Havre.

What is said of the lake sailor is also true of the navigators of the great Western rivers. The Mississippi boatman has changed materially since the days of the flat boat and the great passenger steamers. The railway that annihilates space destroys also the picturesque element of the old days on the Ohio and the Mississippi. But commerce in heavy commodities has greatly increased and the coal and grain of the North go down stream in great quantities while cotton, sugar and molasses come up stream from the South.

Here the "sailor" (who, after all, is not so much a sailor as a deck hand) yields in interest and importance to the engineer and the pilot. The pilots of the great river steamers are practically the only navigators of the Mississippi, the Missouri and the Ohio. "No class of public servants," says a recent writer, "stands in a position of greater trust and responsibility. It is difficult to conceive of a more dangerous task than that of guiding one of these gigantic steamboats along the twisting, shifting, treacherous channel of the river. The pilots are a vastly better set of men than those who followed the profession ten and twenty years ago. The improvement is in their morals, their education and their usefulness."

" Mark Twain's " quaint and characteristic stories of boating on the Mississippi during the old days that have now passed away are full of humor and bristle with interest. His record of his own experience as a "cub pilot" faithfully pictures. even in the midst of the facetiæ with which he surrounds it, the education, the trials and the manly training of the young river-navigator, thirty years ago.

The stories of the coolness, the bravery and the fidelity of the Western pilot are many. In a life of constant care, anxiety and hazard a man who feels the importance of his post and the responsibility that devolves upon him must, if he is really a man. develop the manly qualities.

And what is true of the pilot of one of those light-draught, high-piled river steamers is also true of the engineer. With the pilot he really divides the responsibility that rests upon the officers of those majestic-appearing but all too flimsily-built crafts, so many of which have proved but tinder-boxes and death traps in the hour of fire or collision.

The nerve and faithfulness to his trust displayed by Jim Bludso the hero of one of John Hay's strongest "dialect ballads" is not the mere creation of a poet's brain. The engine room and pilot house are full of just such stories of dogged but glorious heroism.

" Jim Bludso" was a type of the old-time Mississippi engineer of twenty-five or thirty years ago — reckless, careless, and with but few of the amenities of cultured life, but loyal to duty and courageous even to death:

> " A reckless man in his talk was Jim,
> And an awk'ard hand in a row ;
> But he never flunked and he never lied -
> I reckon he never know'd how."

His were the days of rivalry and jealousy on the competing lines of passenger steamers, when desire and the determination not to be beaten were pushed even to the pitch of desperation :

> "All boats has their day on the Mississip
>   And her day come at last, —
> The Movaster was a better boat
>   And the Belle she wouldn't be passed
> And so she come tearin' along that night —
>   The oldest craft on the line —
> With a nigger squat on her safety valve,
>   And her furnace crammed rosin and pine.
>
> "The fire bust out as she cleared the bar
>   And burnt a hole in the night,
> And quick as a flash she turned and made
>   For that willer-bank on the right.
> There was runnin' and cursin', but Jim yelled out
>   Over all the infernal roar,
> 'I'll hold her nozzle ag'in the bank
>   Till the last galoot's ashore.'
>
> "Through the hot, black breath of the burnin' boat
>   Jim Bludso's voice was heard
> And they all had trust in his cussidness,
>   And knowed he would keep his word.
> And, sure's you're born, they all got off
>   Afore the smoke stacks fell, —
> And Bludso's ghost went up alone
>   In the smoke of the Prairie Belle."

There is more of heroism and of real manliness in such a rough, fearless, but loyal fellow as was this typical Mississippi engineer, than in many a so-called "flower of chivalry" of the knightly days or in the blood-stained conqueror of later times.

Equal to the engineer Jim Bludso of the poet in daring and fidelity to his trust, was the pilot James Allen of fact.

" He was," says a brother pilot who tells the story, " my partner during the war days on the steamer Von Phue. He had been in the rebel army but I had known him for many years and trusted his honor when he came under our flag. We started out of New Orleans and had got up as far as Morgan's Point where the river makes a bend. I was in my stateroom and Allen was at the wheel, when I heard a crash of glass in the pilot house and then the sound of a cannon shot. I rushed out, looked up and saw Allen pale as death. ' What's the matter? ' I said, and just then came another shot from the shore smashing through the boat. I knew what it was now. A six-gun rebel battery was trained on to our boat and playing away like mad. ' Are you hurt, Jim? ' I called out. ' No,' he replied, keeping his eyes on the bow of the boat which he was pointing away from the battery. ' I'm all right, but the cap'n 's killed.' I ran up into the pilot house and sure enough there lay the captain and the clerk dead as a door nail. Bang; bang! went the battery again as we rounded the point. ' Can't I help you, Jim? ' I asked between the shots. ' You go below,' was all he said. ' It's my watch. I'll steer the boat.' And I went below. Before we had got past the battery, in those two attacks they had put into our boat sixty-two shots. But we escaped 'em and got by all right. We were saved, but I tell you it was all owing to the honesty and courage of Jim Allen, a rebel pilot."

CHAPTER XII.

EIGHTEEN hundred and sixty-one was an era of crisis in the history of the United States. The great republic was at peace with the world. Her industries were growing, her resources were increasing, her remarkable development in trade, in commerce, in population and in all that makes a nation prosperous and progressive had raised her to a foremost position among the peoples of the world.

In that year came the tragedy. Separating on questions of private opinion but of national importance the republic found itself rent by a great civil feud, its whole southern half resisting the efforts made by its northern counterpart to keep the Union intact. Resistance was succeeded by secession; secession by civil war. The Rebellion from a political threat became a national fact.

War found the nation singularly unprepared. The army was reduced to its lowest peace footing. The navy was even more unavailable. Of its ninety steam and sailing vessels, twenty-one were "unserviceable," and twenty-seven were "out of commission." Of the remaining forty-two, twenty-six were far from home, scattered through the foreign seas and ports of the globe. Of the twelve vessels "at home" only two were available for immediate use, the Brooklyn of twenty-five guns and the Relief of two. Of the seventy-six hundred seamen fixed as the complement of the navy there were, in receiving ships and home ports, but two hundred and seven at the disposal of the Navy Department, while over three hundred of the nation's naval officers "resigned" to take sides with the South when the hour of conflict came. Conspiracy shrewdly planned had been as shrewdly executed.

Once committed to war the nation acted quickly. The president's proclamation calling for volunteers found ready response and army and navy grew rapidly. From town and village, from store and shop, from fishing-boat and forecastle came the strong and stalwart young life of the North eager to fight for the Union. In 1863 there were in the naval service of the nation thirty-four thousand men, and at the close of the war, in 1865, there were nearly fifty-two thousand men in the service and the enfeebled navy of 1861 had grown to six hundred and seventy-one vessels.

The seventy-five hundred naval officers appointed during the war — one seventh of the whole service — were composed of a varied material. "Some," says Professor Soley, "were merchant captains and mates of experience; others had never been at sea. Those employed on the Mississippi were chiefly steamboat men and pilots . . It was no uncommon thing in 1861 to find officers in command of steamers who had never served in steamers before and who were far more anxious about their boilers than about their enemy."

With this mass of undisciplined seamen and equally un-
trained officers it would have been impossible to have successfully withstood an enemy trained to naval warfare and supplied
with ships and sailors. It was the salvation of the Federal
navy that, crude and unprepared as it was for ocean warfare, its
enemy was still more crudely furnished. "Except its officers,"
says Professor Soley, "the Confederate Government had nothing in the shape of a navy. It had not a single ship of war. It
had no abundant fleet of merchant vessels in its ports from
which to draw reserves. It had no seamen, for its people were
not given to seafaring pursuits. Its only ship-yards were
Norfolk and Portsmouth . . . For strictly naval warfare,
where ships of war measured themselves against each other, the
South was never able to accumulate a sufficient force."

The War for the Union, therefore, partook but little of the
character of a naval war. Without facilities of its own to produce or to man naval vessels the South was forced to rely for
assistance in this direction upon its pronounced but not acknowledged ally, England.

Indeed, the water conflict was, from the first, rather the
struggle between jailer and prisoner than of evenly-matched
combatants. The navy of the Confederacy was but a weak as-
sortment of confiscated tugs and steamboats, originally intended
for passenger service and hastily strengthened for war. These
could only harass an enemy they could not hope to defeat and,
until the Confederate rams and English-built cruisers went
into commission in the later years of the war but little damage
to Federal commerce or to Federal war-ships was effected by
the rebel "navy."

The naval vessels of the United States, therefore, during the
early years of the war did little more than patrol duty. Lying

at anchor off the Southern ports or cruising along the Southern
coastboard their chief duty was to keep vessels from entering
or leaving the ports declared to be " blockaded." But this was
no small matter. The South must have food and money. She
must have those necessaries of life and munitions of war that
could only be obtained from the outside. To secure these and
to supply the foreign markets with cotton and other domestic
staples enterprising and desperate men were ready to risk all,
even to life itself. Thus arose the most dramatic episode of the
war, so far as the ocean was concerned, that of blockade running.
The flimsy Southern craft of the early war days — the small
sailing vessels and unseaworthy steamers were speedily captured, wrecked or driven off the seas. But the temptations and
profits of this dangerous traffic were too alluring to be resisted.
English capital and English pluck were enlisted. Swift, Clyde-
built steamers were specially constructed for the service, and
the Federal blockaders along the coast had work in plenty to
watch and waylay these stealthy greyhounds of the sea.

Along the Southern coast from the capes of the Chesapeake
to the mouth of the Rio Grande was the game of ocean hide-
and-seek kept up. Despite its dangers and its risks blockade-
running continued and the merchants of Nassau and Bermuda
waxed wealthy with their ventures. But the persistence and
energy of the blue jackets of the Union triumphed. The
blockade though one of the most difficult ever attempted by a
nation was successfully maintained. Notwithstanding the peculiar formation of the Southern coast — with its net-work of
channels, the nearness of such " neutral " but friendly ports as
Nassau and those of the Bahamas, the desperate need and determination for the cotton of the rebellious States, and the final
introduction of fast-sailing steam blockade-runners — the block-

ade was so successfully maintained that the traffic was at last almost entirely broken up.

As a result of their vigilance the loyal sailors at the close of the war had to their credit a total of 1,149 prizes of which 210 were steamers. 335 vessels were sunk, burned or destroyed, and this work — a greater showing than that of the War of 1812 which had been almost strictly a naval war — was the labor not of privateers but of the American Navy exclusively.

Many were the exciting chases, many the inspiriting captures. The Stag and the Charlotte were decoyed and captured by means of shore lights skillfully displayed; the Kate was disabled and destroyed in the gray of a summer morning by a boat-load of sailors from the Union fleet; the Hebe, boarded in the teeth of a northeast gale, was rendered valueless by a boat-load of sailors who, their own boat being swamped, knew that the exploit was to end for them in victory or death; the Venus, one of the finest and fleetest of the blockade-runners, was overhauled in a stern chase by Lamson in the Nansemond, riddled by four well-directed shells, driven on shore and captured by a boarding crew; the Howquah chased a prize straight through the concentrated fire of the Confederate batteries; and on the Charleston station four boats' crews from the blockading fleet, under cover of the darkness, boarded a blockade-runner as she lay at her dock in fancied security, overpowered the sleeping crew, forced the engineer to get under way at once, and, almost before the dazed captives knew just what had happened to them, the plucky blue jackets were carrying their prize out of the enemy's reach. At five o'clock on a November morning Captain Breck of the Niphon spied a blockade-runner chased by one of the Union fleet. Caught thus between two enemies the plucky runner turned at bay and steered straight for the Niphon as if to cut her down. Breck saw the move and was ready for it. On came the desperate blockade-runner on desperate purpose bent. Breck ordered a boarding crew to form on the Niphon's bow. Straight through a raking shower of canister dashed the stranger. Crash! came her beak into the Union vessel carrying away bowsprit and stem. But the boarding crew was ready. As the two vessels met they leaped the rail regardless of collision or shock and with a rush made themselves masters of a prize that netted them and their comrades a return of $180,000.

These and many similar experiences that might here be detailed show the desperate character of the service alike for runner and for watcher. The blockade - runner's side of the story is quite as interesting and even more exciting, and is proof of the valor and

RECRUITS FOR THE NAVY: DRILLING THE AWKWARD SQUAD.

dash that has been displayed by the American sailor on whichever side he fought.

But it was not alone in maintaining a stringent blockade that the best naval work of the war was done. The lack of what might be called a navy on the Confederate side precluded as has been shown the possibility of actual naval engagements but brilliant work was nevertheless accomplished by Union fleets and cruisers while the daring and, intrepidity displayed on Rebel ram and Confederate cruiser surely demands place in any story of the American sailor.

The doings of this latter craft — the Confederate cruisers — fitly termed by Professor Soley "the commerce-destroyers" — attracted the attention of the entire world. Built mostly in English ship-yards and backed many of them by English capital these trim and fast-sailing Rebel cruisers replaced the "mosquitoes of ocean warfare" which in the early part of the war had essayed the part of an offensive navy. Steering boldly into foreign parts they wrought devastation upon American commerce in every sea. The Sumter, Florida, Alabama, Rappahannock, Georgia, Nashville and Shenandoah were the chief of these commerce-destroyers, only the first-named of these being of American build. All came to an untimely end, but before that end was reached these pests of the seas had inflicted upon the American merchant-marine injuries from which it never has recovered.

The capture of the Florida by the Wachusett in neutral waters, if "unauthorized and unlawful" was still a brilliant piece of sea-work. It called out an official reprimand, but, all the same, it made the name of Commander Napoleon Collins as popular among his countrymen as was that of Captain Charles Wilkes of heroic memory — the "unauthorized" captor of the Rebel commissioners on board the British steamer Trent. The end of the Alabama, when, off Cherbourg harbor, in almost the only naval duel of the war she was sunk after an action of sixty minutes by the Federal sloop of war Kearsarge, raised the name of Captain John A. Winslow to the highest place in the regard of his countrymen, put a "stopper" to the boasted "lucky days" of Raphael Semmes, and freed American commerce of one of its most persistent persecutors. This engagement in fact almost revived the enthusiasms of the old naval glories of 1812. For this victory of the Kearsarge over the Alabama was one in which an English-built vessel supplied with English guns and manned by an English crew was thoroughly beaten and sunk in a sharp fight of less than an hour by American blue jackets, serving American guns in an American-built ship.

Into every sea where defenceless American merchantmen sailed these rebel commerce-destroyers sailed. It was a destructive and one-sided warfare that they waged until the guns of Yankee cruisers or the toils of diplomacy put an end to their careers. But not unfrequently they found their victims not such ready prey as they expected. The Pacific whalers especially, inured to a life of hardship and struggle, often sought to strike back before they would willingly allow their ships and the labor of years to go without a blow. Just such a plucky Yankee skipper was Captain Thomas Young of New Bedford, overhauled in Behring Strait by the cruiser Shenandoah. Deserted by his frightened crew who saw the uselessness of resisting the guns of an armed man-of-war the old skipper stood alone upon the cabin roof determined to defend his vessel to the last. "Stand off, if you know what's good for you!" he yelled to the advancing boat from the cruiser. "Haul down your flag!" came back the order. "I'll see you hanged first," Captain Young replied. "Down with it or I'll shoot you," cried the officer in the boat. "Shoot away; I can shoot too!"

returned the old skipper. Up the chains and over the rail clambered the boarding crew and as they made for their sole adversary on the cabin roof the brave old fellow levelled his pistols and pulled trigger on his assailants. First one and then the other pistol was snapped; but no reports followed. The caps had been removed by his terrified comrades. Then only did the brave old skipper surrender while his captors, unable to appreciate real heroism, clapped him in irons and robbed him of everything he possessed.

Of equal pluck and courage was the bluff old captain of the whaler Ben Scott. Arming his men in haste when the dreaded Alabama overhauled him in far Southern waters he sent back the reply to an order to heave to: "Stand off! We'll go to the bottom before we'll surrender to a rebel!" Volley after volley came from the cruiser as its punishment for such obstinacy, but to every demand to surrender came back the whaler's musket shots. "The Ben Scott don't surrender! Come and take us if you can!" At last, riddled with broadsides, down went his vessel, bow first. Even when the sinking crew had been fished out of the water the old skipper's pluck did not seem to have been cooled by his bath. Walking straight up to Semmes, the rebel captain, he said: "Wal', ef I'd only 'a' had one old cannon aboard, we'd 'a' licked you fellers out 'er yer boots. Here we be; now what you goin' to do with us?"

Recognizing early in the conflict their lack of sufficient sea armament the naval advisers of the Confederacy suggested the encasing of certain stout-hulled steamers in iron enough to render them shot proof. From this crude idea came the iron-clad — a species of sea-fighter that led to the present iron and steel battle-ships and revolutionized the art of naval war. Provided with heavy iron beaks for crushing in the wooden hulls of their opponents these " rebel rams " became dangerous and formidable neighbors in Southern harbors and the scars left by their ponderous beaks were found on the shattered hulls of many a sunken Union vessel.

Two, notably, stand out from the list of a dozen or more of these iron monsters of the Confederacy — the Merrimac and the Albemarle. The career of the first of these rebel rams and her losing fight with that queer little " cheese-box on a raft " (forever famous as the Monitor) is familiar to all. It is a water fight that has become historic, for it revolutionized the methods of ocean warfare and led to the present ponderous iron navies of the world. But though Worden, bruised and blinded in the fight as he worked the little Monitor, is the central figure in that memorable affair, the memory of the gallant Lieutenant Morris, bravely defending the Cumberland to the last is dear to every admirer of the heroic. Of the sailors who stood by him in that losing fight Professor Soley says: " Never did a crew fight a ship with more spirit and hardihood than these brave fellows of the Cumberland while the vessel was going down ; " and Longfellow has immortalized the scene in stirring verse :

<blockquote>

" At anchor in Hampton Roads we lay,
  On board of the Cumberland, sloop-of-war ;
And at times from the fortress across the bay
    The alarum of drums swept past,
    Or a bugle blast
  From the camp on the shore.

Then far away to the south uprose
  A little feather of snow-white smoke.
And we knew that the iron ship of our foes
    Was steadily steering its course
    To try the force
  Of our ribs of oak.

</blockquote>

CUSHING'S DARING DEED: BLOWING UP THE ALBEMARLE.

Down upon us heavily runs,
  Silent and sullen, the floating fort;
Then comes a puff of smoke from her guns,
    And leaps the terrible death,
    With fiery breath,
  From each open port.

We are not idle, but send her straight
  Defiance back in a full broadside!
As hail rebounds from a roof of slate,
    Rebounds our heavier hail
    From each iron scale
  Of the monster's hide.

'Strike your flag!' the rebel cries,
  In his arrogant old plantation strain.
'Never!' our gallant Morris replies;
    'It is better to sink than to yield!'
    And the whole air pealed
  With the cheers of our men.

Then, like a kraken huge and black,
  She crushed our ribs in her iron grasp!
Down went the Cumberland all a wrack,
    With a sudden shudder of death,
    And the cannon's breath
  For her dying gasp.

Next morn, as the sun rose over the bay,
  Still floated our flag at the mainmast head.
Lord, how beautiful was Thy day!
    Every waft of the air
    Was a whisper of prayer,
  Or a dirge for the dead.

Ho! brave hearts that went down in the seas!
  Ye are at peace in the troubled stream;
Ho! brave land! with hearts like these.
    Thy flag that is rent in twain,
    Shall be one again.
  And without a seam!"

Still more remarkable as a daring piece of sailor spunk was the self-imposed task of Lieutenant William Cushing in his attack upon the second-mentioned of these rebel rams. A young fellow of twenty-one, courageous to a fault, enthusiastic to the verge of recklessness, and yet cool, determined and collected in the hour of greatest danger, Cushing determined to destroy the iron ram Albemarle, just then a threatening bar to Union success in North Carolina waters. The hero, already, of one remarkable piece of coolness and audacity in his attempt to capture with but a handful of men the commanding officer of the enemy's forces and to destroy the rebel ram Raleigh, Cushing secured for this second enterprise the use of a steam launch at the bow of which he rigged a spar torpedo that could be lowered into the water and exploded by means of a trigger-line held in the hands of an expert gunner.

On a dark and stormy October night this young lieutenant and his volunteer crew started on their hazardous trip. Past the Rebel pickets and the Rebel shipping the launch crept on, up the river to where at the dock lay the deadly ram. So quietly did they glide along that Cushing even began to entertain hopes that he might board and capture the monster without the need of his deadly explosive when suddenly the warning bark of a dog startled the enemy. Now all was changed. The hope for a surprise was over. Everything depended upon the skill and coolness of the intrepid young leader. Driving his little craft straight at the now aroused Albemarle he dashed alongside through a shower of rifle-bullets, then took a wide sweep out to the middle of the river and, turning again, headed at full speed for the log-encircled monster. Shot upon shot rang out from the defenders of the Albemarle as the audacious little launch dashed on to the attack. But neither

the storm of rebel bullets nor the open ports of the great ram
as the shore fires lighted up the scene could stay the dash or
check the rollicking bravado of Cushing and his men in that
hour of supremest peril. "He went into action," says Professor Soley, "with the zest of a schoolboy at football, and the
nerve and judgment of a veteran." "Hullo, the ram!" he
shouted. "Get ashore or we'll sink you! Surrender; surrender, on your lives! We're going to blow you up!"

The one little howitzer on the launch poured its "dose of
canister" into the open ports of the Albemarle and just as the
launch dashed against the boom of logs that surrounded the
ram the rebels trained dead upon her their big hundred-pound
gun. The launch, forced high upon the logs, was now within
a dozen feet of destruction. Standing in the bow, plain to all
in the glare of the surrounding fires, his right hand already
rendered useless, Cushing held in his left hand the torpedo
lines and almost in the same instant that the great gun
blazed away at him he deftly lowered the spar, drove the
torpedo under the "overhang" of the ram and pulled the
trigger line. The roar of the enemy's hundred-pounder was
echoed by the crash of the torpedo.

The launch, disabled and entangled in the logs, was no
longer manageable. "Jump for your lives!" cried Cushing,
and he and his gallant men leaped into the water. Two went
down in the attempt. One escaped. The rest were captured,
but the plucky young leader swam ashore, hid in the woods
and swamps till daylight and then, weak and wounded, made
his way to the Union picket boat and thus escaped. He had
accomplished his task. The Albemarle, a total wreck, heeled
over and sunk at her moorings. And the daring of Cushing
called out praises both from friend and foe.

Such exploits as these though notable because of their personal daring were by no means phenomenal. Even though it be conceded that the naval arm of the service in the war for the Union was a minor part, its usefulness limited, as Admiral Ammen declares, to the blockade of the coast and effective aid to the army in the capture of forts, it still remains that the blue jackets of 'sixty-one need not yield in heroic example, in valor or in deeds of " high emprise " to the boys in blue with whom they fairly divide the honors and renown. The brilliant passage of the rebel forts by the Union fleets at New Orleans, at Vicksburg and at Mobile secured for the valor of the American seaman the plaudits of a watching world. The victory at Port Royal was secured entirely by the guns of the fleet. At Fort Fisher sixteen hundred sailors and four hundred marines from the Union fleet joined in the land assault, and charged desperately at the solid sea front. Though at first repulsed they turned back again and with dogged determination charged with the land forces on the landward side and wildly cheered as one of their own number pulled down the Confederate flag. The forts at Hatteras Inlet were reduced solely by the guns of the navy, and it was the navy that opened the shackled Mississippi to traffic from Cairo to the Gulf.

There were as has been said but few ocean duels in the course of war. Such however were the actions between the Kearsarge and the Alabama, already noted, and that between the Alabama and the Hatteras off Galveston — the rebel cruiser's first naval battle. The fight between the rebel privateer Savannah and the United States brig Perry, and the destruction of the steamer Petral by the national frigate St. Lawrence would also come into the list of naval battles, but beyond these the open-sea fight did not extend. The only

Confederate vessels afloat were blockade-runners and cruisers and neither of these vessels cared to meet with or engage the war-ships of the Union.

Undoubtedly the most important naval engagement of the war, as, indeed, it is conceded to have been one of the fiercest naval fights on record, was Farragut's memorable passage of the forts at New Orleans. Exposed to the fires of two of the strongest forts in the Confederacy, harassed and raked by the combined shore batteries, gunboats and rams of the rebel defenders the Union fleet made its forward move and within the space of an hour and a half had passed the forts, destroyed almost the whole of the Confederate fleet and held the city of New Orleans at its mercy. Well has Brownell in fiery verses * sung the story of the river fight:

> "Would you hear of the River Fight?
> It was two, of a soft spring night —
>   God's stars looked down on al',
> And all was clear and bright
> But the low fog's chilling breath —
> Up the River of Death
>   Sailed the Great Admiral.
>
> .   .   .
>
> Who could fail with him?
> Who reckon of life or limb?
>   Not a pulse but beat the higher!
> There had you seen, by the starlight dim,
> Five hundred faces strong and grim —
>   The Flag is going under fire!
> Right up by the fort, with her helm hard-a-port,
>   The Hartford is going under fire!
> The way to our work was plain,
> Caldwell had broken the chain,
> (Two hulks swung down amain,

* The lines presented here are but a fragment of Brownell's spirited poem. His rendering of Farragut's "General Orders" in verse is one of the most unique things in rhyme. He also put into rhyme a description of the fight at Mobile, where he was an acting ensign on Farragut's flag-ship the Hartford.

Soon as 'twas sundered) —
Under the night's dark blue,
Steering steady and true,
Ship after ship went through —
Till, as we hove in view,
  Jackson out-thundered.

Back echoed Philip! — ah, then,
Could you have seen our men,
  How they sprung, in the dim night haze,
To their work of toil and clamor!
How the loaders, with sponge and rammer,
And their captains with cord and hammer,
  Kept every muzzle ablaze!
How the guns, as with cheer and shout
Our tackle-men hurled them out,
  Brought up on the water-ways!

First, as we fired at their flash,
  'Twas lightning and black eclipse,
With a bellowing roll and crash —
    But soon, upon either bow,
  What with forts, and fire-rafts and ships —
    (The whole fleet was hard at it now,
All pounding away!) — and Porter
Still thundering with shell and mortar —
'Twas the mighty sound and form
Of an Equatorial storm!

But that we fought foul wrong to wreck
  And to save the Land we loved so well,
You might have deemed our long gun-deck
  Two hundred feet of hell!

For all above was battle
Broadside and blaze and rattle,
  Smoke and thunder alone —
(But, down in the sick bay,
Where our wounded and dying lay,
  There was scarce a sob or a moan.)

THE DECK OF THE HARTFORD — FARRAGUT'S FLAG SHIP.

And at last, when the dim day broke,
And the sullen sun awoke,
  Drearily blinking,
O'er the haze and the cannon smoke,
    That ever such morning dulls —
    There were thirteen traitor hulls
  On fire and sinking!

Lord of mercy and frown,
  Ruling o'er sea and shore,
  Send us such scene once more!
    All in Line of Battle
When the black ships bear down
On tyrant fort and town,
    'Mid cannon-cloud and rattle —
    And the great guns once more
    Thunder back the roar
    Of the traitor walls ashore,
And the traitor flags come down!

There is no grander or more heroic figure in all the war-
pictures of the Great Rebellion than that of David Glasgow
Farragut. A typical American sailor, he had served in the navy
of his country from earliest boyhood; he had stood by the side of
Porter in his splendid defence of the Essex in the war of 1812,
and had lived to add renown and glory fifty years after to
the flag he had then helped to defend. His simple faith,
his sturdy manliness, his sublime courage, his modesty and his
kindliness were at once an example and an inspiration to those
who fought under him. Accomplishing at New Orleans "a feat
in naval warfare that had no precedent," lashed to the shrouds
in Mobile Bay, passing the belching forts at Vicksburg, and the
batteries at Port Hudson — whatever the danger or whatever
the risk he was still the same sturdy, unruffled, courageous
" Old Heart of Oak." Down went the ill fated Tecumseh, done

to death by rebel torpedoes in Mobile Bay. Just ahead of the Hartford flag ship, the Brooklyn halted as if in doubt. From Mobile Point thundered the whole rebel cannonade. "What's the trouble?" came the call to the Brooklyn, from the Admiral lashed to the port rigging of the Hartford. "Torpedoes!" was shouted back in reply. "Damn the torpedoes!" said Farragut. "Four bells! Captain Drayton, go ahead! Jouett, full speed!" The Recording Angel forgave the emphasis. The Hartford passing the halting Brooklyn dashed forward, took the head of the line and led the fleet to victory.

But together with Farragut how many others, brother sailors in the Union fleets, merit mention here. Foote and Dupont, Wilkes and Porter, Boggs and Bailey, Rodgers and Worden, Dahlgren and Davis — these and many others in minor positions deserve equal meed, while the records of the service teem with stories of gallantry, heroism, fidelity and martyrdom. John Davis, gunner's mate of the Valley City, serving the guns during action from an open keg of gunpowder, coolly sat upon the open barrel when an exploding shell set fire to the woodwork and, preventing the sparks from igniting the gunpowder, kept his seat until the fire was extinguished. The Monitor's men, uncertain and dubious as to the safety of their home in that new-fangled "cheese-box" yet went into battle without a murmur although for over forty-eight hours they had been deprived of their rest and had found scarcely anything to eat. "Come and take me!" came back the answer of a Yankee skipper when Semmes on the Alabama ordered him to surrender. "Surrender or I sink you!" the rebel captain signalled. "Attempt it," replied the plucky captain, "and by the living God, I will run you down and we will sink together."

Pilot Collins and Commander Craven met at the foot of the

ladder that, upon the shattered and sinking Tecumseh, was the only way to safety. But one of them could escape. Craven stepped back with heroic courtesy. " After you, pilot," he said. " There was nothing after me," said the pilot as he related the story; " for when I reached the top of the ladder the vessel dropped from under me." Commander Craven was the modern Sir Philip Sidney.

In escaping from the ram Manassas, below New Orleans, the Vincennes grounded, and the order was given to fire the vessel and escape to the Richmond. The train was laid, but as the crew were leaving the stranded ship one old sailor who did not think the order a brave one snatched up the burning slow match and flung it overboard. The next day the Vincennes was floated off, safe and sound.

Freeman, the trusted pilot of Farragut, stood in the ratlines above even his stout old commodore lashed in the top. Lieutenant Commander Gwin, in a fight with the Mississippi batteries left the armored pilot house of his ship, the Benton, to watch the effect of the enemy's fire saying, "with a noble rashness," that the captain's place was on the quarter-deck. And there he died. Captain Henry Walker, three weeks before Farragut passed the New Orleans forts and in face of the opinion that it was certain death to make the attempt, ran the Carondelet past the river batteries, during a heavy thunder storm, — " one of the most daring and dramatic events of the war," says Commander Mahan.

These are but a few of the many instances of pluck and valor that could be cited in proof of the American sailor's daring in the hour of duty and of danger that came so often to him in the battle days of the Civil War.

The thunders of ram and fort, of battery and war ship are

stilled.   The warlike deeds of 'sixty-one are fast becoming a
misty memory and the six hundred war ships of the Union
navy have dwindled to a small and beggarly array.   But the
memory, though misty, is strong and deathless and while time
shall last America will proudly place in the gallery of her
national heroes the men who fought for the honor of the flag
upon the plunging decks of frigate and cruiser, of gun boat
and monitor in the days when the blue jackets of her navy
were brave and zealous defenders of the nation's honor and the
nation's flag.

CHAPTER XIII.

ITH the last shot of the Civil War that w e n t hurtling over blue waters the days of conflict and battle that for generations had marked the sailing courses of America with cannon-smoke and b l o o d came to an end. Henceforth the rivalries of the sea were to be rather those of friendly struggle than of bloody war, and the test of strength was to lie in fleet keels and in bulging canvas — in striving for the silver cup or the fluttering pennant of peaceful rivalry rather than in the boarder's cutlass or the lowered flag.

The desire for display and discipline that seems to be ingrained in the nature of man was transferred from the deck of the war-ship to that of the pleasure craft. Desire grows with endeavor and to-day the ownership of a yacht is the ambition of every prosperous American. The increasing fleets of white wings that with each new summer dot our Northern coasts, the increasing sums of money expended in the building and outfitting of swift and beautiful pleasure boats, the advance made in the science and art of yacht construction, the interest and enthusiasm displayed in every trial of skill and of speed between rival yachts on lake or river, bay or broader sea are proof that the great public loves to watch the graceful exhibitions of water tactics and that the present is, notably, the day of the gentleman sailor.

There have always been "gentlemen sailors" — that favored class of wealthy humanity who are better able to own than to sail their private vessels. But, from the days of the pleasure galleys of Tyre and the regal yachts of the Roman emperors, ownership in these expensive luxuries has never been so universal as it is to-day. In modern times England had long maintained the lead in private ownership, interest and speed. Forty years ago American yachts like American books were unheard of in England, and Sidney Smith's famous query might have been extended from American literature to American yachtsmanship. Major Crowninshield's parti-colored craft of two hundred tons launched at Salem in December, 1816, and known as Cleopatra's Barge was the first American yacht, and was the first to make the ocean trip. But this Yankee pleasure craft was regarded rather as an American eccentricity than as a serious attempt at yacht construction and it was not until the notable triumph of the schooner America over the entire pleasure fleet at Cowes in the year 1851 that England awoke to the fact that it had not only a competitor but a victorious rival in the big republic across the western sea.

The " Hoboken Model Yacht Club " organized in 1840 was the first attempt in America at an association of the owners of private pleasure boats. In 1844 this association became by a change of name the New York Yacht Club and from the incorporation of this organization dates the real growth of American yachting.

The Southern Yacht Club, formed in New Orleans, about 1850 with its racing course on Lake Ponchartrain was the second American club. The Neptune Club on the Shrewsbury

THE "GENTLEMAN SAILOR."

River was the third and the Carolina Club of Wilmington was the fourth.

The first actual regatta was sailed in New York harbor in July, 1845; the first match race (and the first ocean race, as well) was that between Mr. Stevens's sloop Maria and Mr. Perkins's schooner Coquette in October, 1846. In this forerunner of much later sport the victory was won by the Coquette.

From this point interest in this exhilarating ocean sport

steadily increased, and the victory of the America in British waters, already referred to, was the culminating point of the initial era in American yachting.

It was a great day for the American yachtsman; the twenty-second of August, 1851. Amid the hundred yachts that thronged the roadstead at Cowes lay the low black hull of "the Yankee," in model and rig noticeably different from the British craft that surrounded her. In a double line from Cowes Castle were moored the eighteen yachts that were entered for the race. Nine were cutters and nine schooners, the America being among the latter.

At ten o'clock the signal gun from the battery set the yachts in motion and, at once, sheeted in canvas from deck to topmast, they dashed away like a field of race horses, the America a laggard in the start. Very soon however she began to show her mettle, and stood bravely out bowling easily along under mainsail, foresail, fore-staysail and jib while her rivals in the race had every inch of sail set that their club rules allowed.

Soon she began to pass her antagonists. First the cutters dropped behind; then with a freshening wind the America gathered way and forged ahead of the Constance and the Beatrice: but, the next instant, the Volante cutter dashed forward, her great jib catching all the wind, and left the America behind. So the race continued with varying fortune until, when off Brading, the America caught a six-knot breeze, passed with a rush, the four yachts that were leading her, and leaving every vessel in the squadron far behind flew like the wind toward the buoys that marked the turn in the course. Off the Culver cliffs the nearest yacht was two miles astern. Off Dunnose she broke her jib-boom short but gathered in the wreck and, at the Needles, she was fully seven miles ahead of her nearest pursuer.

"Is the America first?" came the hail off Cowes to one of the returning steamers. "Yes," was the reply. "What's second?" rang the anxious English query. "Nothing!" came the honest English answer, and cheers for the blue ensign and white stars of the visitor from over-sea mingled with the regret that England had lost the cup.

But now the breeze died away, further real sailing was impossible, the yachts began to drift, and those that had been out of sight when the America was off the Needles, being of lighter tonnage, now slipped into range; the eight miles' distance narrowed rapidly, but the gun that greeted the finish hailed the America as winner in the race, eight minutes in advance of her competitors. Had the wind held its force the Yankee schooner would have distanced her nearest antagonist by fully an hour. The boasted "national rig" upon which English yachtsmen had relied so implicitly for speed and success yielded to the American design and the defeat led the British boat-builders to a change of model and of rig.

Elated by his success "Commodore" Stevens of the America at once offered to race his boat against any English yacht for a stake of ten thousand guineas, but his challenge was not taken up and after beating the schooner-yacht Titania by an hour's distance in a sea race of forty miles the America returned with the prize "cup" to the United States. That trophy, still known as the America's Cup, has remained in Yankee hands to this day.

The America's success gave a fresh impetus to the yachting interest in this country. The owning of pleasure boats by the wealthier classes began to be recognized as an American luxury, but even with the incentive of an historic victory the growth of the sport was slow and the outbreak of the Civil War

for a time retarded its further development. It is one of the
minor features of that struggle, as showing the patriotism of
the "gentleman sailor," that many of the best of the private

(BUILDER OF THE PURITAN, MAYFLOWER AND VOLUNTEER.)

yachts were loaned or given by their owners to the Government
for use in the naval service of the Union.

It was one of these donated yachts that after the close of
the war gained a victory that has made it historic. This was
the Henrietta, a keel yacht of two hundred and thirty tons,
schooner rigged, built for James Gordon Bennett, Jr., of

New York, by Henry Steers, a celebrated boat-builder. Completed and launched in June, 1861, Mr. Bennett had at once placed her at the disposal of the Government and the "flyer" did duty for four years as a revenue cutter between New York and Florida. In 1866 having returned to the "service" of the New York Yacht Club the Henrietta took part in what has been termed "the most remarkable contest ever entered into either on land or water." This was a trial of speed between three American yachts — the Fleetwing, the Vesta and the Henrietta — for the enormous sweep-stake of ninety thousand dollars. The race was to be made in midwinter and over an ocean course that extended from the Sandy Hook Light Ship, off New York harbor, to the Needle's Light in the English Channel.

The race was won by the Henrietta. But it was a victory obtained rather by superior navigation than by superior speed. The Vesta, though covering the greatest distance, lost the race by eight hours and fifty-five minutes and but for her pilot's blunder might have made first place. The skillful piloting of the Henrietta secured for her the victory by the shortest distance and the quickest time, her record being three thousand one hundred and six miles in thirteen days, twenty-one hours and fifty-five minutes. This remarkable record was almost on a par with the fleetest packet ships of those days and only a little below the steamer average.

The victory of the Henrietta raised the "gentleman sailor" in the scale of pluck and seamanship. For where he had, heretofore, held rather a minor place in the opinion of seamen as one who was only a smooth-water sailor, hugging the land and afraid to venture off soundings, it was now established that he was ready to brave the winter perils of an ocean voyage and was able to hold his own against even the best professional sailors. Captain Coffin declares that this was "certainly, the most remarkable yacht race ever sailed, whether as regards the length and nature of the course, the season of the year, the amount of money involved, or the result of the struggle. It lifted American yachting," he says, "to a level with any in the world and placed the New York Club on an equality with the Royal Yacht Squadron of Great Britain" — the recognized standard of the world's yachting superiority.

In fact, the spirit and zeal of the sportsman were beginning to infuse themselves into the skillful handling of American pleasure craft. Pluck and daring were alike entering into the sport, and the dash made through Plum Gut by Mr. Bennett in the race around Long Island — a short cut deemed especially hazardous and seldom attempted by yachtsmen — together with the record of the Henrietta in the ocean race of 1866 materially changed the old ways and increased alike the desires and the risks of the American yachtsmen. They became each year still more adventurous. The safe and quiet Elysian Fields Course no longer satisfied them. The tests must be made in part on the ocean. The Sandy Hook Light Ship thus became the turning point of an "inside" course, while the "outside" course, a windward and leeward one, stretched away twenty miles to sea. This yielded, in turn, to the Atlantic itself where sailing courses of hundreds of miles were mapped out; one race, as we have seen, circumnavigated Long Island, and the height of hazard was attained when stout and well-appointed racers laid their courses across three thousand miles of sea.

The interest in the exciting sport grew materially after the close of the war. English yachts, restless so long as the America's Cup remained in Yankee keeping, began to come across the ocean to fight for its possession. The plucky struggle made for this trophy in the summer of 1870 by the British schooner Cambria, against the American fleet of twenty-five sail came very near to being a victory for England. The little schooner Magic won; the Cambria was tenth at the finish, but, according to Captain Coffin, "she was beaten because she was clumsily rigged and canvased. I think I am correct in saying," he adds, "that with a modern suit of canvas the Cambria, in 1870, would have carried home the America's Cup."

But she did not, and hence ensued that series of international races for the possession of the coveted trophy that have served to heighten public interest in ocean sports and to enrich the annals of endeavor with some of the most brilliant and closely-fought water-struggles in the history of amateur seamanship.

If, however, the Cambria did not win the cup she showed herself determined to maintain the honor of England's pleasure navy against all comers. The Americans responded to her challenge and the season of 1870 was a notable one in yachting history, the August races at Newport being especially brilliant and interesting. The Cambria, however, came off victor in one only of all her matches and this result, as it emphasized the defects in English rig, led to a new departure in "canvasing" among British riggers.

So great was the advance in the interest in yachting as an American sport that in the year 1872 the membership of American yacht clubs had grown from the nine members of 1844 to a round thousand, owning yachts valued at five millions of dollars. In 1875 there were in the United States thirty-four regularly organized clubs registering six hundred and ninety-two vessels, and in 1885, forty years after the commencement of this expensive sport, there were over one hundred clubs registering seventeen hundred and ninety-seven yachts. The number of additional yachts and private pleasure vessels not officially registered would largely increase this total.

Official figures, indeed, cannot mark the limit of a sport that is steadily growing in popular approval. Wherever, on ocean, lake or river, a land-locked harbor affords relief from breaker, surf or sudden storm there now ride at anchor through the sunny summer days the trim and tidy craft that skim the waters only at the pleasure of the favored "gentleman sailor."

Of every size and of every conceivable make and model, from cat boat to schooner and from canoe to steamer, the white wings of the American pleasure fleet dot the sun-lit waters. The breezes that fill the sails or stir the picturesque awnings bear with them also vigor, health and manliness to thousands who but for the practical development of this noble sport would lack the incentive to a sturdy and symmetrical growth. To this result the organizers of American yacht clubs and the patrons and votaries of yachting as an American pastime have largely contributed. And even the negative side of the sport — its risks, its dangers, its tendency to degenerate into a vehicle for unlawful betting and disastrous gambling on issues — can neither neutralize nor outweigh the positive advantages that must result from so healthful and invigorating a sport.

But healthful amusement is not the only outcome of an indulgence in the owning and sailing of yachts. A desire to excel creates a demand for improved methods that only skilled labor can supply. Improvements in model, build and rig have led to a systematic and constant development of naval architecture. The William Tooker, the George and Henry Steers of 1849 are the Hereshoffs, the Charles J. Paine, and the Edward

OFF SANDY HOOK.

Burgess of 1889, while that interval of forty years has given popularity and renown to many a clever designer and successful boat-builder.

More than this, the growth of yachting as a national sport has not only yielded employment to skilled and ambitious workmen; it has supplied occupation and the means of livelihood to thousands of seamen in manning and managing the constantly increasing fleet of pleasure boats. From the ranks of fishermen, coasters and pilots has come a class of expert seamen who have developed into professional yachtsmen. This, in turn, is of national benefit. An augmented pleasure service keeps in continual training a large force of men and of vessels as a reserve that can at once be drawn upon for efficient service in any emergency that shall call for nautical knowledge, experience and skill.

Although most owners of small pleasure yachts are their own skippers and often their own crew few vessels beyond the tonnage of yawl or cat-boat but must depend upon the assistance of others as master, mate or crew. Less owners, proportionately, are their own skippers than in the early days of yachting. For a sloop of thirty-five tons a crew of five men is deemed a necessity and the number of sizable pleasure craft now afloat calls into service a large and ever-increasing contingent of strong and sturdy helpers. Here alone is a navy in embryo. At least six thousand sailors to-day find employment on the decks of American pleasure vessels. The official complement of the United States navy at the outbreak of the Civil War was but seventy-six hundred men, and this, by intentional neglect, had fallen far below the yachtsman's six thousand.

The "gentleman sailor" has, therefore, called into existence a new class of American seamen — the professional yachtsman.

He must be a skilled sailor, thoroughly familiar with soundings, currents, channels and the devious ways of harbor, bay and sailing course.　He must be reliable, ready and alert, courteous, willing and handy, with less of the proverbial roughness of the regulation "old salt" and with more, perhaps, of the valet in his composition than belongs to the merchant sailor.

But this need for a diversity of gifts is offset by the substantial results.　The professional yachtsman commands much higher pay than does the common sailor.　In 1872 the twenty-five hundred men employed on board the registered pleasure craft in actual service during the four yachting months created an outlay in wages and "keep" of over twelve hundred thousand dollars.　There are now in the United States an ever-increasing number of competent skippers who, in their summer service as captains or sailing masters on the big yachts or the still larger steam yachts, earn a sufficient sum to enable them to revel in the sailor's luxury and "lay by" during the stormy and uninviting winter season.

This last-mentioned pleasure craft, the steam yacht, while of comparatively recent development is forcing its way into a prominence that demands recognition not alone as the most expensive of all American luxuries but because it is a most practical and beneficial luxury.　The steam yacht is one of the strongest incentives to progress in naval architecture and one of the factors in nautical education that may be relied upon as a feeder for the navy of the future.

"Your regular old yachtsman," says Mr. Jaffray, "has a profound contempt for steam yachts.　He considers that all the romance and pleasure of yachting consist in the uncertainties, dangers and difficulties attending sailing.　He glories in the storms which compel the shortening of sail, the lying to, the scudding

before the wind under a staysail and all the other vicissitudes
which attend excess of wind; while, on the other hand, he takes
dead calms, with sails idly flapping against the masts and the

THE MAYFLOWER.

reflection of his vessel in the mirror-like water, with philosophy
and contentment."

But time is, unfortunately, a matter of too much importance
to busy Americans to be thus "wasted" when the same ground
— or, rather, the same water can be more quickly covered by
other and more rapid methods. " In this happy country," says

Mr. Jaffray, "we have neither time nor inclination to be becalmed on the glassy ocean for hours and days, or to creep along at three knots indefinitely. Steam yachtsmen can go where they please and when they please and, what is more important, they know when they will get back."

Hence the evolution of the steam yacht. It is not an American idea. Originating in France it has been developed by American ingenuity to its present perfection. Mr. Aspinwall's crude little fifty foot Fire-Fly of thirty years ago, with its single paddle-wheel working in the centre of the boat and encased in an air-tight box, has grown into the palatial private steamer of to-day — magnificent yachts like the Atalanta and the Nourmahal, beside which the old-time galleys of the Roman emperors with their baths and hot houses and jewelled porticoes would be but crude and ungainly affairs.

From the steam launch of forty feet to the Atalanta of two hundred and fifty feet, the steam yachts run the scale of dimensions, tonnage, appointments and crew. The Nourmahal, probably the handsomest steam yacht afloat, is constructed entirely of steel and fitted to circumnavigate the globe. The Atalanta can show a record of seventeen knots an hour, the Corsair and Stranger of fifteen, and the limit of cost and speed have not yet been touched.

This species of pleasure craft, even more than the sailing yachts, call for the services of skilled and reliable sailors. The smallest steam launch must have a pilot, an engineer and at least one deck hand. The Namouna carries a crew of fifty men and her pay roll when "in commission" is not less than twenty-five hundred dollars a month. The crews of the steam yachts are "the pick of the seamen." They are well-housed, well-fed, and consider their employment "a soft berth." To man and run an average steam yacht — that is a well-built and well-equipped decked steamer of from seventy-five to one hundred feet long costs, according to the modest estimates of Mr. Jaffray, at least ten thousand dollars for a season of five months and calls for the services of eight or ten men. This is, as has been said, a modest estimate. The cost of running such floating palaces as the Namouna, the Nourmahal and the Atalanta creeps far into the tens of thousands. It has, indeed, been placed at from six to twelve thousand dollars a month. Truly, it was not out of place to denominate this princely pleasure as the most expensive of all American luxuries.

And yet yachting is not, necessarily, an expensive amusement. If conducted, as Mr. Benjamin puts it, "without regard to the national weakness, ostentation," the sport is one which can be shared alike by the millionaire and the American of moderate means while the legacy of health that it bequeaths can be monopolized by neither. Whether threading the creeks and bays of the New England coast in the little "single hander" wherein the yachtsman is often captain, crew and passenger combined — "three single gentlemen rolled into one" — or standing upon the bridge of some thirty thousand dollar steam yacht — monarch of all he surveys — or striving for the America's Cup in some swift-sailing Mayflower or Volunteer, the gentleman sailor is taking to himself fresh supplies of health and strength and helping to build up America's interest in a noble and invigorating sport.

And when this same gentleman sailor casts off the conventional "gentleman" and becomes for the cruise a simple son of nature what a store of comfort and pleasure does he not enjoy. "To him," says Mr. Benjamin, "the humblest fare seasoned with the ozone of the salt, breezy ocean is enough. He delights to leave behind the swallow-tail coat and white choker, the desk, the postman and the morning paper, and is never happier than when perched on the weather rail in a blue flannel shirt conning his lively sloop and puffing at his brier-wood pipe. . . . He hears the halliards slatting against the mast in the night wind, or feels the yacht jerking at her anchors and anon the rattling of a cable or the creaking of blocks as another yacht runs in to her anchorage. He recks not that his wee bark is neither long nor costly, for the spirit that inspires him is the same which fired the Vikings of old to deeds of heroism and glory on many a stormy sea."

Of all the deeds of " heroism and glory " in the annals of American yachting none excel in interest the three remarkable contests for the possession of the famous America's Cup that occupied public attention during the three successive seasons of 1885, '86 and '87.

English ingenuity had been at work. A swift-sailing cutter with a wonderful record was sent across the water and the hopes of British yachtsmen centered upon the Genesta. But American genius had not been idle. In reply to this English challenge was launched the sloop Puritan — a centre-board yacht in which says Captain Coffin, " from stem to stern, from keel to truck, all things about her were closely calculated." Three races were arranged for, and the winner of two out of the three was to take the cup. Both races were won by the Puritan — the first on September 14, 1885, by a lead of sixteen minutes and nineteen seconds over an all-round course of thirty-eight miles to the Sandy Hook Light Ship and return; the second over an ocean course twenty miles to leeward and return on September 16, by one minute and thirty-eight seconds. American ingenuity won, but it was by so small a

margin that it was conceded that, had the Yankee yacht been
any other than the Puritan, the Genesta would have sailed in
victor.

In the next year the fight was renewed. Across the sea
came the Galatea, sister cutter to the Genesta, but presumably
an improved and faster craft. But again Boston's clever builder
was ready. The centre-board sloop Mayflower — eighty-five
feet seven inches water line, twenty-three feet six and one half
inches beam — was built and launched. In a trial race she out-
sailed the Puritan, victor of the year before, and on the seventh
of September, 1886, lay at anchor off Owl's Head in the inner
bay below New York awaiting the signal to test her rival's
speed. At ten o'clock came the warning whistle. With club
topsail, staysail and jib all set the Mayflower dashed across the
starting line, carrying her boom to port and breaking out her
jib topsail as she crossed the line. With equal alacrity the
Galatea obeyed the starting signal; by a smart and seamanlike
manœuvre she " hauled to " and with a great headway rushed
in between the Mayflower and the stake boat thus getting the
weather gauge and " blanketing " her antagonist. But this
device did not work. With a celerity that was bewildering
to the English tars the Yankee sloop " ran from under the
Englishman's lee " and having the advantage of lighter
draught in shallow water stood straight on for a full half-
minute after the British boat had been forced to tack and
then, coming about to windward, had so much the advantage of her rival that no manœuvring on the Englishman's
part could win back the lead and when the Galatea touched
the home line the Mayflower had already preceded her by
twelve minutes and two seconds. On September 11, over
the outside course, an even worse defeat was experienced, for

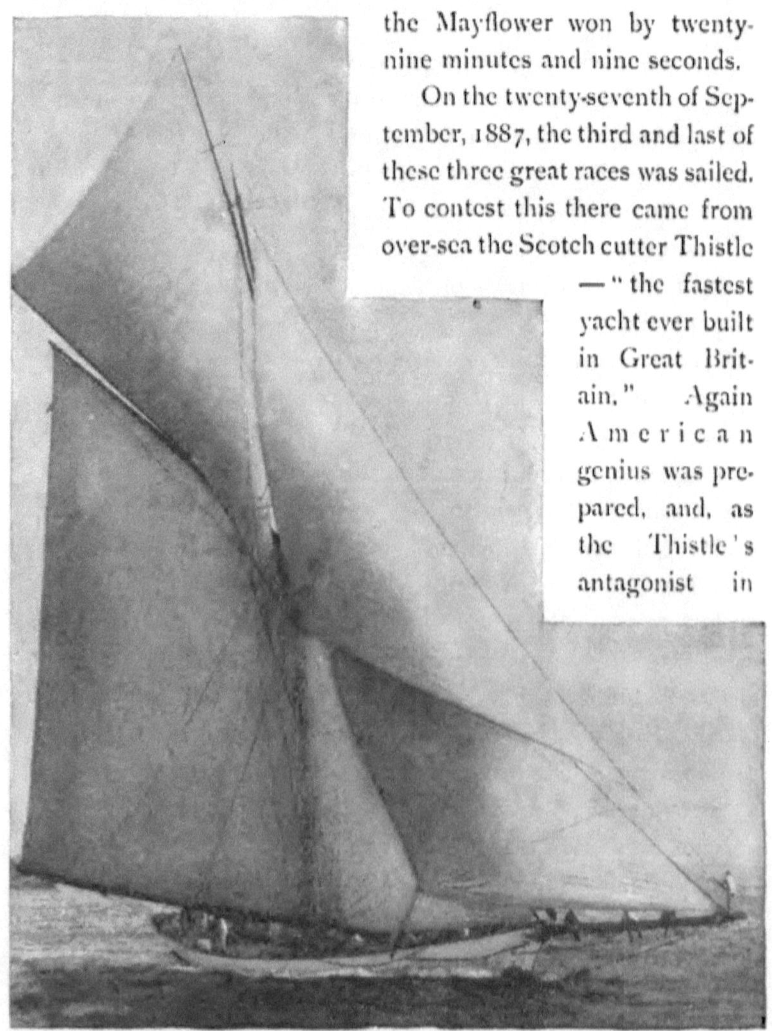

the Mayflower won by twenty-
nine minutes and nine seconds.

On the twenty-seventh of September, 1887, the third and last of
these three great races was sailed.
To contest this there came from
over-sea the Scotch cutter Thistle
— " the fastest
yacht ever built
in Great Brit-
ain."   Again
A m e r i c a n
genius was pre-
pared, and, as
the   Thistle's
antagonist   in

THE VOLUNTEER.

the race, sailed the Volunteer, a steel centre-board sloop
designed and built by Mr. Burgess especially for this contest.

Already in a trial of speed had she proved victor over both the Mayflower and the Puritan.

A more beautiful boat and rig than the Thistle, say enthusiastic yachtsmen, was never seen in New York Bay. It was the most hotly contested race of the three seasons. As the starting gun boomed the Thistle crossed the line, with sails trimmed aft and "drawing" beautifully, while the Volunteer was "jibing" round astern. It seemed an evil omen. For the first time in a struggle for the America's Cup a British cutter had led her Yankee rival. But at once the Volunteer seemed to waken to the responsibility. Crossing the line nearly two minutes behind her antagonist she kept straight on toward the Staten Island shore and when the Thistle came about she still kept on her course undismayed. It was the British mistake of 1886 repeated, for when a little later the Volunteer did come about she crossed the Thistle's bow and took away her rival's wind. On she forged, a mile ahead of the Scotch cutter. She rounded the Spit Buoy that marked the turn in the course fully two miles ahead of the Thistle and crossed the line a winner of the race by nineteen minutes twenty-three and a quarter seconds. Two days after, on the twenty-ninth of September came the second race. By a piece of bold seamanship the Thistle won the windward berth, but by a still more remarkable exhibition of sailing skill the Volunteer luffed twice before she crossed the line and gaining by this a tremendous headway dashed grandly on and when the signal for the start boomed from the flag ship the Volunteer lay fully twenty lengths to windward of the cutter. Then ensued five minutes of marvelous sailing, anxiety and enthusiasm. Five minutes only; for at the end of that time the struggle for the lead was practically over and the Thistle was a beaten boat. And so it proved; for when the home run was finished the Volunteer came in victor eleven minutes forty-eight and three quarter seconds ahead and the America's Cup still remains in the hands of its captors.

Surely such sport as this is thrilling, inspiring, invigorating. Such victories are a tribute alike to American genius and American pluck and the great reception and testimonial given in Boston after the final success to the, three times, inspirer and designer of the victorious boats in the three international races—General Paine and Mr. Burgess—were at once a recognition of energy and genius and an exhibition of pardonable pride in the supremacy of American keels.

The yacht is a school of patriotism. To win a race is a laudable desire; to come in victor over foreign rivals develops, as Mr. Benjamin says, that "enthusiasm of patriotism which is now kindling once more through the republic and welding our various races into one great homogeneous people."

It is this sentiment that gives fresh impulse to the yachtsman's muscle as he hauls away at the sheets, runs up the topsails and sets the giant spinnaker; it was this, too, that prompted Captain Joe Ellsworth of yachting fame to reply when asked to pilot the Thistle in the last international race, that he had "never yet sailed against his own flag and never would."

The yachtsman has become a prominent feature in American sea life.* The custom of summer cruising on ocean, lake and river is increasing with each new year and though the question of superiority as between keel and centre-board is still undecided the growth of this gallant pastime is of even greater

---

* It is a significant fact, as showing how closely the amateur touches the professional sailor, that there are in America many yacht clubs known as "Corinthian" in all of whose races the "crews" are restricted to amateurs. In the great international races the crews of the Puritan, the Mayflower and the Volunteer were composed in a considerable part of amateur yachtsmen — "gentlemen sailors."

importance than the minor questions of build and rig and model. The benefit of an out-of-door life on board a swift-sailing yacht as the keen and strengthening breezes come freshening over the white caps of some great lake or of the greater ocean is not to be computed in figures but it is certain to tell in the manlier because healthier life of America's youth. Not even the most sea-detesting of landsmen but will join in a godspeed and good voyage to the enthusiastic and daunt-less gentleman sailor as he stands out to sea, his club pennant flying at the peak and his heart, if not his lips, joining in the inspiriting song of the yachtsman :

> " Up with the anchor! the white-crested billows
>   Are leaping like dolphins our swift keel to greet;
> Awake! all ye sluggards, throw by your soft pillows,
>   Make sail on our darling, the Queen of the Fleet.
>
>   .   .   .   .   .   .
>
> She welcomes the breeze with ripples of laughter,
>   And shows her white teeth at each wave that we meet;
> She flings back the spray at crafts that come after;
>   Ah! none can compare with our Queen of the Fleet."

CHAPTER XIV.

IT is useless to evade the facts. Disguise it as we may the simple truth remains that the American sailor, conconsidered as an American, is but a relic of the past. American commerce still exists. Its statistics for 1887 show a record of twenty-three thousand and sixty-three craft (embracing steam and sailing vessels, canal boats and barges) with a total carrying capacity of over four million tons.* The tonnage we employ, including all that floats on salt water and fresh, is the largest in the world. Our commerce, foreign and domestic combined, is greater than that of any other nation. Our foreign commerce alone reached in 1887 a total valuation of over fifteen hundred millions of dollars. The domestic commerce very largely exceeds this amount.

But the registered tonnage of the Unites States — the vessels actually sailing under the stars and stripes — is decreasing rapidly. While American commerce has grown to enormous

* The exact figures are 15,735 sailing vessels, 5,481 steam vessels, 910 canal boats and 917 barges.

proportions, American transportation has as marvelously declined. Of the "goods, wares and merchandise" exported and imported into the United States of America in the year 1821, eighty-eight and seven tenths per cent. were transported in American vessels and eleven and three tenths per cent. in foreign "bottoms." In 1887 American vessels carried but thirteen and eight tenths per cent. of America's commerce while foreign vessels carried eighty-seven and two tenths. In 1855 the ship-building industry of the United States produced an aggregate tonnage of 583,450. In 1886 the same industry produced a total tonnage of but 95,453. This decrease has been especially marked in the past four or five years. In 1883 there were built in the United States 1268 vessels of all descriptions. In 1886 there were built but 715.

It is in no sense the province of this book to enter into a discussion of the reasons for this decline in the once proud "merchant marine" of America. Politicians and political economists have warred over the question for a quarter of a century. Advocates, now of Free Trade and now of Protection, have engaged in wordy conflict over the matter and discharged against each other arguments, figures and statistics more formidable than the crashing broadsides once exchanged by the old-time line-of-battle ships. And still the decrease goes on while each year's statistics prove only more and more clearly the actual decline in numbers and in *morale* of the American sailor.

Of the sixty thousand seamen employed upon United States shipping more than one half are foreigners. Lascars and Portuguese, Germans and Scandinavians, British and Italians largely make up the crews of American vessels, and the recent exhibit of our fishery statistics show how meagre is the real Yankee element even in this domestic industry.

" The men that sail out of New York before the mast," says Mr. Heywood, "are beyond doubt the most ruffianly in the world. They are of all nationalities and seldom article for the voyage, but for the run, leaving the ship as soon as she touches the dock."

"When I was a boy at sea," writes Mr. Nordhoff, "the American flag was to be found literally on every sea, and the American ship was the tautest, the best fitted, the best sailer and made the most successful voyages. The American ship-master was by far the most intelligent of his class. He had the air as he had the habit of success. He had not only seamanship, but brains and a commercial education."

It is far different to-day. Yankee ships, in foreign ports, are, as one old sailor has testified, "as scarce as hen's teeth." The commerce of America sails in foreign "bottoms" and observant seafarers allege, with reason, that "the flag that once floated over the fastest ships and shielded the best sailors in the world will, in a few years, be a stranger on the ocean."

" Why, bless my heart," cried a waggish English captain when, not long since he spoke the stars and stripes on the South Pacific course, "that must be a Yankee ship. I remember seeing that flag when I was a boy. The poor fellow must have drifted off the coast and got lost. Hadn't yer better chalk the reckoning on the head of a barrel, Mr. Buntline, and give it to him and tell him to get home as fast as he can ? "

And if the character of the sailors, as a class, is low so too has that of the captains deteriorated. Mr. Jewell, formerly United States Consul at Singapore, is authority for the statement that " not one sea captain in ten is a just and conscientious man. He is low in origin, low in education, low in impulse." Spite of the protections thrown about seamen by the

THROUGH THE GOLDEN GATE.

American shipping laws the tyranny of the quarter-deck is still unmitigated and absolute. The reputation of American skippers among sailors is that of a "slave-driver" and, in truth, on far too many merchant ships brutality and injustice are the governing forces.

"If you hear a story of brutal outrage committed on some foremast hand," says Mr. Heywood, "whether perpetrated in China, on the burning slave coast or in frozen Labrador, in nine cases out of ten you will learn that the principal is an American skipper." "It is a source of wonder to many who have donned the blue and served a term before the mast," declares Mr. Skinner, "that mutinies do not occur on half the merchant ships afloat. Were day laborers compelled to work as long, fare as hard and be treated as cruelly as are sailors, the press of the land would ring with protests, labor leagues would organize to fight for justice, and legislative action would be sought to put a stop to further brutality." But, so both these last-quoted observers declare, there is no law for a common sailor in the ports of the United States. Courts do not often declare in favor of the illiterate seaman when he seeks redress from his more influential captain. Complaint therefore being useless poor Jack seldom appeals from the tyranny of the quarter-deck. Low diet, unclean quarters, kicks, hard labor and hard words he has come to regard as "all in the day's work." His nature becomes changed, his habits degraded, his manliness disappears and the American sailor of to-day is no longer the "jolly Jack Tar" of thirty years ago when, so Mr. Nordhoff tells us, "we Yankees counted ourselves the best men that sailed the seas."

Of course this is the darkest side of the picture. There are still fine ships, considerate captains and decent seamen in the

American merchant service, but they are, unfortunately, the exception rather than the rule and American seamanship has with the decrease of American tonnage visibly declined.

For both these waning conditions there exist reasons other than those advanced by economists and politicians. First and foremost the American sailor is the victim of the advance of science. The practical application of steam as a motive power on the water and the substitution of iron for wood in the construction of vessels, as these have reduced the proportionate number of ships needed to transport the world's commerce have also reduced the need for able seamen and the number as well. Your true sailor heartily detests the steam service. The mercantile marine of to-day, he declares, does not need sailors; "any pier-head loafer will serve its turn." The pay and the work are those of the stevedore while the chances for life when one is in peril on the sea are materially lessened. A wooden ship, even when wrecked, will float but your iron shell, as one old seaman puts it, " washes under and goes down like a stone." No sailor, Mr. Heywood asserts, will, " if he can help it, ship on a commercial steamer and 'pot-wallop' about her decks in grease and dirt."

Again, as has been shown, the American merchant marine has never recovered from the blow inflicted upon it by Confederate cruisers during the days of the Civil War. The carrying of ocean freights passed to foreign vessels and the lost ground has never been recovered. The discovery of petroleum and the use of gas and electricity as methods of illumination affected the great whale-fishing industry so disastrously that where once fortunes were made in a few years by experienced whalemen the whale fleets have now practically disappeared and the returns even of a successful whaling voyage scarcely repay the time and money invested. As to the other causes cited by students of America's maritime decline — the existence of a protective tariff, the indisposition of Government to grant subsidies, mail contracts and other fostering helps, and the backwardness of America's development of her coal and iron mines — these must be left to the wisdom of national legislators for settlement and need not here enter into the recital of the story of the American sailor.

But with hope in the future — which always means progress and not retrogression — it is for us in this closing chapter of the Yankee seaman's story to gather the stray scraps of his record that have not yet found a place herein — the flotsam and jetsam that, if he is scuttled and breaking up, float in upon us as we seek to save from the wreckage of the past some indication of his manliness, his courage, his frailties and his customs in the days gone by.

The American sailor, in his better days, had always a pride in his profession. He was brave; he had a strong sense of duty and although accustomed to think, as Mr. Nordhoff says, that "the man who could hand, reef, steer and heave the lead was the best of created beings," he had a love for his calling and a loyalty to his ship that made him a hearty comrade, a sure reliance and a firm friend. "Be true to your ship," was the sailor's eleventh commandment. He might sometimes fracture the other ten, but this one he ever kept intact. Though in his "growly" moments (and your real "salt" always holds as one of his inalienable rights the privilege to grumble) the sailor might abuse his vessel as "an infernal old bucket" he is quick to resent criticism of his floating home by a stranger. "I have known," says Mr. Heywood, "a surly, silent mate who had a growl for every one and a good word for no one, stamp and

clap his hands with delight at overhauling and passing some
rival ship, and sarcastically order the cook to 'git out yer
bellers and make a wind for that there craft on the port-
quarter.'"

On board a good ship there was plenty of good will. From
master and mate to cook and cabin boy there was a desire to do
one's duty and an ambition to do it well. Despite the vices
that confinement breeds there was both clean thinking and
clean living on a well-manned vessel. "A ship's forecastle filled
with an able crew," says Mr. Nordhoff, "is a very respect-
able place compared with a country store on a winter evening.
Such a crew — and there are such yet, O sea! — such a crew
usually knows how to take care of itself. It is when half a
dozen good sailors are, by the carelessness of owner and captain
and the rascality of agents and boarding-house keepers, mixed
up with a dozen or a score of skulking scoundrels, that the forecastle and the whole ship presently becomes a place fit only for
devils."

Good-will as it breeds comradeship creates too an equality of
labor. With a good crew it is share and share alike and where
this develops a spirit of independence it also contributes to the
growth of manliness. A sea life tests the virtues as it fosters
the vices of humanity. This latter quality (the desire to appear
manly, whatever happens) is often pushed to extremes. "An
overstrained sense of manliness," says Mr. Dana, "is the characteristic of sea-faring men. If a man comes within an ace of
breaking his neck and escapes it is made a joke of; no notice
must be taken of a bruise or cut. Any expression of pity or
any show of attention would look sisterly and unbecoming a
man who has to face the rough and tumble of such a life."

Off Cape Horn, on a dark and stormy night, the men on an

American ship were reefing topsails. Every motion was fraught with danger and a plunge overboard meant no rescue. One of the younger lads lost his hold of the reef point and slipped from the foot rope. He would have gone down to his death in an instant had not his nearest neighbor, a powerful seaman, caught him by the collar and hauled him back on the yard. Neither sympathy nor concern were expressed by the rescuer, however much he may have felt for the lad. " Hold on another time, you young monkey," he growled as he "yanked " the boy up. And that was all that was said of the affair.

Once, in the China Seas, while their vessel was pitching bows under with every sea two men went out to stow the flying jib. As they were working their way back the ship gave a tremendous pitch and both men lost their hold. But as they fell they grabbed the foot ropes and hanging thus to a tossing ship, between wind and water, they managed to work their perilous way hand over hand to the bowsprit shrouds. " H'm !" grunted a tough old salt as his half-drowned comrades clambered on deck again, "you fellers wanted to show how smart you were — cuttin' about on the foot-ropes; didn't you ? A little more and you'd 'a' gone to Davy Jones." And when they tried to explain matters they were only met with jeers and became for days the laughing-stock of the forecastle.

Out of the comradeships of the forecastle comes also the closer bond of personal friendships. Two men who " take to each other " will have a community of interest alike in goods, in plans and in work. This, in forecastle language is " chummy-ship " and " to have a good chum," says Mr. Nordhoff, " is one of the pleasantest parts of a voyage." To lend an oil-jacket is the highest test of friendship; for the generosity of a sailor though it may apply to every other article he owns stops, for some reason or other, at the oil-jacket. The loan of this piece of waterproof property is therefore considered as the surest indication of "chummy-ship."

The ever-present dangers that encompass a sailor's life make him active and alert, obedient to the word of command and ready in every emergency.

"Jump! jump, you scoundrel!" shouted the captain to that adventurous sailor-boy who, foolishly daring, had crawled out to the end of the main-royal yard and clung there for his life. The lad, trained to obedience, leaped from that cruel height and was saved. And it is this readiness to "mind orders" that is a sailor's salvation in many a moment of peril. The "Stand by the royal halyards!" that indicates the rising storm and the "Hoist away the top-gallant yards!" that tells of the passing of the squall alike find men alert to respond. And, whether to accompany the "slip-slap" of the windlass as the anchor of the homeward-bound ship comes up from foreign soil or to inspirit all hands when, in a gale of wind, they mast-head the topsail yard or set to work at the halyards, the inevitable "shanty" is yelled out at the top of strong and vigorous lungs.

Song lightens labor and has always been one of the sailor's most potent helpmeets. It is asserted that there is less singing among American sailors than with those of other nationalities, but be this as it may the American sailor has his own share of "shanties" and scraps of sentimental doggerel. There is a song and chorus for almost every piece of shipwork. "Whiskey makes a poor old man — O whiskey, whiskey!" hauls up the mainyard; "Away, haul away — haul away, Josey," hauls taut the weather mainbrace as also does "Haul the bowline — Kitty, you're my darling;" "A Yankee ship came down the river — Blow, my bully boys, blow," heaves up the anchor and

A VICTORY OF PEACE: BLUE JACKETS TO THE RESCUE.

" Lorenzo was no sailor, — 'Renzo, boys, 'Renzo," hauls up the foretopsail yard. " A song," says Mr. Dana, " is as necessary to sailors as the drum and fife to a soldier. They must pull together as soldiers must step in time and they can't pull in time, or pull with a will, without it. Many a time, when a thing goes heavy, with one fellow yo-ho-ing a lively song — like ' Heave to the girls!' 'Nancy O!' 'Jack Crosstree,' 'Cheerily, men,' etc., — has put life and strength into every arm."

As song is the sailor's labor-lifter so is story-telling his time-killer. Your old-time sailor, with a life filled with vicissitude and adventure, was a regular storehouse of stories and the long hours of the watch or the Sunday leisure were given largely to listening to his "yarns." Says Mr. Nordhoff: " With the good ship hove-to under a close-reefed maintopsail, or a storm-mizzen, the helm lashed down hard a-lee, and everything snug, alow and aloft, the watch gathers together under the topgallant forecastle or on the forehatch spinning long yarns of past gales, or sprees on shore, and the few hours slip away before one knows it."

The "sprees on shore" have ever been the sailor's bane. Rum is and always has been his chief root of evil. Despite the incessant work of temperance people among our seamen, despite the watch that is set upon those "carrion of the shore" the keepers of sailors' boarding-houses, their runners and their aids, despite the abolition of the "grog ration " on our men-of-war (according to Commodore Matthew Perry "one of the fomenting causes of evil on shipboard") and all the other attempts that have been made to stay the tide of drink this foulest enemy of manliness is still the sailor's greatest curse — sapping alike his energy, his usefulness and his life. Boston's " Black Sea " and New York's Cherry Street with their rows of vile dens and their still viler inmates have done to ruin many a gallant tar.

But the gallant tar has still another weak spot. This, though not a plague spot like the curse of rum, is one that influences many a stalwart sailor and has not unfrequently turned even his bravery into cowardice. It is his superstition.

Bred to a life that has to do with many of the phenomena of nature while at the same time he has neither the intelligence nor the indifference that governs the more preoccupied landsman, the speculations of the sailor upon the things he sees and hears and so often experiences run naturally into superstition. To him as to all simple folk a thing that seems to defy explanation is of the supernatural. The sailor's shifting horizon of sky and wave incloses many an uncanny apparition, many a sign and portent. Here again the introduction of steam as a motive power and the innovations of modern life have caused a marked decrease in the sailor of the old type, but there are still enough of these picturesque elements left, among those old-time seamen who remain, to make the decline of superstition slow even if it be sure.

There are still many firm believers in the mermaid, the sea serpent and the phantom ship. One of these marine visions — the phantom ship — has afforded the poets of to-day themes for verse and romance. Whittier's Orr's Island legend of "The Dead Ship of Harpswell" out-flies even the Flying Dutchman itself, while his poem of the lost Palatine that, lured on the rocks by wreckers, and plundered and burned by them, still sails its ghostly course across Long Island Sound, is almost tragic in its startling outlines :

> " For still, on many a moonless night,
> From Kingston Head and from Montauk Light
> The spectre kindles and burns in sight.
>
> Now low and dim, now clear and higher
> Leaps up the terrible Ghost of Fire,
> Then, slowly sinking, the flames expire.
>
> And the wise Sound skippers, though skies be fine,
> Reef their sails when they see the sign
> Of the blazing wreck of the Palatine ! "

So, too, as the American sailor's Flying Dutchman has for himself and his mates a real existence, do they tell of mermaids and of mermen seen as lately as 1881, while the perennial sea-serpent is to them an ever-present reality.

Believing in phantom ships they have also an unshaken belief in ghosts. The " shrieking woman " of Marblehead still haunts the rocky coasts about that typical sea-port town while the Block Island natives see even to this day the ghostly refugees of Revolutionary days struggling to make a shore they can never reach. The phantom crew of the foundered Johnson still haunt the deck of the ghostly Hascall that ran them down and Bret Harte's beautiful Greyport Legend keeps alive the story of the lost children of Portsmouth.

The minor superstitions are well-nigh legion. A playful cat on shipboard is a sure sign of a storm — "a cat," says the forecastle tradition, " has a gale of wind in her tail." A dead body kept on board ship always brings ill-luck. A shark following in a ship's wake is a most fatal omen. Ill-luck when explainable by no other cause is by the sailor ascribed to the presence of some guilty or objectionable person on board — the " Jonah " of the crew or the cabin. So, too, if a person may not be himself objectionable his name may be and woe to the shipmate or the passenger who brings an unlucky name on board. It is still the sailor's firm belief that a sick man cannot die until the tide begins to ebb, and every seaman can appreciate with peculiar force that sentence in "David Copperfield" (for New England no less than old England holds to this

A "YARN" OF THE SEA.

theory) that describes the death of Barkis: "And it being high water he went out with the tide."

Even modern science has not entirely dispelled the belief in the influence of the St. Elmo lights — malign or helpful according as the light may settle on the lower rigging betokening a storm or play around the tops foretelling good sailing weather. The "corposant" (as many sailors, torturing the old

Spanish, call this uncanny ball of light) if it plays about the yard-arm and throws its pale light full in any one's face is a sure sign of death and even now the most intelligent sailor regards this electrical freak of nature as a solemn and certain warning.

But with all his failings and with all his frailties the American sailor is entitled to the praise and gratitude of his countrymen and his story is replete with deeds of heroism, self-sacrifice, fidelity and chivalry.

The peaceful records of humane societies are fully as eloquent as the martial Roll of Honor. He who pulls the life-boat is often as grand a hero as he who wields the boarding cutlas, and the brave fellows of the coast stations are among the sea's victors of peace. No fishing craft but can tell its story of courage, self-sacrifice and humanity; no merchant vessel but has its traditions of bravery in storm and stress, of helpfulness, fidelity and self-denial; and even upon a humble canal boat a future president of the United States once made a record for pluck and manliness.

Not alone upon bloody decks, murky with the smoke of cannon and horrid with the din of battle, have the seamen of America proved their right to the title of heroes. The bravery of Reuben James, who in one of those bloody fights with the pirates of Tripoli, deliberately thrust his head beneath a descending Moorish scimiter and saved Decatur's life almost at the expense of his own, finds its parallel in the heroism of black George the Savannah negro-sailor who drew into his own body the Indian bullet intended for his captain. The determination of Perry who in reply to the remonstrances of his officers that the wind gave the British ships the advantage exclaimed, " I don't care ; leeward or windward they shall fight to-day," is equalled by the pluck and resolution of the

Salem merchant, Captain Nathaniel Silsbee. Unjustly detained by the French consul in a neutral port in 1798 he demanded an investigation. "You cannot have it under two months," said the consul. "That is the extreme of unjustice," declared Silsbee. "I'll not leave this office until my case has been called." And there, with a doggedness that was heroism, he sat for twenty-four hours without food or sleep until the consul in simple admiration of his obstinacy gave him a free discharge. "Why did you discharge the Yankee so quickly?" the consul was afterward asked. "*Parbleu,*" replied the Frenchman, "I found I must either dismiss him or bury him and I preferred the former."

When in the harbor of Marseilles in May, 1872, in the dead of night an Italian ship with a cargo of petroleum took fire there was consternation both on ship and shore. The burning vessel was surrounded by hundreds of valuable craft and they and the town were equally in danger. The citizens seemed paralyzed with fright; the sailors were equally unmanned. Suddenly from the flagship of the little American squadron then in port sounded the shrill notes of bugles calling away the boats of the fleet. At once they were manned, twenty in number, by the Yankee blue jackets and pulled rapidly toward the burning ship. Over the side of the Italian scrambled officers and men. The flaming vessel was speedily scuttled though the roaring flames almost drove the brave fellows off. Then the moorings were cast loose and, lashed stern to stern, the twenty American row boats towed the scuttled and blazing ship into the broader bay. Here she speedily sank and Marseilles and her shipping were saved. Truly —

" Peace hath her victories
No less renowned than war."

Upon the future of the American sailor it is vain to speculate. While the risks of the shore prove so much less hazardous than the risks of the sea and the development of America's resources afford an easier path to fortune than does her foreign commerce the young life and the young strength that formerly sought opportunity upon the water will find it on the land. But a change for the better may come at last. The fast declining tonnage of the United States may be stayed and made to increase again by one or by none of the remedies proposed by politicians and economists. Out of the noble harbor of New York or in through the beautiful Golden Gate of the far Western sea-port the ships of America may bear the products of the fatherland in greater number than ever the past has seen, and the stars and stripes may again be met and honored upon every sea.

Already the navy of the Union from being the laughing stock of the world has taken to itself new life. Legislators begin to appreciate that a navy, as has been said, is a source of economy. New cruisers are being builded. Since 1883 Congress has passed appropriations for the completion of five double-turretted monitors, the building of two sea-going iron clads and fourteen unarmored steel ships of varying sizes, and the arming of all these with the best and most powerful modern weapons of naval warfare. May there never be use for these in actual conflict. But preparation is always better than humiliation. There is a moral argument in the steel cruisers Newark and Charleston, and the armored battle ships Texas and Maine that foreign powers will appreciate and respect more effectively than arguments and apologies backed only by worm-eaten monitors and "obsolete war-veterans."

But whether in war or peace, in naval or mercantile commission, on errands of mercy, on voyages of research, of discovery or of scientific exploration the American sailor has a record for courage, pluck and ability that should not be lost sight of by his brethren of to-day and must not be forgotten by the seamen of the future.

Dim forecastle and plunging yard, breezy pilot house and throbbing engine room have their heroes and their inspirations quite as worthy imitation as the more exalted quarter-deck and bridge. And whatever the future of the American sailor, so far as increase in numbers or commercial strength are concerned, the world will hold him recreant if he fails to emulate the virtues, the heroism, the loyalty and the manliness of his prototypes and predecessors in a glorious past.

THE ACHIEVEMENTS OF THE AMERICAN SAILOR

WITH CERTAIN HAPPENINGS THAT HAVE AFFECTED HIS STORY

PRESENTED IN CHRONOLOGICAL ORDER.

As the American sailor we must here count only the native-born or strictly American resident of the United States dating from colonial times. The Mound Builder of prehistoric days, the Indian, the early discoverer and explorer can hardly be given place in this chronological survey of America's sea-happenings in war and peace. From Leif Ericson to the landing of the Mayflower must be omitted as belonging rather to the pre-American period, though a few of the important events in "boat-building" preface the later chronology.

1004. Thorvald the Norseman repairs his ship on Cape Cod.

1509. Diego de Niccusa, shipwrecked on one of the West India "Keys," builds a "raft" to escape to the mainland.

1510. Lope de Olano commences to build a caravel at the mouth of the Belen River.

1516. Vasco Nunez de Balboa builds four brigantines (two of which were successfully launched) on the Pacific side of the Isthmus of Panama.

1520. Martin Lopez builds two brigantines for Cortes on Lake Tezcuco.

1521. Cortes's fleet of thirteen brigantines (built at Tlascala by Lopez) launched on Lake Tezcuco — April 28.

1528. Panfilo de Narvaez built five unseaworthy brigantines on the Florida coast.

1542. Luis de Moscoco (successor of De Soto) builds two large boats to escape down the Mississippi — June.

1562. Nicholas Barre and his comrades build a pinnace on the South Carolina coast to escape to France.

1607. Thomas Digby builds the pinnace Virginia at the mouth of the Kennebec.

1613. Captain Samuel Argall of the Virginia colony attacks and captures DuThet's vessel at Mount Desert.

1614. Captain Adriaen Block builds the Onrust (Restless) at the Manhattans (launched in the spring).

1624. The Plymouth Colonists built two shallops for the coasting trade.

1627. A pinnace built at Buzzard's Bay for trade with the Dutch at the Manhattans.

1631. The Blessing of the Bay "the first American man-of-war" built on the Mystic River near Boston — launched July 4. The great Nieuw Netherlands, of eight hundred tons burden, built under the supervision of the Director Minuet at the Manhattans (New York).

1632. A ship from Virginia brings two thousand bushels of corn to Boston.

1636. A vessel of one hundred and twenty tons built at Marble Harbor near Salem. Governor Endicott sails against the Block Island Indians.

1639. A "Boston ship" attempts the Northwest Passage.

1640. Master Hugh Peters, a Salem shipbuilder, builds a vessel of three hundred tons and Master Bourne, of Boston, one of one hundred and sixty tons. Raymbault and Jogues pass in a birch canoe around the North shore of Lake Huron to the Sault Sainte Marie to meet a council of the Chippewas.

1644. Expedition from Boston sails to the help of French governor LaTour against his rival D'Aulnay.

1645. A ship of four hundred tons built at Boston.

1647. Master Edward Bangs launched at Plymouth a bark of fifty tons. The first vessel " of size" built by the Plymouth colony — January 24.

1654. Fur traders from Montreal penetrate the Western lakes. Expedition sails from Boston Harbor for the subjugation of Acadia.

1660. René Menard coasts the southern shore of Lake Superior.

1663. One hundred and thirty-two vessels reported in Massachusetts.

1665. Claude Allouez passes along the southern shore of Lake Superior.

1671. Captain Henry Morgan, the buccaneer, conquers Panama.

1673. Marquette and Joliet descend the Mississippi River to within three days' journey of its mouth; first river journey on record — May and June.

1678. La Salle and Tonty cross Lake Ontario in a little vessel of ten tons, the first ship that sailed upon that fresh-water sea — November 18.

1679. La Salle launches the Griffin on Lake Erie — May. Sails to Green Bay — August. Griffin sent back and La Salle and his men paddle up Lake Michigan — September.

1680. Hennepin sails northward on Mississippi and is taken by the Indians.

1682. La Salle descends the Mississippi River to the Gulf of Mexico.

1683. The Revenge, a pirate ship, Captain Cook, sets sail from Chesapeake, Virginia — August 23.

1685. Captain William Phips of Boston discovers the Spanish treasure-wreck.

1686. Henri Tonty descends Mississippi to meet La Salle.

1687. James II. sends a fleet which with the aid of the colonists should go against the pirates in the West Indies.

1690. Sir William Phips commands an expedition to Nova Scotia — March 22. Captures Acadia. Leads an unsuccessful expedition against Quebec — August.

1691. Captain William Kidd received one hundred and fifty pounds from New York for protecting the colony against pirates.

1696. Captain Kidd entered New York harbor with a French fishing vessel he had captured — July 4. Sails for Madagascar — September 6.

1699. Captain Kidd, turning pirate, is seized in Boston which he boldly visited with his alleged piratical crew.

1700. Coast of Carolina infested by pirates. Nine captured.

1704. Captain Church fails in an expedition against Port Royal.

1707. Captain Southack fails in an expedition against Port Royal.

1710. Colonial squadron capture Port Royal (Annapolis), in Nova Scotia.

1711. Admiral Sir Hovenden Walker commands an unsuccessful expedition against Canada — August 22.

1713. Vessels built at Cape Ann Point rigged as schooners.

1714. First out-and-out schooner built at Cape Ann.

1717. Bellamy, a noted pirate, wrecked on Cape Cod and one hundred men drowned. Six of his crew who survived taken to Boston and executed.

1718. Captain Maynard of Virginia defeats the pirate " Blackbeard."

1723. Twenty-five Rhode Island pirates taken by Captain Solgard, found guilty and executed.

1740. Governor Oglethorpe of Georgia leads an unsuccessful expedition against St. Augustine.

1741.   Report of sixty fishing vessels in Marblehead of fifty tons and more.

1742.   John Howard said to have sailed down the Ohio River.   Governor Oglethorpe of Georgia successfully attacks the Spanish fleet of invasion at St. Simon's Bay.   Sails to St. Augustine and forces the Spaniards to submission.

1744.   New York fishermen burn an English frigate in revenge for press-gang cruelties.

1745.   Ship Massachusetts of four hundred tons built at Boston.   Louisburg taken in June.
The fleet of ten vessels, the largest mounting twenty guns, sailed from Boston in April.   In the siege of Louisburg a French ship, sixty-four guns, richly laden with military stores, having on board five hundred and sixty men, was taken.

1746.   Admiral D'Anville's expedition for the capture of Boston scattered by storm — June.

1753.   Philadelphia schooner Argo, Captain Swaine, attempts the Northwest Passage. Captain Taylor of Rhode Island attempts a similar voyage.

1754.   A second Arctic expedition under Captain Swaine loses three men on Labrador coast and accomplishes nothing.

1755.   Troops embarked from Boston in forty-one vessels for Nova Scotia.

1758.   Captain Atkins of Boston sails along the coast of Labrador and makes discoveries.

1764.   Power given to commanders of British ships-of-war to seize vessels supposed to have goods and articles subject to duty.

1768.   Officers of Customs seize a sloop belonging to John Hancock and lying at his wharf.   Great excitement — June.

1771.   Virginia ship Diligence sails for exploration to the Arctic regions.

1772.   A British armed vessel burnt by Providence sailors, under Whipple — June.   James Wilder, of the ship Diligence, fitted out in Virginia by subscription, goes in search of the Northwest Passage and sails to 69° 11'.

1774.   Boston is deprived of its rights as a port by the Boston Port Bill.

1775   John Adams defends John Hancock for smuggling — April 19.   Capture of the Falcon sloop-of-war by the seamen of New Bedford — May 5.   Capture of the King's sloop Margaretta by the boatmen of Machias — June 12.   Washington issues commission to American privateers — September 2.   Congress legalizes his action.   Washington details two companies of the Marblehead regiment (under Broughton and Selman) to man two American war ships and attack the enemy — October 16.   London brigantine Nancy captured by American schooner Lee — November 29.   Esek Hopkins appointed commander-in-chief of American navy — December 22.

1776.   Spirited naval battle on Lake Champlain ; masterly escape of Arnold — October 11. Hopkins with a squadron of eight small vessels makes a descent on the Bahamas.   Fights the ship of-war Glasgow — April 6.   John Paul Jones appointed to command of the Providence — May 10.   During the summer he takes sixteen prizes.   Congress fixes the rank of Captain in the navy — October 10.   The Andrea Doria captures two armed transports and many merchantmen.   John Paul Jones captures armed ship Mellish and frigate Milford (autumn).   Three hundred and forty-two English vessels captured by Americans during this year.

1777.   John Paul Jones starts on a cruise in the Ranger — the first vessel to display the American flag — November.   Austin in Boston brigantine Perch carries news of Burgoyne's surrender to Europe.   Wickes carries the first national cruiser, with Franklin on board, across the ocean.   Conyngham makes a raid on English shipping.   Dolphin captured by British man-of-war Alert.   467 English vessels captured by the Americans during the year.   American brig Cabot (one of the first American cruisers) captured by British.

1778.   Destruction of American frigates Washington and Effingham and capture of the Delaware and Virginia.   D'Estaing arrives off the capes of Delaware with large French fleet. Capture of British war-ship Drake by Jones.   He raids the Scottish coast.   D'Estaing attacks British at Newport — April.

1779. Hopkins' squadron captures eight British transports off the Southern coast. Whipple in the Providence captures a British convoy of ten merchantmen. American cruiser Tyrannicide captures the Revenge. American cruiser Hazard defeats the Active. American cruiser Protector blows up the Revenge. Eighteen prizes brought into New London by American privateers. Paul Jones in the Bon Homme Richard fights and captures the British frigate Serapis — September 23. Mutiny on board the Alliance (bearing Lafayette on board) revealed by an Irish-American sailor and prevented. American expedition against Penobscot sails from Boston — July 19. Defeated by Clinton — July 27.

1781. American cruiser Alliance captures the Mars and Minerva — April. Captures Atalanta and Trepasy — May 28. English capture American ship Confederacy — June 22. Capture ship Trumbull — August. Captain Barney captures the British ship General Monk. American cruiser Congress captures the Savage — September.

1782. Alliance makes a successful cruise. Captain Manly makes a brilliant cruise in West Indian waters.

1783. First Fisheries Treaty. Captain Mooers in Nantucket ship Bedford first displayed the American flag in British port — London, February 6.

1784. Ship Empress, of Boston, three hundred and sixty tons, Captain John Green master, sailed to China. The first vessel to display the American flag in the Eastern seas.

1786. Clark ascends the Wabash to the Vermilion River.

1787. The ship Columbia started from Boston on a voyage round the world; the first circumnavigation performed by an American vessel. Sailed via Cape Horn to Northwest coast of America then to China, and returned via Cape of Good Hope to Boston. Arrived in 1790. Thomas Paine proposes steam navigation in America.

1789. Massachusetts Humane Society makes first attempt at organized succor to seamen. Placed huts for shelter of wrecked mariners on desolate portions of coast. First hut erected on Lovell's Island near Boston. Northwest coast of America first visited by Captain Gray in the Washington.

1792. Captain Kendrick in the Washington discovered Columbia River — May 7. Killed by a Spanish salute of welcome at Sandwich Islands. Captain Bunker in whale ship Washington first displayed American flag in a Spanish Pacific port — Callao, July 4.

1794. Six frigates built for service against the Algerines. Cod-fishery very largely pursued in New England. Keel of the frigate Constitution laid. Act passed creating a new navy. Six frigates ordered — March 27.

1796. The sloop Detroit, bought of N. W. Fur Company, first carried the American flag on Lake Erie.

1797. Frigate Constitution launched — October 21. Sloop Betsey (Captain Fanning) carried the stars and stripes round the world. Frigate Constellation launched at Baltimore — September 7.

1798. Act passed for the construction of twelve vessels — April 27. Navy Department created. British squadron attack American sloop of war Baltimore. Benjamin Stoddert appointed first secretary of the Navy — April 30.

1799. Fight between the Constellation and French frigate Insurgente — February 9. Founding of Marine hospital of U. S. at Fort Independence.

1800. Fight between Constellation and French frigate Vengeance — February 2. Ship of war Boston captured French corvette Berceau — October 12.

1801. The sloops Washington and Wilkinson were the first vessels built on South shore of Lake Erie. First American Squadron under command of Commodore Dale sails against Tripoli. Enterprise, Lieutenant Sterrett, captures a Tripolitan cruiser.

1802. Commodore Morris blockades the ports of Tripoli. Captain Rodgers destroys the Meshouda — June 22.

1803. Commodore Preble blockades Tripoli — October 15. Frigate Philadelphia taken by the Tripolitans — October 31.

1804. Decatur destroys frigate Philadelphia, after re-taking it in a very daring manner — February 15. Preble's squadron fights the Tripolitans. Constitution bombards Tripoli — September 3. Lieutenant Somers blows up Tripolitan magazine — September 4.

1805. Peace with Tripoli. Pike ascends and explores the Mississippi above St. Anthony's.

1807. English armed vessels refused admission into the ports of the United States — July 2. A general embargo is declared by the U. S. Government — December 22. U. S. frigate Chesapeake resists the British claim to right of search. Fulton's first successful trial of steamboat on the Hudson — September 14. Massachusetts Humane Society established the first life-boat station at Cohasset.

1808. American vessels captured and confiscated by both English and French.

1809. The general embargo repealed — March 1.

1811. Fight between ships President and Little Belt — May 16. The first steamboat on Western waters left Pittsburg for New Orleans — October 20.

1812. War declared against England — June 12. Commodore Rodgers in frigate President fires the first gun — June 22. Constitution escapes from five British frigates. Frigate Guerriere, Captain Dacres, captured by U. S. frigate Constitution, Captain Hull — August 19. U. S. frigate Wasp takes the English sloop Frolic — October 18. English frigate Macedonian taken by U. S. frigate Constitution — October 25. British frigate Java surrenders to U. S. frigate Constitution — December 29. Embargo laid for ninety days — April 3,

1813. U. S. ship Hornet takes the English sloop Peacock — February 25. U. S. frigate Chesapeake taken by the Shannon — June 1. Growler and Eagle taken by the English — June 3. English ship Pelican seizes U. S. sloop Argus — August 14. Perry's victory on Lake Erie — September 10.

1814. U. S. frigate Essex surrenders to Phœbe and Cherub — March 28. British ship Avon sunk by American sloop Wasp — September 1. Macdonough captures English squadron on Lake Champlain — September 11. Captain Reid in privateer General Armstrong fights six British war-vessels off Fayal — September 26. Lafitte and his band of pirates captured by Commodore Patterson.

1815. Attack on Algiers for breach of treaty. Lafitte and his Gulf pirates help the American forces at New Orleans. British ship Endymion captures the frigate President. Captain Biddle on ship Hornet fires last shot of the war — March 23.

1816. Private yacht, Cleopatra's Barge, launched at Salem. The owner and commander, Major George Crowninshield, made the first yacht trip across the Atlantic.

1817. First steamboat ascends the Mississippi above the mouth of the Ohio — the General Pike, Captain Jacob Reed. It reached St. Louis August 2. The second — the Constitution arrived October 2. Amelia Island off East Florida taken by a squadron under the command of J. D. Henley from certain marauders who had seized it.

1818. Fishery Treaty of 1818. Steam vessels first appeared on the Lakes.

1819. First passage of the Atlantic by steam effected by the Savannah from New York to Liverpool. The Walk-in-the-Water, first steamboat on Lake Erie, began her trips through Erie, Huron and Michigan. The Independence entered the Missouri River — May 13. U. S. Steamboat Western Engineer under command of Major S. H. Long went on an exploring expedition up the Missouri — June 21. The same month a military expedition of twelve boats sailed up the River.

1821. Gulf pirates defeated and scattered by American navy. Captain Palmer, of Connecticut, made Antarctic explorations and discoveries.

1824. David D. Porter commanded an expedition against West Indian pirates.

1825. Opening of the Erie Canal. First barge reached Albany — October 20. Major-General La Fayette ascended the Ohio River.

1826. The man-of-war North Carolina, Commodore M. C. Perry, defends American commerce from Greek pirates in the Mediterranean. First steamboat navigates Lake Michigan.

1829. Commander M. C. Perry enters Russian waters in command of the sloop Concord. This was the first entry of an American man-of-war.

1830. Treaty with Turkey securing the free navigation of the Black Sea — May 7. Ports reopened to British commerce — October 5.

1832. Piracy of Malays punished by U. S. frigate Potomac. First steamboat at Chicago.

1836. Nicollet explores the Mississippi to its source.

1837. U. S. steamer Caroline is burned by Canadian Royalists near Schlosser for having brought assistance to the "rebels." Brig Creole sails from Hampton Roads for New Orleans laden with slaves and tobacco — October 27. Slaves obtain mastery of Creole, murder their owner and wound several of the crew, and sail for Nassau, New Providence — November 7. The English governor liberates all the slaves except those concerned in murder and mutiny. American brig Morrison driven out of Yeddo Bay, Japan, by cannon shot. The Fulton, the " pioneer of the American steam navy," launched at Brooklyn. Commodore M. C. Perry takes command — October 4.

1838. Great Western steamship first sails from Bristol to New York.

1839. Pilot-boat Flying Fish carried the stars and stripes further south than the ships of any other nation had gone — March. Wilkes expedition to the Antarctic. The first steamboat arrival at Sault Sainte Marie — the Lexington.

1840. Organization of Hoboken Model Yacht Club. Wilkes discovers land supposed to be a continent.

1841. The twin U. S. war-steamers Missouri and Mississippi launched.

1842. First submarine cable laid from Governor's Island to Battery.

1843. United States Government send an eighty gun squadron under Commodore Perry to Africa to carry on a powder-and-ball policy against the Beribees (Africa) and secure a decent burial-ground for American sailors.

1844. Hoboken Model Yacht Club became the New York Yacht Club.

1845. U. S. Naval Academy opened at Annapolis. First regular Yachting Regatta in New York Harbor in July.

1846. First match yacht race between Maria and Coquette. In July Commodore Biddle, in command of the U. S. steamers Columbus and Vincennes, made an unsuccessful attempt to negotiate a treaty with Japan. Commodore Stockton and his naval brigade capture Los Angeles, the capital of California — July. Commodore Sloat seizes Monterey and Commodore Montgomery Yerba Buena. Commodore Shubrick captures Mazatlan. Conner and Perry blockade the Mexican Coast and capture Tampico, Tabasco, Alvarado and Tuspan.

1847. Congress made its first appropriation in assistance to shipwrecked mariners. Commodore Perry in the frigate Mississippi rescues two shipwrecked crews on Green Island — March 21. Bombardment of Vera Cruz — March 24. Surrender of Vera Cruz and San Juan d'Ulloa — March 26. The Britannia defeats the Washington in the first steam ocean race — June. The Sitka is the first steamer to appear in California waters. Lieutenant Lynch sails for Smyrna in the Supply, as commander of the Dead Sea Exploring Expedition.

1848. Commander Glynn sent in the brig Preble to Japan to reclaim twenty-three American sailors imprisoned there. He was successful. Lieutenant Bailey, of the Lexington, takes San Blas. The first steamboat communication between San Francisco and the interior, by the Pioneer, on the Sacramento river — April. Lieutenant Lynch performs the journey from Lake Tiberias to the Dead Sea in two metallic life-boats.

1849. Lopez's expedition to Cuba organized in New York frustrated by proclamation of President. The Southern Yacht Club was formed with headquarters at New Orleans. The first steamer between New York and San Francisco is received with great rejoicing — Jan. 19.

1850. Grinnell equipped two vessels commanded by Lieutenants De Haven and Griffith and accompanied by Dr. Kane. Lopez organized a second expedition to Cuba. Landed and took possession of Cardenas — May 19. First steamboat above Falls of St. Anthony, Mississippi River.

1851. Ship Cleopatra seized for assisting Lopez. Yacht America built, sails across the ocean and beats the whole Royal Yacht Squadron, winning the famous America Cup. Lopez fitted out another Cuban expedition against Cuba in New Orleans. The Pacific crosses the ocean in nine days, ninteen hours and twenty-five minutes. Considered very fast — May 20.

1852. U. S. ship Crescent City boarded at Havana and not allowed to land her mail or passengers. Act of Congress approved calling into existence the lighthouse board of United States — August 31. Perry's expedition sails to Japan — November 24.

1853. Dr. Kane led an Arctic expedition in the Advance. William Walker set sail from San Francisco on his first filibustering expedition — October 15. Commodore M. C. Perry delivered the President's letters to Japan and gave notice of his return the following year — July 14. Clipper ship Dreadnaught beats the Cunard steamer Canada in an ocean race.

1854. U. S. vessel Black Eagle is seized by the Spaniards at Cuba. Captain Hollins of the corvette Cyane bombards Greytown in Central America. Reciprocity treaty between Great Britain and United States regarding fisheries — July 13. Commodore M. C. Perry appeared in Japanese ports with a fleet of twelve vessels and negotiated a treaty — February 12. Carolina Yacht Club organized. N. Y. Club sailed first race at Newport.

1855. Dr. Kane abandoned his ship — May 17. Same year Lieutenant Hartstene sent out to search for Kane. Commodore John Rodgers explores Alaska Coast and Behring Strait — August.

1856. The Arctic ship Resolute formally presented to Queen Victoria by U. S. Government — December 16.

1857. William Walker, the filibusterer, surrendered to Commodore Davis of U. S. sloop-of war St. Mary's — May 1. Same year organized another expedition in New Orleans, but surrendered again to Commodore Paulding — December 8.

1858. Lieutenant Moffat seizes the American slave ship Echo and takes her to Charleston. William Walker attempted another filibustering expedition, but was seized at mouth of Mississippi River. Jersey City Yacht Club organized.

1859. Dreadnaught made the fastest run across the Atlantic then ever made by a sailing vessel (3000 miles in 13 days, 8 hours).

1860. The Great Eastern arrives at New York — June 23. Dr. Hayes set sail for the Arctic Regions in schooner United States — July 10. Charles F. Hall set out on polar expedition — September 7. The Connaught from Galway to Boston, largest vessel then afloat except Great Eastern, caught fire a few hundred miles from Boston. A small American brig came up and though of only 198 tons burden succeeded in saving every one of six hundred persons on board — October 7. William Walker makes his last filibustering expedition — June 27.

1861. Bombardment of Fort Sumter — April 12. Blockade of Southern ports — April 19. Mason and Slidell taken from the English mail steamer Trent — November 8. Steamer Star of the West fired upon in Charleston Harbor — January 4. Confederate steamer Nashville burns the Harvey Birch — November 21. U. S. Naval Academy removed from Annapolis to Newport.

1862. Rebel ram Merrimac destroys Cumberland and Congress in Hampton Roads — March 8. Monitor compels Merrimac to retire — March 9. Farragut attacks and passes the New Orleans forts. Capture of New Orleans — April 24. Confederates blow up the Merrimac — May 11. Farragut's fleet passes the batteries at Vicksburg — June 28. Monitor sinks off Cape Hatteras during a storm — December 30. Burnside's Expedition sails — January 11. Takes Roanoke, N. C. — February 8; Newbern — March 14. Confederate cruiser Alabama captures many vessels — October to December. Clipper Dreadnaught beats her own record in the run from Queenstown (2760 miles in 9 days 17 hours).

1863. Federal iron-clad fleet passes the batteries at Port Hudson — March 14. Charleston, S. C., attacked by monitors and gunboats. The Keokuk, a monitor, sunk — April 7. Vicksburg surrendered — July 4.

1864. The Federal war steamer Wachusett captures the Confederate cruiser Florida in the port of Bahia. The Confederate steamer Alabama attacked and sunk by the U. S. corvette Kearsarge near French coast — June 19. The Tallahassee destroys many U. S. merchantmen — July. Farragut passes the defenses of Mobile Bay and conquers the Confederate fleet — August 5. Charles F. Hall started on second Polar expedition. Rebel ram Albemarle blown up by Lieutenant Cushing — October 27.

1865. The Confederate cruiser privateer Shenandoah surrendered to the English government after destroying many Federal vessels. U. S. Naval Academy moved back to Annapolis. Boston Yacht Club organized.

1866. The Henrietta arrives at Cowes, winning the Ocean Yacht Race.

1868. American yacht Sappho was beaten off the Isle of Wight by the English yacht Oimara — August 25.

1870. American yacht Sappho won two out of three races with the English yacht Cambria — May 10-17.

1871. An American fleet arrives at Corea to conclude a treaty; trouble ensues. The Corean forts are attacked and destroyed and negotiations renewed. Charles F. Hall commands an Arctic expedition sent out by U. S. and Smithsonian Institute in ship Polaris. Organization of the life-saving system. English yacht Livonia beaten by the Columbia and Dauntless — October 16-25.

1872. Sailors for the American fleet board and scuttle a burning ship in Marseilles harbor and prevent great destruction — May. Announcement of the Geneva award on Alabama Claims — September. Fishery treaty called the Washington Treaty. Tigress, Commander Greer, sailed to relieve Polaris — July 14. Commander Braine sent on same errand. The Polaris voyagers are rescued by the Scottish steamer Ravenscraig — June 23.

1874. Arctic voyage of the Pandora (afterwards the Jeannette), Captain Young commander. James Gordon Bennet bore large share of expense. Nathaniel Bishop makes a voyage of two thousand miles in a paper canoe.

1876. Navigation relieved by the blowing up of the obstructions at Hell Gate, near New York City — September 24. Loss of twelve American whaling ships in Arctic ice — October 12. Alfred Johnson, a young man, started from America in the Centennial, a boat twenty feet long — June 15. Landed at Alercastle, Pembrokeshire — August 11.

1877. Canadian and United States Fishery Commission meet at Halifax — June 15. It awards five million dollars damages to Canada — November 20. Fourteen Gloucester fishing schooners lost and fifty lives — January 11.

1878. U. S. Life-Saving Service formally established by an act of Congress — June 18.

1879. The Jeannette Arctic Exploring Expedition sailed from San Francisco. Lieutenant DeLong, commander — September 26. Same year, Arctic Expedition of Lieutenant Schwatka.

1880. U. S. revenue steamer Corwin goes in quest of the Jeannette.

1881. Arctic exploring steamer Jeannette crushed in the ice — June 11. In June the Rodgers, Lieutenant Berry, sailed in search of the Jeannette. Lieutenant Greely sailed on August 11, 1881, for Lady Franklin Bay. Two young sailors crossed the Atlantic in the City of Bath, a boat fourteen feet long, arriving at Falmouth — August 24.

1882. A four-oared race on the Thames between the Hillsdale Club of Michigan and an English Rowing Club, ended in the defeat of the Americans — September 14. Lieutenant J. B. Lockwood of the Greely Expedition carried the American flag to the furthest point north yet reached by man — May 18.

1884. The Nourmahal, first American steel yacht, launched. Steamers Thetis and Bear sail to the relief of Lieutenant Greely. The ocean race between the Cunard Line steamer Oregon and the National Line America from New York to Queenstown won by the Oregon in six days, twelve hours and twenty-seven minutes, beating the America six hours — October 15.

1885. The first International Yacht Race for the America's Cup sailed by the American sloop Puritan and the English cutter Genesta — September 7. The vessels fouled and the race was put off to the fourteenth, when the Puritan won. The Puritan won in a second race on the sixteenth, thus settling the contest. A storm off the coast of Labrador wrecked eighty vessels — October 11. Washington Fishing Treaty expired — December 31.

1886. The second International Yacht Race, September 7, between the American yacht Mayflower and the British yacht Galatea. The Mayflower won in this, also in second race on eleventh, thus deciding the contest. In a schooner yacht race American Sachem defeated English Miranda — October 1. In sloop yacht race American Thetis beat English Stranger.

1887. Third International Yacht Race between British cutter Thistle and the American sloop Volunteer won by the Volunteer — September 27. Congress orders construction of five new steel war vessels.

1888. In yachting season: Volunteer wins Eastern Yacht Club regatta — June 27. Stranger wins American steam yacht regatta. Pappose outsails everything — July 21. Launch of dynamite cruiser Vesuvius. Launch of U. S. war cruiser Baltimore — October 6. Launch of Gunboat Petral — October 13. International canoe race at Stapleton N. Y., won by American canoe Eclipse — October 13.

THE BEST HUNDRED BOOKS ON THE AMERICAN SAILOR.

It is no easy task to select from the multitude of books devoted to the life of the American sailor afloat a list that may be presented as really the "best hundred." Naval and mercantile biographies, economic, statistical and scientific treatises, romances, tales and sketches, sober histories and humorous narratives exist in great number and many of them are of sufficient excellence to warrant place in such a list. The books that, limited to one hundred, upon examination have appeared to treat in most detail and diversity the experiences, history, romance, duties and life of the American sailor have been set apart and their titles are here presented as an attempt toward a comprehensive but by no means complete list of the naval and maritime portions of America's story. Many more might rightly claim admittance, some already included might properly give place to others, but taken as a whole the list will, it is hoped, serve as a basis for selection or reference for such readers as may desire to go more fully than this book has been able into the always suggestive and entertaining story of the American sailor.

Abbott (John S. C.).

Captain William Kidd, and others of the pirates or buccaneers who ravaged the seas, the islands and the Continents of America two hundred years ago. 12mo. Ill. 373 pp. New York, 1874.

Includes the stories of the careers of Kidd, Stede Bonnet, Teach (" Blackbeard "), Barthelemey, Lolonois, Mary Read, Anne Bonny, Sir Henry Morgan and Montbar. Told in the customary "Abbott" vein, but a healthy and entertaining volume.

Abbot (Willis J.).

Blue Jackets of '76 — a history of the naval battles of the American Revolution together with a narrative of the War with Tripoli. 8vo Ill. 301 pp. New York, 1888.

Blue Jackets of 1812. A history of the naval battles of the second war with Great Britain to which is prefixed an account of the French war of 1798. 8vo. Ill. 409 pp. New York, 1887.

Blue Jackets of '61. A history of the navy in the war of secession. 8vo. Ill. 318 pp. New York, 1886.

Mr. Abbot's books are graphic, picturesque, reliable and entertaining. He has a trenchant style and tells his story well.

Agassiz (Alexander).

Three cruises of the U. S. coast and geodetic survey steamer Blake in the Gulf of Mexico, in the Caribbean Sea and along the Atlantic coast of the United States, from 1877 to 1880. 2 vols. 8vo. Ill. 314 + 220 pp. Boston, 1888.

Strictly scientific but very interesting as detailing a peculiar phase of sea-work.

Ammen (Daniel).

The Atlantic Coast. 12mo. 273 pp. New York, 1883. Illustrations and maps.

This is the second volume in the valuable series detailing the services of "The Navy in the Civil War —" Professor Soley's sketch being the first and Commander Mahan's the second volume in the series.

Bowen (Francis).

Life of Sir William Phips, Captain-general of the Province of Massachusetts Bay. 12mo. 102 pp. New York, 1839.

In Vol. 7 of Sparks' "Library of American Biography." A life of Phips was also written by Cotton Mather and included in his "Magnalia." Both accounts furnish an interesting study of the first American sailor of historical note.

Boynton (C. B.).

History of the Navy during the Rebellion. 2 vols. 8vo. New York, 1868. Ill.

Bridge (Horatio).

Journal of an African Cruiser. New York, 1845. 179 1 p. Small 8vo.

Written by an officer of the U. S. navy and edited by Nathaniel Hawthorne.

Browne (John Ross).

Etchings of a whaling cruise, with notes on Zanzibar and a brief history of the whale fishery. 8vo. London, 1846. Ill. 580 pp.

Burgess (Edward).

American and English Yachts. 4to. Ill. New York, 1887. 70 pp.

This is a description by the now famous American yacht builder of the most famous modern yachts in English and American waters with a treatise on yachts and yachting.

Carter (Robert).

A summer cruise on the coast of New England. Boston, 1870.

"A delightful book. Full of humor, description, sentiment, natural history and almost perfectly written." — *Literary World.*

Clark (H. H.).

Boy Life in the United States Navy. 12mo. Ill. 313 pp. Boston, 1885.

A capital description of life in the navy on training-ship and man-of-war, told in story form by a naval officer.

Clark (Thomas).

Naval History of the United States from the commencement of the Revolutionary War to the present time (January, 1814). 2 vols. Philadelphia, 1814. 12mo.

"The first book to treat the subject as a whole and a very creditable book for the period." — Soley.

Clemens (Samuel L.). "Mark Twain."

Life on the Mississippi. 8vo. Ill. Boston, 1883. 624 pp.

Underneath all its humor and nonsense lies much valuable information as to Western steamboat life before the Civil War.

Cleveland (H. W. S.).

Voyages of a merchant navigator of the days that are past. Compiled from the journals and letters of Captain Richard J. Cleveland. With portrait. 12mo. 245 pp. New York, 1886.

A remarkably entertaining account of the voyages and experiences of a Salem sea-captain in the first quarter of the nineteenth century.

Coggeshall (George).

History of the American Privateers and Letters of Marque. 422 pp. New York, 1861. Ill.

Cooper (James Fenimore).

History of the Navy of the United States of America. (To 1851.) 3 vols. in one. 8vo. New York, 1853. Portraits.

The standard "unofficial" history of the U. S. naval service. "It is written in the somewhat pompous style of the period (1839) and although it has a strong fascination as a sea-story its historical value has been somewhat overrated." — Soley.

Lives of Distinguished American Naval Officers. Philadelphia, 1846.

"Brief but of considerable merit." — Soley.

Cooper (James Fenimore), *continued.*

SEA TALES.

Cooper is the Marryatt of America. His "sea tales," says the *Literary World,* "are classics of their kind." These are as follows:

The Pilot; a tale of the sea.   12mo.   New York.

" Long Tom Coffin is probably the most widely-known sailor in existence." — DUYCKINCK.

The Red Rover; a tale of the sea.   12mo.   New York.

" Surpasses the Pilot in animation and romance." — *Literary World.*

The Water Witch.   12mo.   New York.

A story of the Dutch occupation of New York.

The Two Admirals.   12mo.   New York.

Founded on the French naval service in the old French war.

Wing and Wing; or le Feu-Follet.

The Mediterranean during the Napoleonic wars.

" Both the above are," says the *Literary World,* "spirited tales of naval warfare for which Cooper's previous studies of the naval history of the United States had given him abundant material."

Afloat and ashore.   12mo.   New York.

Miles Wallingford.   12mo.   New York.

These two stories deal with the days of search and impressment before 1812.

Jack Tier; or the Florida Reef.   12mo.   New York.

" Has resemblances to the Water Witch." — *Literary World.*

The Sea Lions; or the Lost Sealers.

A tale of the Antarctic.   "While not accounted one of Cooper's best, it has strong friends." — *Literary World.*

Homeward Bound.   12mo.   New York.

Home as Found.   12mo.   New York.

These two are a sea tale and its sequel, devoted to a study of American society.   The offence that their sarcasms occasioned Americans at the time of their publication would scarcely be possible now.

Ned Myers; or Life before the Mast.   12mo.   New York.

Corbin (Diana Fontaine Maury).

Life of Matthew Fontaine Maury.   Portrait.   8vo.   New York, 1888.   326 pp.

The personal, domestic and scientific life of an eminent officer of the United States and Confederate navies, best known as the author of the " Physical Geography of the Sea."   Written by his daughter.

" It has neither table of contents, nor index, but apart from these drawbacks the book is one of absorbing interest, and is a valuable addition to our library of American biography." — *The Critic.*

Cozzens (Fred S.) and others.

Yachts and Yachting.   8vo.   Ill.   200 pp.   New York, 1888.

Comprises a detailed history of American yachting by Captain R. F. Coffin, and records of recent yachting seasons.

Crowninshield (Mary Bradford).

All Among the Lighthouses, or the Cruise of the Goldenrod.   8vo.   Ill.   392 pp.   Boston, 1886.

An excellent description of the lighthouses and the lighthouse service on the northern coast told for young people in story form.

Dahlgren (Madeline V.).

Memoir of John A. Dahlgren, Rear Admiral of U. S. N.   Boston, 1882.   660 pp.   8vo.   Portrait and illustrations.

Dana (Richard Henry).

Two years before the Mast.   A personal narrative.   New edition.   12mo.   470 pp.   Boston, 887.

A remarkably vivid and practical record of life before the mast thirty years ago.   It leads all others as the book best descriptive of the life of the American sailor and has, deservedly, become a sea classic.

Davis (William M.).

Nimrod of the Sea; or the American Whaleman.   12mo.   New York, 1874.

" One of the most minute and satisfactory stories of whaling life.   Full of information and very readable." — *Literary World.*

De Long (Emma).

The Voyage of the Jeannette. 2 vols. Boston, 1883. Portraits, maps, illustrations.

A wife's tribute to a husband's enthusiasm and faith. The book is edited by Mrs. DeLong from the journals of her husband, G. W. DeLong, "lost in the Arctic."

Disturnell (J.).

The Great Lakes or Inland Seas of America. New York, 1863. Minneapolis, 1887. 16mo.

Elliott (Charles B.).

The United States and Northeastern Fisheries.

A comprehensive history of the fishery question.

Emmons (George F.).

Navy of the United States (from 1775 to 1853). 4to. Washington, 1863.

"The best American work on the American navy and especially on the War of 1812. Unfortunately it is merely a mass of excellently arranged and classified statistics, and while of invaluable importance to the student is not interesting to the average reader." — ROSSEVELT.

Farragut (Loyall).

The Life of David Glasgow Farragut, First Admiral of the United States Navy. By his son. 8vo. Ill. 586 pp. New York, 1882.

> "Oh, while old ocean's breast bears a white sail,
> And God's soft stars to rest guide through the gale,
> Men will him ne'er forget, old Heart of Oak,
> Farragut, Farragut — Thunderbolt stroke!"
> — MEREDITH.

Fishbourne (E. G.).

Our ironclads and merchant-ships.

Foote (Andrew Hall).

Africa and the American Flag. 12mo. New York, 1854. 390 pp. Ill.

"An all-important work on the protracted labors of the navy in the suppression of the slave trade by Commodore, afterwards Rear-admiral Foote." — SOLEY.

Greely (A. W.)

Three years of Arctic service. 2 vols., 8vo. New York, 1886. Portraits, maps and charts.

A graphic account of a harsh and bitter experience in the frozen north.

Griffis (William Elliot).

Matthew Galbraith Perry; a typical American naval officer. With portrait. 12mo. 459 pp. Boston, 1887.

"One may help to build up character by pointing to a good model. To the lads of my country, I commend the study of Matthew Perry's career." — From Author's Preface.

"Mr. Griffis' name is a guaranty of accuracy and his work shows literary taste and skill." — SOLEY.

Hale (Edward Everett).

The Naval History of the American Revolution. In vol. 6 of Winsor's "Narrative and Critical History of America." 41 pp. Boston, 1888.

The most complete and impartial sketch of the doings of American men-of-war during the Revolution.

Stories of the Sea, told by Sailors. 12mo. 302 pp. Boston, 1880.

Extracts from the narratives of the actors themselves, edited for young people. The American part of the "stories" deals with Columbus, Sir Richard Grenville, the Buccaneers, Paul Jones, and certain of America's naval battles.

Hart (J. C.)

Miriam Coffin, or the whale fishermen.

A graphic description of Nantucket and the whale fishermen in the palmy days of that industry.

Hawks (Francis L).

Narrative of the Expedition to the China Seas and Japan, in 1852–54, under Commodore M. C. Perry. 3 vols. Quarto. New York, 1856.

Tells the story of the achievements of Commodore Perry in opening Japan to civilization. The first volume contains the general narrative of the expedition and this has been published separately.

Hayes (Isaac I.).

An Arctic Boat Journey in the autumn of 1854. 8vo. 375 pp. Boston, 1860. Maps.
The Open Polar Sea. 8vo. 434 pp. New York, 1867. Ill.

Headley (J. T.).

Farragut and our Naval Commanders (1861–65). 8vo. 316 pp. New York, 1867. Ill.

Hepworth (George H.).

Starboard and Port.

A yachtsman's book by a yachtsman. "Rich in nautical information and spicy anecdote." — *Literary World.*

Heywood (Philip D.).

An Ocean Tramp. 12mo. Ill. 233 pp. Boston, 1888.

Describes a phase of ocean life during the transition from sails to steam and the voyages of an American sailor in foreign seas. "A modern ' Two Years Before the Mast.' "

Higginson (Thomas Wentworth).

A book of American Explorers. 12mo. Ill. 367 pp. Boston, 1877.

Describes for young people the early days of American discovery by the old navigators from Columbus to the Mayflower and Governor Winthrop.

Travellers and Outlaws; Episodes in American history. Boston, 1887.

The sea "episodes" treated in this entertaining volume are "Old Salem Sea Captains," and "The Maroons of Jamaica."

Hunt (C. E.).

The Shenandoah; or, the Last Confederate Cruiser. 1867. 12mo.

James (William).

Naval History of Great Britain from 1793 to 1827. 6 vols. 8vo. London, 1837.

The sixth volume of this work is devoted almost entirely to a British account of the war of 1812. "An invaluable work," says Roosevelt, "written with fullness and care, but also a piece of special pleading by a bitter and not over-scrupulous partisan."

Jewell (J. G.).

Among our Sailors, with regulations governing the U. S. Merchant Service. 311 pp. New York, 1874. 12mo.

Kane (Elisha Kent).

Arctic Explorations. 2 vols., 8vo. . Philadelphia, 1857. Portraits and Maps.

One of the most notable, as one of the most interesting records of arctic endeavor.

Kingsley (Charles).

Westward ho! or The adventures of Sir Amyas Leigh, Knight, of Burrough, in the County of Devon, in the Reign of her most glorious majesty Queen Elizabeth. 12mo. London and New York, 1881.

One of the noblest, gentlest, most romantic and most manly of sea stories and tales of adventure. Based on the achievements of the sailors of the days of Drake and Raleigh and Grenville, on the Spanish main.

Lanman (Charles).

Life on the Lakes. New York, 1836. 2 vols. Ill. 8vo.

Lindsay (W. L.).

History of merchant shipping and ancient commerce. Ill. 4 vols. 8vo. London, 1876.

Lossing (Benson J.).

Pictorial Field Book of the War of 1812. 8vo. Ill. 1084 pp. New York, 1869.

"Notwithstanding their ' popular' and pictorial character the great value of Mr. Lossing's books is well known to students. For topographical details he is invaluable and he gives attention to a multitude of side-points that throw much light on the main subject." — SOLEY.

The Story of the United States Navy. 12mo. Ill. 418 pp. New York, 1880.

The history of the navy told for young people in Mr. Lossing's attractive style. It covers the period from 1775 to 1865.

Loubat (J. F.).

Medallic History of the United States of America, 1776–1876. Folio. New York, 1878. 170 etchings. 2 vols.

A luxurious volume, very valuable. Details the medals presented for bravery at sea.

Lynch (Wm. T.).

Narrative of U. S. Expedition to River Jordan and the Dead Sea. Maps and illustrations. Philadelphia, 1849. 8vo. 508 pp.

Mackenzie (Alexander Slidell).

Life of John Paul Jones. 2 vols. 12mo. New York, 1848.

"Written at the instance of Jared Sparks. Its merit is that it has sifted all the existing material and made a more readable and better constructed narrative than the others." — HALE.

Life of Oliver Hazard Perry. 2 vols. 18mo. New York, 1843.

Life of Stephen Decatur. (In Vol. XXI. Sparks' American Biography.)

"An excellent memoir which has the advantage of coming from a professional hand." — SOLEY.

Mahan (A. T.).

The Gulf and Inland Waters. 12mo. 267 pp. New York, 1883. Maps.

This is the third volume in the "Navy in the Civil War" series, Professor Soley's being the first and Admiral Ammen's the second volume in the series.

Melville (George W.).

In the Lena Delta. 8vo. Ill. Boston, 1885. 497 pp.

This is Chief-Engineer Melville's narrative of the search for Lieutenant DeLong and his companions and is followed by an account of the Greely relief expedition.

Melville (Herman).

Omoo, adventures in the South Seas (a sequel to Typee).

Moby Dick; or the Whale.

Melville's books are strongly American, romantic and full of incident and the flavor of the sea. "Omoo," says Douglas Jerrold, "has much of the charm that has rendered Robinson Crusoe immortal."

Morris (Charles). The Autobiography of Commodore Charles Morris (from 1799 to 1840).

Annapolis, 1880. 111 pp. 1vo. Portrait.

"It is unique. It is the only narrative published by a naval officer of the older period giving in his own words the story of his own life. . . . It offers a graphic picture of life in the service during that period." — SOLEY.

Nordhoff (Charles).

Cape Cod and all along shore. 12mo. Boston, 1868.

Short stories of sea-faring scenes, life and character on the New England coast.

Sailor Life on Man-of-War and Merchant Vessel. 2 vols. in one. 8vo. Ill. 733 pp. New York, 1884.

The first part details a boy's experience in the United States Navy, forty years ago; the second portion tells of a sailor-boy's voyages to see the world on a merchant-vessel of the same period.

Whaling and Fishing. 16mo. Cincinnati, 1856. 3 vols. in one. Ill. 957 pp.

Nourse (J. E.).

American Explorations in the Ice Zones. 8vo. Ill. 624 pp. Boston, 1884.

Describes the Arctic expeditions of DeHaven, Kane, Rodgers, Hayes, Hall, Schwatka and DeLong, the relief voyages of the Corwin, Rodgers and Alliance, the cruises of Long and Raynor, the Greely expedition, the discoveries of Lockwood and the naval explorations in Alaska. It also notices the Antarctic cruise of Wilkes and the U. S. Signal Service Arctic observers.

Parker (William Harwar).

Recollections of a Naval Officer from 1841 to 1865. 12mo. 372 pp. New York, 1881.

The recollections of a naval officer in the United States service until 1861 and in the Confederate Navy until the close of the war of the rebellion. Gossippy and diffuse but full of pictures of the life of American men-of-war's men.

"His style is anecdotic and racy, but his facts are faithfully presented, his judgments are sound to the core and his impressions are sharply outlined." — SOLEY.

Parkman (Francis).

LaSalle and the Discovery of the Great West. 12mo. 483 pp. Boston, 1880. Maps.

A noble work largely descriptive of the enterprising French explorer who first sailed the great lakes and built and launched the first vessel that navigated America's inland seas.

Parsons (Usher).

Life of Sir William Pepperell. 12mo. Boston, 1856. 352 pp. 12mo. Map.

A fairly good life of the American leader of the "mettlesome enterprise" that captured Louisburg and led to the downfall of French dominion in Canada.

Phelps (W. D.).

Fore and Aft; forty years experience of a Boston shipmaster.   Boston, 1870.

" Realistic, lively and wholesome." — *Literary World.*

Porter (David D.).

Memoir of Commodore David Porter.   Albany, 1875.   8vo.   427 pp.   Ill.

Qualtrough (Edward F.).

The Sailor's handy book.   16mo.   Ill.   New York, 1883.   594 pp.

A guide to yachting and sailing for amateurs and professionals.

Reed (Sir Edward J.), and Simpson, Edward.

Modern Ships of War.   8vo.   Ill.   284 pp.   New York, 1888.

The portion of this work devoted to American war ships and artillery was written by Rear-admiral Simpson of the United States Navy.

Roosevelt (Theodore).

The Naval War of 1812, or the History of the United States Navy during the last war with Great Britain; to which is appended an account of the Battle of New Orleans.   8vo. 541 pp.   New York, 1883.   Ill.

The latest and by far the best account of the war of 1812.   Vividly written and worthy to be esteemed a standard.

Ruschenberger (William S. W.).

Voyage Round the World, including an embassy to Muscat and Siam in 1835, 1836 and 1837. 8vo.   Philadelphia, 1838.   559 pp.

An excellent description of foreign service in the navy by a navy surgeon.   His " Three Years in the Pacific " is also a good contribution to the story of life in the American navy.

Sabine (Lorenzo).

Life of Edward Preble.   (Vol. 22 of Sparks' American Biography.)

" An invaluable book by far the largest part of which is taken up with a full and satisfactory examination of Preble's Tripoli Campaign." — SOLEY.

Semmes (Raphael).

Cruise of the Alabama and the Sumter.   2 vols.   London, 1864.   8vo.   Ill.

Service Afloat.   Baltimore, 1869.   8vo.   Portrait and illustrations.   833 pp.

Both books are experiences at sea written by the daring commander of the Rebel privateer Alabama.

Sheppard (F. H.).

Love Afloat; a story of the American Navy.

" One of the best sea stories of the last decade; spirited, truthful and finely told.   It never, we suspect, has had the reading it deserves." — *Literary World.*

Soley (James Russell).

The Blockade and the Cruisers.   12mo.   257 pp.   New York, 1883.   Maps.

This is Vol. I. in the series " The Navy in the Civil War," Admiral Ammen's sketch being the second and Commander Mahan's the third volume in the series.

The Sailor Boys of '61.   8vo.   Ill.   Boston, 1888.

The Boys of 1812.   8vo.   Ill.   Boston, 1887.

Professor Soley is a very interesting and painstaking writer.   His books are the fruit both of nautical knowledge and experience.

Starbuck (Alexander).

History of the American Whale Fishery to 1876.   8vo.   767 pp.   Waltham, 1878.   Ill.

Thornbury (George Walter).

The Monarchs of the Main.   London, 1876.

Details the story of the Buccaneers.

Tilton (Theodore).

Tempest Tossed; a Romance of the Sea.   12mo.   New York.

An interesting though somewhat overwrought story of sea and wreck, with a unique development.

Wells (David A.).

Our Merchant Marine; how it rose, increased, became great, declined and decayed.   12mo.
219 pp.   New York, 1885.

A careful though not a dispassionate study, from a free-trade standpoint, of the history and decline of the American merchant marine.

Wilkes (Charles).

Narrative of the United States Exploring Expedition (1838–42).   8vo.   London, 1845.

This London edition is abridged into one volume from the large Philadelphia edition of five volumes.   It records the antarctic expedition of Captain Wilkes.

Winsor (Justin).

Narrative and critical history of America.   8 vols.   8vo.   Ill.   Boston, 1886–89.

This important work seems to merit a place in this list even though all other distinctive histories of America are excluded.   It is so thoroughly a student's work, contributed to by leading American historians and full of the results of careful record and research that it is one of the best factors in the study of the growth and story of the American sailor as well as of America itself.

INDEX.